BEGIN AGAIN

HOME IN YOU SERIES
BOOK TWO

Crystal Walton

Impact Editions, LLC
Chesapeake, VA

Printed in the United States of America

Impact Editions, LLC
www.crystal-walton.com

Book Layout ©2013 BookDesignTemplates.com

Cover Design ©2017 Victorine Lieske

Author Photo by Charity Mack

Name: Walton, Crystal, 1980-
Title: Begin Again / Crystal Walton.
Identifiers: LCCN 2017900514 (pbk) | ISBN 978-0-9862882-8-9 (pbk)
BISAC: 1. FICTION / Clean & Wholesome Romance 2. FICTION / Contemporary Inspirational Romance

Library of Congress Control Number: 2017900514

PROLOGUE

Anchor

Cracks of thunder over the Pamlico Sound had nothing on the adrenaline pounding in Drew Anderson's ears. With his knees pressed into the pier's wet, grainy boards, he stilled a hand over his dad's. "We should wait for the Coast Guard. You don't know what conditions you're facing."

"No time." Dad finished untying the rope tethering his old skiff to the dock. "A family's stranded in this storm. What else is there to know?"

Just like Dad to put complete strangers first.

A gust of wind chased another clap of thunder. The grooved wrinkles bookending Dad's compassionate eyes softened. "Sacrifice doesn't build character, son. It reveals it." He squeezed Drew's arm, climbed in the boat, and cranked the motor. "They have a home to return to."

So do you. The thought of losing one more person in his own home nearly knocked Drew upside down like the capsized sailboat on the horizon.

Lightning lit up the tumultuous waters. "Daddy?" From the top of the pier, Drew's five-year-old daughter, Maddie, tore free from Grandma Jo and sprang for him.

He swept her into his arms and nestled her head under his chin. "It's okay, Sea Monkey." After holding on with all he had, he tightened her hood and kissed her forehead. "Grandma Jo's gonna take you back to the house. Daddy and Grandpa will be home soon."

"In time for good-night prayers?"

His heart cinched. "Always, sweetie. I promise." Drew transferred her to Grandma Jo and looked between his dad and baby girl—his past and future. Two anchors that steadied him through every storm. That wasn't about to change now.

He boarded the skiff and nodded for Dad to motor them away from the docks. Once out of the harbor, their boat felt more like one of Maddie's bath toys, rocking in the waves as they approached the sailboat.

Drew lowered the anchor and turned as Dad was emptying his pockets—his wallet, two pieces of saltwater taffy. He stalled with the shop's keys in his hand. Drew had his own set, but Dad's were the original ones from the day he and Mom first opened their store in Ocracoke.

"For safe keeping." He set the keys in Drew's palm, curled his fingers over them, and turned to the water.

"Dad, let me. I'm—"

"No. I need you here to pull them in." Leaving no room for argument, Dad dove in and swam to the sailboat like a fit petty officer instead of a retired vet.

Drew readied the life jackets. Within minutes, Dad returned with a trembling teenager under his arm for Drew to tow aboard. It didn't matter if they were strangers. The young girl clung to Drew as if she'd known him all her life.

He cradled her head to his chest while Dad returned for the next rescue. "You're going to be okay. I need you to put this life jacket on, okay?"

With a shaky nod, she reluctantly loosened her hold around his waist. A swell pitched the skiff to the left. Drew gripped the edge of the boat to steady them. "I've got you—"

A woman's scream whipped his head toward the waves smacking the side of the sailboat into Dad's back. The sight alone almost knocked the wind from Drew. He launched for the edge, but Dad held up a hand to stop him. Powering through, he brought a woman in reach for Drew to lift to safety. "Dad, that's enough."

"My husband." The woman clenched Drew's sleeve, her frayed plea coiling around him. "Please."

Raindrops thrummed into the silence he knew Dad wouldn't leave unanswered. Every ounce the hero he'd always be, he cut through the dangerous waters for one more save.

Rain blended into tears of shock and fear as the girl rushed to her mom.

A guttural howl of wind pierced the sound and lurched Drew into the skiff's opposite rail. Darkness festered. Muddled yells swarmed. He rubbed the base of his head until a hand grasped the boat's ledge.

Drew's pulse kick-started enough energy to propel him to his feet. He reached over the side. The husband. As soon as

Drew hauled him aboard, the guy backed against the inside of the boat and gasped for air.

Drew scanned the choppy water. "The man who rescued you." He searched the guy's face. "Where is he?"

"The sail. I don't know. I..."

Drew didn't hesitate. He plunged into the cool waves, muscles burning with tension. Unforgiving winds spun the capsized sailboat into his path. No sign of Dad. Drew banged a palm to the wood and swam to the opposite side. Nothing.

Panic surged. He sucked in a giant gasp of air and dove under the boat. There, tangled in the sail. Drew pushed against the current with a strength he didn't know he had.

Heartbeats struck his ears like a shot clock. One strike. Two. Pressure seared his lungs as he heaved to break Dad's motionless body free. Three. Four.

Out of air, Drew wrenched them both to the surface.

Thunder growled. Rain pelted. But nothing roared louder than Dad's lack of breathing. Drew buoyed him against the boat. Five. Six. "Come on, Dad. I made Maddie a promise." He pinched Dad's nose and released air into his mouth. "Come on!"

The wind raged in response, hurling them both off balance. Waves beat them into the side of the boat, but a whirlwind of fury and fear kept Dad clutched in his arms.

He scanned for the skiff. Seven. Eight. No more time. He had to make it. Adrenaline fueled him through the dark swells. He hefted Dad aboard and cleared the edge in one swing. Raindrops pounded against the bottom of the boat like a military drum.

Nine. Ten. Drew dropped to his knees. “Don’t do this.” Eyes blurry with rain and unshed emotion, he laced his shaky hands over Dad’s chest and pumped. Again. And again.

The young girl clung to her mom and released a cry Drew felt to his bones. He transferred breath to Dad and leaned an ear to his soundless mouth. Praying. Begging. *Please.*

Wind tore across the sound and thrust the sailboat straight for them. The girl screamed this time as the husband lunged for the wheel. Drew grasped the ledge, scraped an arm under Dad’s back, and pulled him to his chest.

Shot clock, drained.

Chaos brewed around him in slow motion. Every heartbeat amplified. Every second further out of reach. Drew rocked Dad in his arms, his voice a hoarse whisper. “I promised.”

A dangerous mix of emotions building inside him craned his head to the perilous sky. One mangled yell followed another until his lungs fully emptied. Movement flickered from all directions. But in the eye of the storm, he could only manage to hold Dad tighter—his world unhinged, his anchor lost.

CHAPTER ONE

Enigma

Five Years Later

The waves pulsing against Ocracoke's shoreline echoed every reason Drew Anderson should turn away from this door.

He raked a hand through his just-washed hair, wishing for the familiar feel of sand and salt instead. He should be in the water, chasing an answer he was running out of time to find. Not wasting an evening at a summer party.

For the twentieth time tonight, concerns about his daughter being away from home at a sleepover knotted his stomach. He rotated his neck. Maddie hadn't had a flare-up in weeks. She'd be fine. If anything came up, Winnie's parents had his number.

Checking his cell just in case, Drew scrolled to the text Maddie had sent earlier. Leave it to his carefree baby girl to urge him to have fun tonight.

Inside, conversations coming from a small den to the right competed with laughter and music trailing in from a sliding door leading to a pool. Drew took one look at both options and headed into the kitchen instead. Other than the faint sound of a girl singing nearby, only the churn of the ice maker filled the quiet room.

He leaned against the counter, closed his eyes, and massaged his temples.

"You shouldn't try so hard." From behind a cute pair of glasses, blue eyes met his. A blonde in an off-the-shoulder, white cotton dress and an unabashed gaze stood in front of him.

Where'd she come from? Drew glanced behind him. To what, the wall? Of course she was talking to him.

When his vocal cords caught up, he cleared his throat. "Excuse me?"

A lot of good unclogging his voice did. If it got any more pubescent, he'd take that windpipe right out and knock some sense into himself with it.

She reached for his hand and lowered it from his throbbing temple. "De-stressing. You're trying too hard."

Drew stared at her warm fingers against his. "I'm sorry, and you are?"

"Ti Russo." A series of bracelets jingled down her arm. "Pleasure."

He'd never met a girl who went by an initial.

Looking down, she ran the back of her bare foot along her calf. Waiting.

Now would be the appropriate moment for southern hospitality. Or at a minimum, basic manners in returning the introduction. Yet Drew just stood there like a washed-up piece of seaweed languishing under a sunrise he couldn't look away from.

She was probably a few years younger than him. Twenty-eight at best. But her eyes carried the experiences of someone twice her age, along with an artistic flair he knew better than to entertain.

"Thanks, but I'm fine." He strode to the opposite counter.

"If you really want to work on something, you might try honing your lying skills."

Drew turned, jaw slack. If the girl's accent wasn't enough confirmation she was from the Big Apple, her lack of a filter just eliminated any doubt. Unbidden, thoughts of New York triggered memories that had been festering beneath the surface all day. He tamped them back down where they belonged.

Ti dipped her head in front of his, brow raised as if waiting for him to divulge his inner thoughts. Like that was happening.

"Don't you have a hot yoga class to go to or something?" He scanned the kitchen for a drink. Or maybe a pail of ice to dump over his head.

"What do you know about hot yoga?"

Way to open himself up for that one. Drew pressed his tongue to the inside of his cheek. "Isn't that what you girls do on vacations?"

A trace of something unreadable passed her eyes before she batted it away. Fear? She covered a moon-shaped scar on her arm when Drew's gaze strayed to it. "I might be here for business," she rambled off way too fast.

"Then I'm sure you need to get back to it." As he should've been doing.

Drew swiped one of the pre-filled cups of Coke on the counter, took a giant swig, and almost spewed it back out. Not Coke. Dr. Pepper. He pivoted around in search of something clear to wash out the aftertaste. The water filter on the fridge looked like the only option.

That reminded him. He remembered to tell Winnie's mom Maddie couldn't have soda, didn't he?

Right beside him again, Ti propped a never-ending leg against the fridge. "Rose."

"Sorry?"

"Rose. It's the queen essential oil for de-stressing. Expensive, but totally worth it. You should try it with a little lavender, maybe some bergamot."

Wow. He must've really looked pathetic if some hippie chick was trying to push herbal remedies on him. He snagged an empty cup from the counter.

"Ooh. Or how about a little painting therapy? I met a girl at Down Creek Gallery earlier. We talked about doing some acrylics one morning this week. You should come."

Her unassuming smile curled around him while errant strands of hair mingled with her long dangling earrings. Drew pressed the cup in the general direction of the lever, but he didn't tear his gaze from her until something churned louder than his stomach.

Ice. Tumbling over the cup and spilling everywhere. Great. Drew turned to the sink.

She followed. "C'mon, it'll be—"

Her high-pitched squeak spun him around in time to avert her collision with the scattered ice cubes melting on the floor. She gripped his sleeve, and he secured one stabilizing hand to her waist, the other to the fridge. This close, heady fragrances swirled up from her hair and tangled around his voice again. "You all right?" he managed.

A hint of satisfaction gradually colored over the fleeting embarrassment in her eyes. "See what a little distraction does? Gives that uptight stance of yours an elastic stretch." Her lips crept to the side. "Or is that from the yoga?"

Without answering, he let go, grabbed a towel from the sink, and knelt to the floor.

Ti was right behind. "Seriously, you should come tomorrow. It'll at least get your mind off whatever's got your forehead all scrunched like that."

Not likely. Aromatherapy? Painting on the beach with a starry-eyed artist? Negative. The only thing he needed to do was get back to figuring out how to meet the bank's deadline.

Drew dumped the ice in the sink and turned for the front door. "I hope you have fun on the island, but I really need to go."

His momentum ushered him into the briny air, up the walkway, and into a breeze waiting for him like a friend. What was he trying to do by coming here tonight?

Hunched against the garage, Drew looked back at the house and released a long breath. He shouldn't have been short with that girl. She wasn't the one he was upset with.

Flashes of unwelcome memories stormed in. He glared at the dark sky until the call of the waves beckoned him to race the riptide. To taste the salty water, feel the rush of the surf, and cling to the only consolation that had gotten him through these last several years.

In the morning, a new day would begin again.

The memory of his dad's voice breezed through him. Trouble was, even with the sunrise coming, Drew was no stranger to how long a single night could be.

Ti stood in the kitchen with her heart lodged somewhere in her throat while the door closed behind Mr. Enigma.

His green eyes had gripped her the minute she saw the torment they held. She didn't have to know the specifics. She had experienced enough turmoil of her own to recognize the signs.

The pain hit her dead in the chest again. What was wrong with her? She'd come to the party to fade into the background and forget what'd driven her all the way to North Carolina from Queens last night. She was supposed to be clearing her head, not clouding it.

So, maybe trying to get someone else to de-stress helped her do the same for a few minutes. Still, her impulsive decision to come was probably a mistake. She grabbed her shoes.

Outside, humidity fogged her glasses but didn't keep her from overlooking the dark-haired, tan-skinned guy from inside leaning against the garage. Their eyes met long enough to make it clear he thought she was following him.

Before Ti could alleviate his worries, a couple strolled up from the opposite direction.

The dude's white blazer, complete with brown chest hairs curling over his V-neck shirt, screamed *Miami Vice.* To top it off, his hair-sprayed do had about as much give as his haughty grin. "Drew Anderson. Joanna and I were just talking about you."

So, Mr. Enigma had a name. And clearly had a beef with the Don Johnson wannabe. Whatever was brewing between them was none of Ti's business, but something about the weary strain across Drew's shoulders made her want to take up for him.

Drew blocked the walkway in an obvious effort to shield her from the conversation.

V-neck Boy didn't seem to miss it. His gaze zinged past Drew to Ti before slithering back to its primary target. He curled an arm around the brunette at his side, his grin feigning confusion. "We'd love for you to clear something up. For the life of us, we can't figure out why you'd turn down my offer to buy your struggling shop."

"Not now, Marcus." Drew clipped the guy's shoulder on his way past him.

"Time's running out." Marcus turned. "I know you don't want to go another tourist season barely breaking even. Especially with your little girl needing—"

Drew was up in the dude's face in two seconds flat.

Without thinking it through, Ti sprang forward and wedged between them. "Easy, boys." She warned Marcus away with her best you-don't-want-to-bring-out-the-New-

York-in-me look. "Drew must not've told you yet. I'm a consultant here to help his business." *Consultant? Um, okay, this could go bad fast. What am I doing?*

Drew's raised brows obviously had the same question. She darted him a go-with-it expression. They'd figure it out later. Right now, they had to get V-neck Boy off his back.

"A consultant?" The guy looked her up and down and then dipped his chin. "Good luck with that." Without the slightest bit of concern on his face, he prodded his date forward.

The minute they disappeared inside, Drew glowered at Ti. "What was that?"

"Um ..." She twirled her earring around. "An intervention?"

"Thanks, but I already told you, I'm fine."

Ti rubbed bits of gravel off the bottom of one foot while contemplating ten different ways to rid Mr. Enigma of his pride.

His guarded stance didn't budge.

"Okay, fine. I'm not really a consultant, but I have my own business. I know what it takes to make things run. Let me at least offer some suggestions." A project to keep her mind occupied would be a lifesaver right now.

"You don't even know what kind of shop I have."

Ti peered around the small beach town. "I'm gonna go with souvenirs for $500, Alex."

Drew cocked his chin. "I thought you were here for work."

"Sort of." She switched hands and let her slingbacks hang from her fingers. "I'm visiting a friend for a while."

"What's a while?"

"Haven't decided yet."

He edged in, as if proximity would burn a hole through the wall keeping her from telling him the full truth. Face right below his, Ti begged the heat mounting her body limb by limb to stop below her neckline.

Drew stretched a palm against the siding behind her. She glanced from his eyes to his ringless left hand and back. If he noticed her quick appraisal, he didn't show it. "And you can just walk away from your business for an indefinite amount of time?"

This close, an unruly section of hair above his ear stole her focus. Probably an overlooked result of bed head. Ti pushed the visual away and accomplished another swallow. "Like I said, I know how to make things run."

His hand dragged down the wall, his countenance with it. "I can't pay you."

"I wasn't asking." She matched his backward stride. "It's fine, really. My business is pretty self-sustaining. And I happen to have some money saved up from another life."

"Another life." His mouth quirked. "Do I want to know?"

"You could guess."

He turned to leave, bait untaken.

A group of four-wheelers zoomed down the beach with whoops and hollers trailing them. Slightly redneck-ish, maybe, but at least those guys knew how to have fun. Unlike *some* people.

All right, so the guy obviously wasn't the playing around type. Fine. Ti caught his arm. "Relax, Yoga Boy. I was just trying to feel you out. Look, I'm here for ... *a while.* I need inspiration for new art pieces. Your shop obviously needs some new inventory—"

She didn't give him the chance to interject when he balked. "We're talking about a mutual benefit here." Along with a diversion. If she could keep the nightmares at bay for a few weeks, maybe she'd have a shot at figuring some things out.

Offering her best disarming smile, she swayed from side to side. "No harm, no foul."

The look on his face begged to differ.

"Drew." A shirtless guy in board shorts jogged up from the beach, carrying a surfboard with a strap hitched to his ankle. "You're not bailing already, are you? We're just ..." A glance from Drew to Ti sprawled into a Cheshire Cat smile. "Sorry, hoss. Didn't mean to interrupt."

Drew looked like he was suppressing an eye roll. "You weren't. Cooper, this is ..."

"Ti Russo." She extended a hand.

The door behind them opened, and her friend Livy joined them on the walkway. "Oh, brilliant. I get to introduce you all at once."

Hearing the random British vernacular Livy had picked up while living in the UK would've been funny if Downer Drew's expression weren't ruining it.

"You know this girl?" he deadpanned.

"We modeled together in London." Liv curled an arm around Ti's. "Been friends ever since."

Drew rolled up his sleeves. "Why didn't you tell us you had a friend coming?"

"Didn't know. She surprised me last night."

That was one way of putting it. Ti chewed her lip. Couldn't they talk about anything else?

Obviously not.

Skeptical eyes led Drew a step closer. "You really did just pick up and leave your job."

Ti raised a nonchalant shoulder. "Everyone needs a breather now and then."

"Sure you're not running away from something?"

Her heart thudded against her chest, but she kept her voice casual. "Aren't we all?"

"Some of us have responsibilities."

The pavement burned into her skin almost as much as his attitude. "Thanks for clearing that up. I always wanted to meet a real-life Paris Geller."

Intense green eyes roved over her until a visible ache creased his face. Yet rather than respond, Drew backed up farther, turned, and walked away.

"Good talk," she called to his retreating backside. Uptight much?

Livy squeezed Ti's arm. "Don't worry. It's not about you."

Could've fooled her. Didn't matter. Her offer to help was a means to an end for them both. Plain and simple.

Cooper peeled off his surfboard's Velcro strap from around his ankle and looked her over again as though assessing the situation. "Why don't you crash at my place while you're here?"

Livy let go of Ti and whacked him in the bicep. "While *you* crash on Drew's couch."

His dimples sank in as he rubbed his arm. "Of course."

"Hold on a sec." Ti looked from Cooper to Drew's distant silhouette, their similar features just then hitting her. "Are you two brothers?"

"I got Dad's charm. Drew got his ..."

"Anal retentiveness?"

Cooper laughed. "You pick up quickly." He rubbed the back of his hand under his scruffy chin, looking hesitant to say more.

He didn't have to. She'd already gotten a good enough picture. Which meant she probably shouldn't make things worse by being all up in Drew's space. Especially if she was going to follow through on this consultant deal. "Liv, you sure I can't stay with you?"

"Only if I want an ear-bashing. I already told you. Mr. Fiazza will flip if he knows I snuck you into my flat last night. No one but waitstaff is allowed in those quarters."

"Then I'll get a room somewhere else."

"Not this time of year, you won't." Livy shared a knowing look with Cooper. "Every motel on the island will be booked solid through August."

Fantastic. Ti peered across the sleepy town, the fear of going home closing in.

"We're your best option." Cooper dragged a piece of wax over his surfboard. "I have a trailer on Drew's property. It's not huge, but you'll have your own space. And we'll be close enough if you need anything."

Ti studied him. Good-looking? Definitely. A charmer? Probably. But he carried a hint of the same integrity she saw under his brother's armor. "If you're positive you don't mind."

"Not at all." An assuring smile warmed over her.

"Smashing." Livy stretched with a yawn. "Because I've got to call it a night."

Ti peeked at her cell. "When did you start going to bed so early?"

"When I started having to get up at the crack of dawn to wait tables."

Though playful, her tone hid a note of sadness. Regret, maybe. They'd kept in touch after Ti left London when her best friend, Cassidy, needed help with a camp she inherited, but Livy never explained why she ended up leaving, too. How'd she go from a high-dollar model career overseas to barely scraping by as waitstaff in North Carolina?

Maybe Ti wasn't the only one with secrets to hide.

CHAPTER TWO

Intentions

Morning sunlight sifted through the bathroom window in Cooper's trailer. Ti scrubbed a washcloth over her body, desperate to erase lingering memories left from the dream that had awoken her. Saddest part was, she would've sworn she'd blotted out her nightmares for good.

Until two days ago.

Thirty seconds. Hearing the message on her home voice mail for thirty seconds was all it had taken. She hadn't stopped to think. She ran. What was new?

The haunting voice on the recording snaked to mind all over again.

Wings flapped right outside the window. Her shoulders hit her ears. Ti dropped the washcloth and squelched a gasp. Stupid seagulls.

Torn between fear and agitation, she got dressed and curled up on the bed Cooper had graciously offered her. The window A/C unit wheezed against the heat, memories against her chest. She jolted off the mattress and grabbed her cell instead.

A groggy version of her longtime best friend's voice answered on the fourth ring. "Ti, it's six a.m. Everything all right?"

Hard to blame Cass for asking. It would normally take a Mack truck slamming into Ti's bedroom wall to get her up this early.

"Yeah, sorry. I'm fine. Just having a hard time sleeping." Before Cass could probe, Ti added, "I'm calling for a favor."

"Of course. What's up?"

Ti traced her fingers along a shelf littered with books on the stock market. "Would you mind keeping an eye on my bank account? Just pop online every other day or so to make sure there are no big withdrawals." Cass was the only person on the planet Ti trusted with her finances.

"Um ... o-kay." Cass dragged out the word. "You want to fill me in on the reason why?"

Not really.

"What aren't you telling me?"

Ti thumbed through a book. "Nothing. I just need to go off the grid for a while. A mini vacation." Sort of.

The charged pause from Cass's end of the line stood in for the wary glare she would give Ti if they were in person. "Where are you?"

Ti peeked out the window toward the harbor. "It's probably better if you don't know."

"Ti—"

"I'm fine, Cass. You don't need to panic."

"Then maybe you shouldn't have led with 'I need to go off the grid for a while.' What's going on? Is Murray looking for you?"

Her ex from London? Yeah, right. It had taken him a whole week and five other chicks to get over her. No surprise Cass would assume Ti was running from one of her loser boyfriends. Story of her life. Probably better to let her think that. Ti didn't want to get into it, anyway.

"Just check the bank account, okay? And give that sweet hubby of yours a hug for me. I'll be in touch. Love you, babe."

"Ti, don't—"

She ended the call and powered down her cell. She didn't need a lecture. She needed deflection. Fast.

After slipping on a pair of heeled sandals, Ti wound her hair up into a loose side bun and cast a quick glance in the mirror. It would do for now.

Puddles outside stopped her in front of the door. It must've rained sometime last night. She traded her heels for her rain boots and left her cell on the nightstand.

Toting an easel and paint supplies, she bustled out of the trailer and into the one distraction that always promised escape. At least her past hadn't robbed her of that.

Yet.

Drew shook the sand from his hair while jogging up to his house with his surfboard. The bright yellow smart car parked at the curb garnered a chuckle out of him, just like it had on his way out to the beach at sunrise. Somehow, it was exactly what he would expect Ti to drive.

Not for the first time since leaving the party last night, a pang of mixed feelings lurched in his stomach. An ex-model, up and leaving her business without any forewarning? Something didn't smell right. True, maybe he came off a little too defensive at times. But if it meant protecting Maddie, so be it. Someone had to look out for things around here.

"Part of being a man is knowing where to draw the line around your family. The harder part is admitting when you've crossed it yourself."

Dad had been gone five years, and his words of wisdom still found a way to cut to the surface at the exact moment he would've said them if he were here.

Drew unwrapped a piece of saltwater taffy, bit off a chunk, and chewed on what he knew he had to do. As soon as Ti got up, he would apologize for his behavior … and then free her of her *consultant* duties. Being polite was one thing. Being naïve was another.

He set his board on the porch and brushed the rest of the sand off his feet before stepping inside. Their Jack Russell, Jasper, soared down the stairs as if guarding the White House. In less than thirty seconds, his expectant pant turned into a pout when Maddie didn't waltz in behind Drew.

He rubbed the dog's bristly brown and white head. "I know the feeling, buddy."

Jasper moped into the living room and lolled on the carpet with an exaggerated sigh. Drew stifled a laugh. He probably looked just as pitiful. The thought of Maddie without supervision from the few people he trusted with her health had kept him up half the night.

A snore rang from the couch. Cooper.

Drew's gaze zipped from his brother to Jasper, a grin following. "Want a treat?"

Jasper's ears perked up. Drew grabbed a Milk-Bone from the kitchen and dangled it above Cooper's snoring body. Jasper rocketed three feet across the room straight onto Drew's intended landing zone.

Cooper flung forward at ninety degrees and sent a drool-soaked throw pillow onto the carpet. A sleepy gaze zeroed in on Drew. "Real funny, hoss." Cooper chucked the pillow at his head.

Dodging it, Drew laughed. "That's what you get for drooling on my couch." He patted his leg, and Jasper flew to his side with the prize treat in his mouth. "Good boy."

Unimpressed, Cooper fell back against the cushions and dragged a palm down his face.

"Shouldn't you be shacked up in your trailer with that hippie girl?"

Cooper glared through his fingers. "I'm not like that."

"Right." Drew leaned against the doorway between the two rooms. "What? Ti's not your type?" Like he had to ask.

"She seems . . ." Cooper sat up and swayed his head. "Complicated."

"And yet, you have no problem letting a *complicated* stranger stay in your place?"

Cooper shrugged. "She's a friend of Livy's. That's all I need to know."

Ignoring the inkling of truth in that tiny detail, Drew headed into the kitchen. Tea was calling. No telling what he was in store for today.

Cooper stumbled toward the fridge while Drew got the teakettle going. "Was the sun still there today?"

Drew ignored his brother's sarcasm. Cooper didn't get why he needed the sunrise each morning, and Drew wasn't about to bother explaining it.

At the sink, he opened a Tupperware container and recoiled at the rank odor oozing out of it. He slammed the lid back on and fought a dry heave. "Jeez, Coop, did ya let something die in here?" Even Jasper wrinkled his nose while retreating into the living room with a whimper.

Cooper took a swig from a leftover cup of coffee in the fridge and flashed a sheepish look. "I might've left it in my trunk ... for a week."

"Yeah, well, you left your life of luxury a year ago. There's no maid service here." Drew thrust the container into Coop's stomach. "So, do us all a favor next time, and pitch the whole thing in the garbage, huh?"

The moan of the front door opening intercepted whatever witty remark was about to leave Cooper's mouth.

"Jasper?" Maddie tossed her backpack to the side and knelt to the tiles.

The dog reached her in seconds. With his front paws propped on her knees, he licked her face to his heart's content. That Milk-Bone had nothing on the excitement of seeing his best friend. Apparently, the feeling was mutual.

Maddie squealed, falling backward while Jasper slobbered her with a night's worth of overdue kisses. "Did you miss me, boy?"

As if that was even a question. Barking an energetic *Yes*, the dog zipped around the living room, stopped to lick her face again, and sprinted in another spastic circle.

Two red French braids bobbed to the rhythm of Maddie's laughter.

Drew's throat closed as it did every time he saw his girl come to life like that. How was she ten years old already?

He dug for a playful tone. "Hey, no love for your dad?"

One glance at the half smile that looked way too much like her mom's finished off his heart.

"I missed you, too," she said on her way into the kitchen.

Hands on his hips, he tilted his head. "How much?" She'd outgrown this bit years ago, but she graciously still humored the tradition he wasn't ready to let go of.

Maddie stretched her arms as wide as they'd go and flung a glance at both ends. "*This* much!"

Drew extended his arms, too. "Well, I missed you *this* much."

She hopped up to tap his hands. "You only win 'cause your arms are longer than mine."

Not long enough. He wrapped them around her and pretended he could fend off the day when she wouldn't need them anymore.

"Hey, Freckles. Ready for some fun in the sun with Uncle Coop?" Cooper ruffled her bangs.

Maddie's face lit up. "Always."

Cooper might've made bad choices regarding women, among other things, but Drew couldn't deny he knew how to take care of his niece.

The teakettle's whistle cleared a second knot in Drew's throat. What was his deal today? He dropped a green tea bag into his largest travel mug. After hesitating half a second, he plunked a second tea bag in and filled the cup to the brim. He needed all the help he could get.

A yellow sticky note with a message from Mr. Parsons at the bank glared up at him from the counter.

And there went any chance of de-stressing.

Drew set a bowl on top of it. He'd deal with that later. "Ready for some breakfast, Sea Monkey?"

A flash of color outside on the patio separating the house from Cooper's trailer caught Drew's eye. In bright pink rain boots, cutoff jeans, and a frilly cream sweater over a black tank top, Ti ferociously whipped a paintbrush across a canvas. *What in the world?*

"On second thought." Drew caught Maddie by the shoulders, steered her around, and funneled her to the stairs. "Why don't you run up and take a shower first?"

Once she disappeared up the steps, Drew cast a sidelong glance at Cooper. "Can you get her oatmeal ready?"

Cooper nodded as Drew eased out the back door.

Scratching his jaw, Drew trotted down the steps toward Ti and the sound of singing. He looked around. No speakers. No music. Just a melodic voice—the same one he'd heard last night when he'd first arrived at the party.

Did she always sing to herself? And who randomly started painting in someone's backyard first thing in the morning... in rain boots? Pink ones, no less.

Not good. Maddie would latch on to her in seconds. He knew his extroverted daughter. Knew how eager she was to have a female presence in her life. Which meant Drew had to guard who got too close.

One of Ti's back-and-forth glances between the sky and the canvas intersected with him. Sunlight glimmered over a pair of silver studs in her ears. "Did the seagulls wake you up, too?"

He blinked. "Uh, no. I'm always up early."

"Right." She swiped a rogue strand of hair caught in her lashes and curved it behind her ear. "The whole responsibility thing."

"Yeah, about that." Drew stuffed his hands in his shorts' pockets. "Listen, I'm sorry for being curt last night. I appreciate your offer to help out around here. And I trust Livy, but—"

"You don't trust me." It wasn't a question.

He gave a small shrug.

Her smile faltered only for a moment. Going back to her painting, Ti dabbed the brush against a small palette. "I promise I don't sniff the paints."

It shouldn't be this hot out at seven in the morning. Ignoring logic, heat scaled his cheeks. "I didn't mean to imply—"

"No, I'm pretty sure you did."

Okay, this wasn't exactly going as planned. Drew tugged his ear. "My daughter..."

"I get it." Ti kept her attention on the canvas. "You think I fit the stereotype. A reckless model-slash-artist who's into the party scene." With a flick of her lashes, her gaze met his. "You might be wrong, you know."

"Or I might not be."

"Only one way to find out." Another flutter returned her focus to the painting. And once again, Drew simply stared.

Not solely at her beauty, but at her boldness and drive. Her intense connection with the painting. The way she swayed in unison with the brush as if it were an extension of something inside her, needing to come out.

His chest constricted. But instead of following the voice in his head, shouting for him to walk away, he angled around the easel. One look at the canvas caught him in the gut.

The sunrise, captured from the vantage point of his own backyard. No embellishments. No abstract interpretations. Just unfiltered wonder inspired by the one thing that centered him day after day. He hadn't been moved by art like this since …

Longings he'd banned himself from ever feeling again clawed in from two directions.

Swallowing was enough of a feat. Speaking was off the table. Complicated? Cooper didn't know the half of it.

Drew backed up and turned toward the house.

"Where you going?" Ti called.

"To the shop." At the stairs, he peered over his shoulder. "You coming?"

Her smile rivaled the sun. "You won't regret this."

Drew plodded up the steps without looking back. *Already do.*

Inside, Cooper handed him his travel mug and a smirk.

"What?"

Cooper splayed his hands out. "You tell me, hoss."

Drew shouldered past him. "Why don't you just worry about keeping an eye on Maddie today."

"I'm not the one who needs to worry about what his eyes are on."

"You're barking up the wrong tree."

"Oh, yeah? Then tell me what you're thinking about right now."

"Other than how to end this conversation?" Drew trekked toward the staircase.

"Fine, but hey," Cooper called. "You're coming to the bonfire tonight, right? Nine o'clock on the north end."

"Do you have a party every night?"

"Only when I can help it." Cooper lounged against the counter, a grin sliding around his coffee cup. "You should bring a date. It'll be good for you."

More like the death of him. This whole thing was a very bad idea.

CHAPTER THREE

Puzzle

Painting earlier had been exactly what Ti needed to clear her head. As long as she stayed busy with a project the rest of the day, she'd be fine.

She traded her rain boots for her black heeled sandals and shorts for a pair of dark-washed capris. Surely, even Mr. Uptight had a relaxed dress code for work. He lived on an island, for Pete's sake.

Sure enough, when Ti rounded the corner of the house, Drew stood by the curb in khaki cargo shorts and a green button-down that should have been outlawed for matching his eyes so well. Too bad those beauties came with a bite.

She was used to gruff exteriors. Used to the layers people kept themselves buried underneath. But something told her the hurts Drew guarded ran deeper than most.

Still trying to make sense of him, Ti studied her temporary business comrade. Tall and defined, he had a body any other guy would strut. Yet he didn't seem interested in pursuing or being pursued. A family man with a past. A business owner with a story. One thing was for sure. Drew Anderson was more than intriguing.

The same patch of messy hair drew her focus again as confident strides led her toward him. Maybe it was more than bed head.

His gaze lingered over her when she approached.

Ti circled a finger along one of the hoop earrings she'd swapped with her studs. "I can give you some tips if you want."

Drew blinked. "What?"

"Style. You're checking out my outfit like you're looking for pointers." She waved a hand over his clothes. "I assume this combination was a happy accident."

Really? Not even a smile? Jeez, this guy was stiff.

Head down, Drew fiddled with a travel mug. "No, you, um ... aren't wearing glasses today. It threw me for a minute."

All right, he might not know how to loosen up, but that adorable flustered look made up for it tenfold. "They were just a cute accessory."

His mouth pulled sideways. "Of course they were. As is the camera, I assume." He nodded at the bag slung over her shoulder.

"Nope. That's for business. I like to study my projects before diving in. You'd be surprised how much more you see from behind a lens. Things you'd miss otherwise."

A swarm of thoughts colored those gorgeous eyes of his. What she'd give to hear just one of them when he looked at her like that.

Breaking contact, he lifted the lid from his travel mug and blew inside it.

Now he was speaking her language. "I'll tell you what. If you give me that cup of coffee, I won't give you a hard time about the cowlick you've got going on."

Drew patted his hair while following her fixation on his mug. "Sorry, I don't drink *cauffee.*" He exaggerated her New York City accent. "How about green tea instead?"

Um, how about no. Ti peeked in his mug and scrunched her nose. "Thanks, but I actually already choked down a handful of grass on my way over, so I'm all set for the day. And you really don't want to start joking on accents, buddy."

He cocked his chin. "I don't have an accent."

"You kidding me?" Ti drew herself up to his stature, cupped a hand over her eyes, and peered out to the water. "It looks like *hoi toid's* coming in." She couldn't even get out his version of "high tide" without cracking up. "I mean, seriously, what is that? Some kind of Irish-English brogue?"

This time, real laughter tumbled out. "I don't sound like that."

Ti perched her hands on her hips. "First of all, congratulations on laughing. It sounds good on you. And—"

"Hey, Anderson." An older guy with a red bandana tied around his head and a scraggly beard down to his chest hobbled across the street like a pirate who'd shipwrecked at Woodstock. "You ready to sell your boat to me today? A hundred dollars more on the table. C'mon, kid. Help an old man live out his glory days before it's too late."

Ti spun toward Drew. A boat owner, too. Impressive.

He shook his head. "The skiff's not for sale, Lenny. Same as the last five hundred days you've asked me."

A wiry laugh echoed across the street. "I'll wear you down someday, kid."

Drew waved him off and looked at Ti. "Accent or not, at least I don't sound like an old haggler."

"Hey, as long as you tell me there's an actual coffee joint somewhere on this island, you can talk however you want."

Nodding in concession, Drew motioned behind her. "Off Sunset Drive."

Hallelujah, somebody had mercy on her. She started for the street. "I'll meet you at the shop."

"You don't even know where it is."

Ti turned but kept shuffling backward. "I'll find my way."

Drew stared at her like a puzzle he couldn't figure out. "You swipe a tourist map when you first got here?"

She returned his grin. "The village is, what, a whole four miles long? If I can manage navigating Manhattan, I think I'll be fine tackling this small town."

His face dropped. He screwed the lid back on his mug, his jaw just as tight.

Jeez, this guy's mood swings were giving her whiplash.

Ti adjusted her camera bag. "Sorry, am I mis—?"

An unknown ringtone chimed from her pocket. She'd almost left her cell in the trailer. Probably should have. The nameless number on the screen gripped her muscles. Without warning, the raspy voice from her messages replayed in her head. If he'd gotten a hold of her cell number ...

Shoving the phone back down, Ti ignored the call and the thought. She couldn't go there right now. Especially with Drew's shrewd gaze boring through her walls. The last thing she needed was Andy Hardy prying into her broken past.

Ti hooked a thumb over her shoulder and backed up. "I'm gonna go grab that coffee." And pull herself together before Drew figured out how to pull her apart. They all had layers, but hers weren't the kind he'd want to uncover. Not if he knew what lay beneath.

Twenty minutes later, and one iced coffee down, Ti strolled past another lodge with a no vacancy notice in the window and a store with a rusted tin sign that read, *Open from 9:00 a.m. to 8:00 p.m., or so.* Or so? Classic island lifestyle, right there. Shame it hadn't rubbed off on Drew.

A right-hand turn led her along a street with a series of picket-fenced yards landscaped with old skiffs, net floats, and driftwood. A far cry from Queens, but the village couldn't get any more charming. Well, other than the washed-out shop in front of her, screaming for a makeover.

Ti shielded her eyes from the sun to read the overhead sign. *Anderson's Soundside Treasures.* The woman in the café was right. If Ti looked for the building with faded shutters and zero curb appeal, she'd find Drew's shop.

Chuckling, she shot a handful of takes with her camera and scrolled through the drab images. And Drew didn't need her help? Please. *Wait till I'm done with this place.*

She withdrew her cell right as Drew strode through the door.

"Thought you were getting coffee."

"Already finished it."

"And found the place without any problems." He tipped his head as if praising an accomplishment.

"Well, I managed to dodge the nonstop stream of beach cruisers and golf carts just fine. The brazen crab scurrying across the road, on the other hand, just about got me. Close call."

Winking, she opened the voice recorder app on her phone and surveyed the property. "Storefront makeover. I'm thinking Grecian Isle colored shutters, decorative walkway, some kind of centerpiece." She tapped the phone to her chin and studied a picture on her camera. "Ooh, a swi—"

"Sorry, what are you doing?"

She gave him a no-brainer look. "Taking notes. I told you, I study my projects before tackling them."

Drew kneaded his shoulder blade like he was wrestling over what to say. "You really don't have to go to a lot of trouble."

Was he still worried about paying her? Ti set a reassuring hand to his sleeve. "I want to."

His gaze gravitated to her fingers above his taut arm.

Can someone say tense? She brought her cell to her mouth while trying not to laugh at his awkward expression. "Owner's uncomfortable with personal touch."

That jaw-half-opened expression got her every time.

She raised a shoulder. "I take notes on my clients, too. Helps me know how to cater art pieces better."

Drew's voice caught up three blinks later. "I'm not a project."

"You're tied to one." Ti jutted her chin at the pitiful looking storefront. "Trust me. You *both* could use some TLC."

Drew followed her to the porch. "You haven't even been inside yet."

"Doesn't matter what's inside if you can't draw anyone in to check it out. As if living on Back Street isn't bad enough, you're tucked away at the very end. Believe me, the outside's your first problem to deal with."

He stopped her at the door with another whirlwind of thoughts streaming past his eyes.

Unable to help herself, she raised her cell again. "Owner likes to brood."

Drew chased her through the door on the heels of her laughter. He bumped into her three steps inside, where one look around the store jerked her to a halt.

She lowered the phone. "Uh, you got any legal pads instead?"

"What's wrong with the inside?"

"You mean, besides feeling like someone just dumped me into a shipment from China?"

He grabbed a piece of taffy from a container by the register. "There's nothing wrong with my inventory."

"Yeah, if you want to offer the same dollar-store trinkets every other beach souvenir shop in America offers." She lifted a shell nightlight and gawked at the overpriced tag. No wonder he was struggling.

His jaw twitched. "Not artsy enough for you?"

"You've really got something against art, don't you?"

Evading, Drew rearranged a row of starfish on a shelf until they fit perfectly.

She had to admit, his OCD quirks were kind of cute.

A horsefly that must've snuck in with them buzzed past her ear.

Ti sidled alongside Drew and picked up a shot glass from the next shelf down. "You know, lemon eucalyptus oil is as effective as DEET. You should put a diffuser in here. Not that your cologne doesn't smell amazing, but that's not going to relax anyone. Especially the ladies coming through here. Believe me. By the way, you mind if I buy you some new shirts? We should go to J. Crew tonight. Tell me you know what J. Crew is."

He peered up from the display. "How do those thoughts even coincide?"

"You'd have to be in my head to understand."

"I'm not that brave." Drew returned the glass she was fidgeting with and strode for the register.

"At least get a diffuser."

"Hard pass."

"Oh, c'mon. It's a great way to unwind." She flitted into his path. "You're telling me this shop doesn't stress you out?"

"At this exact moment?" he deadpanned. "You have no idea."

She swept a glance over his lumberjack size and brusque exterior. "I gotta tell ya, Drew. The Luke Danes vibe really works for you. We should pick up some flannel shirts tonight. Ooh, and a backward hat would totally hide that cowlick of yours."

He brushed her hand away from his hair. "What is it with you and *Gilmore Girls?*"

"Ha. I knew you'd be into chick shows. The hot yoga thing tipped me off."

"I'm *not* into chick shows. And I'm not shopping for flannels tonight. Or ever."

"All right, forget the flannels." Ti caught his hand as he turned. "But I just want you to know, where you go …" She flung her arms in the air and belted out the *Gilmore Girls* theme song in all its cheesy glory.

With the perfect Luke-grunt, Drew trucked toward the counter. He made this way too fun.

"Aw, c'mon. Where you going?"

"I have real work to do."

"Tell me about it," she mumbled. Her laughter petered out a little more with each glimpse around the shop. All joking aside, the place truly needed a major overhaul. And a diffuser.

One battle at a time.

Ti set her camera on the counter and meandered around the room, recording voice notes while passing displays. Working hard wasn't his problem. Drew exuded drive and commitment. Getting him to see how to work as an artist was the real challenge.

But maybe that was exactly what Ti needed.

A twinge of anticipation pulled her across the floor with ideas swirling.

On the wall behind the register, a rickety framed photo of a man handing Drew a set of keys stood out among the other pictures. Drew must've inherited the family business. That would explain why he didn't want to sell it. Was his dad still around?

Ti spun toward the sound of a bell chiming over the door and smacked into a cloud of old lady perfume.

A woman with gray roots chasing her blonde highlights strolled in, wearing lipstick to match the bright pink, oversized flowers on her blouse. "Morning, Drew."

"How you doing, Mrs. Cunningham?"

The woman fluttered a hand at him like she had an imaginary handkerchief in it. "I'd be better if I were out on the water today."

"Roger still hasn't fixed your boat?"

An airy sigh punctuated her eye roll. "He's off on one of his business trips again." She hefted a giant purse onto the counter and leaned forward on both forearms till wrinkly cleavage ran into a fuchsia rose stretched across the middle of her shirt. "I'll take you out for a spin if you come work on it today. Roger won't be back till tomorrow."

And people said *Ti* was bold. Lipstick Mama was working it.

Drew's face turned a hundred shades of red. "Thanks for the offer, Mrs. Cunningham, but I, um, have, uh ..."

"Work to do," Ti peeped up from around the corner.

Mrs. Cunningham's gaze danced over her like a strobe light. "I see." Dismissing Ti, she fanned through a rack of stationery beside the register. "I thought you might need a little ... distraction. With all that's been going on, I can't imagine dealing with the anniversary of your dad's death, too." She set one sun-aged hand over his and the other on her chest. "My heart goes out to you."

Drew freed his caged fingers. "I'm managing just fine."

"And how about Maddie? That poor girl." Mrs. Cunningham shook her head. "My goodness, she gave us all quite a scare. I don't believe my nerves ever recovered from the first hospital call."

Drew stretched his neck while keeping his attention on the computer screen. "Maddie has a lot of fight in her."

"Growing up without a mother, of course she does. And to think, Ann—"

Drew shot up. The teetering stool behind him cut her off, no words necessary.

Without a mother? Drew lost his wife? It made total sense now why he was so guarded and protective. Ti would be too if she had to raise a child as a single parent.

The meddlesome woman gently set a lighthouse notepad on the counter and slid a five-dollar bill beside it. "Well, now, you be sure to let me know if there's anything I can do for you, you hear?"

He rang up her stationery and managed a tight-lipped, "Yes, ma'am."

As soon as she left, Drew returned to sorting through a stack of bills.

Lipstick Mama wasn't entirely off base about Drew needing help keeping his mind off things. Ti just had to figure out how to break through his closed-off shell. Sympathy was out of the question. Too prideful. She ambled over and picked at a chip on the counter. "That was a pity sale, in case you missed it. She didn't really need that notepad."

Drew lounged back. "Is mind reading on the résumé you pitch to all your clients?"

"It's easy to read people if you're willing to look past the surface." At least, it was easy to read *most* people. He needed to give her something to work with if she was going to help him.

When he didn't bite, she twirled away from the counter toward a winding staircase. "What's up—?"

"That's off limits." Already beside her, Drew blocked the stairs.

"Wow, look at you. Secret chamber?" She raised a wry brow at his chiseled expression.

"Next topic."

"Touchy." Holding his gaze, Ti lifted her cell between them. "Owner has a mysterious side."

His jaw rippled. He hedged her backward with a sharp glance at her phone. "I'm not the one hiding something."

She almost snorted. "You serious?" Her exaggerated peek up the stairs tacked on a dozen exclamation points, but his stern eyes kept inching her away. She crossed her arms and peered back at the photo behind the register. "Fine. Then tell me about the shop. Did your dad pass it down to you?"

Drew stopped, face crinkling.

She'd take that as a yes. "If you can cook, you could always turn it into a diner."

His eyes reached for the ceiling. "Does it ever end?"

"Wit happens to be the greatest skill on my résumé. Right after mind reading, of course."

He wheezed. "I walk right into these things, don't I?"

"And never see them coming." Ti nudged him with her elbow. "For real, though, what's the story with the shop?"

"No story."

"There's *always* a story."

A tangle of emotions contorted his expression. "Only if you're always chasing one."

"How else are you going to find adventure?"

"What if all you find is disappointment?" The torment in his eyes pierced through again.

"That's part of the risk."

He prodded her farther back. "Maybe I'm fine with the way things are."

"And maybe you're lying."

If her bluntness tripped him up, it wasn't long enough to stop him from advancing. "Do you always say what you think?"

"I just call it like I see it." Something behind her pressed into her back.

Drew studied her, his gaze more powerful than any touch. He had a way about him—this intense-yet-broken hero pull she'd have to be dead not to find attractive.

Ti searched for her breath. "You do that a lot, you know. Look at me like a math problem you can't figure out."

"Sorry. You're not like most vacationers who come through here."

"Is that a good or bad thing?"

"I'm still deciding."

This close, she wasn't sure herself. She was used to guys' fast words and even faster hands. But Mr. Enigma baffled her. All she knew was those green eyes needed reins before she lost the ones keeping her from running her fingers through his tousled cowlick right now.

Thirty seconds of charged silence felt more like thirty minutes.

He finally released her gaze. "The second story's off limits. As are all personal discussions. We're here to work."

A pent-up exhale leveled out Ti's shoulders. "We *are* working."

"No." He backed up. "I'm trying to work. You're ..." He waved at her, his face crestfallen with something she couldn't read. "Distracting."

Of all the adjectives he could have used, of all the ones she'd heard from other guys, the most benign one shouldn't have felt like a sucker punch.

Buffering the sting, Ti adjusted the strap on her heel and straightened. The emotions from the week were obviously throwing her off her game, but Drew wasn't the only one who could be hard-nosed. He wanted to work? Fine. He'd just better hope he was ready for what he asked for.

CHAPTER FOUR

Undertones

Another restless night put a serious strain on Ti's makeup the next morning. Any more nightmares, and she wouldn't be able to camouflage the bags under her eyes.

Coffee in hand, she strode up the walkway to the shop. At least she'd put the sleepless hours to work forming a plan. Drew's brusque exterior wasn't going to back her down.

She skipped the first two stairs up to the porch. The Don Johnson lookalike from the party came through the shop's front door at the same time Ti went to open it.

What was he doing here? Taunting Drew again? The guy didn't know when to quit. Or maybe he just didn't know who he was up against.

He slid his sunglasses down his nose without moving to let her pass. "Miss New York, right? From the other night." His gaze careened from her tan trilby hat down to her matching ankle boots and skimmed back up her sundress. "I wouldn't waste your time on a business about to fold. But if you're looking for more action while you're here, I can give you my number."

She'd rather get her stomach pumped. Yet instead of gagging in his face, she played along. "Do you have a card?"

His smug grin was almost as disturbing as the curls poking out of his T-shirt. "Of course."

"Awesome." She tapped his shoulder with the business card he gave her. "I was looking for something to burn off the heebie-jeebies you give me. This will be the *perfect* fire starter. I owe ya one." *Creep.* Ti shouldered past him into the shop without waiting to see her response sink in.

A minute later, squealing tires echoed a revved engine. Talk about overcompensating. Little did V-neck Boy know, his instigation tactics only fueled her determination to see him lose.

She marched up to Drew, seated behind the counter, and handed him the list of ideas she'd scribbled down last night, along with a budget.

Drew sized up the sheet. "That's a decent chunk of money."

"The return on investment will be worth it. You have to spend money to make money. Business 101."

He stared at her so intently, the papers in his hand mindlessly slipped to the desk.

Ti mimicked his curious pose. "Seriously, if you keep looking at me like that, I'm gonna paint monkey ears on you and call you George."

Scratching his clean-shaven jaw, Drew laughed softly. "Sorry. You have a way of catching me off guard."

"So I've noticed." She set her coffee down, ran her hands along her arms, and avoided his gaze. "I know you think I'm just a flighty model, but—"

"That's not what I think."

A residual pang left from his comment yesterday crept back to the forefront. She tilted her head. "Just distracting?"

A slow-building flush colored his neck. "I didn't mean that the way it sounded."

"We've been down this road already." He'd made his impressions of her loud and clear. No need to keep backpedaling. "We're here to work, right? So, how about we agree to shoot it straight with each other? I'm not as fragile as I look." At least, not that she'd show him.

Drew lowered his chin. "It's not—"

The overhead bell rang, followed by an adorable voice chattering away. Cooper and a girl probably in her early twenties entered the shop, bookending an elementary-aged girl between them.

A small cluster of freckles on the girl's nose complemented the strawberry blonde braids swaying as she relayed a grand-gestured story. "... And Winnie said Fletcher told her he saw Mrs. Godfrey's ghost at the Island Inn, but I told her not to believe *anything* boys say." Her hazel eyes found Drew across the room and turned ten times brighter.

Drew scooped her up. "Hey, Sea Monkey." With a kiss to the cheek, he set her back down. "I thought you were going paddle boarding with Uncle Coop today."

"We are." Cooper strolled up to the counter and picked through a container of mints. "But we ran into Chloe on the way, and Maddie couldn't pass up giving her a play-by-play of her sleepover."

"It's not something *boys* would understand." The girl in skinny jeans and dark-rimmed glasses winked at Maddie on her way behind the counter to the register. She must be one of Drew's employees. What a trooper. She got major points for that alone.

Cooper adjusted his Tar Heels hat, leaned back on both elbows, and smiled at Ti. "So, what's the prognosis?"

The two girls must not've noticed Ti when they first walked in. Now, someone might as well have plastered a spotlight on her. She slipped off her hat and ruffled her bangs. "I just gave Drew a list of things we should start with, actually."

Hipster Girl cleared her throat in an obvious nudge for Drew to make introductions.

He looked between them. "Oh, sorry. Chloe, this is Ti Russo. She's going to be helping out around here for *a while.*" No one else appeared to notice his inflection, but it gave Ti enough of a laugh to relax her shoulders.

Chloe turned from Ti to the patron-less store. In a matter of seconds, her expression transitioned from confusion over what in the world Ti could do to occupy her time to relief over seeing someone with a clue finally stepping in.

Ti liked this chick already.

And little Miss Sunshine in the glittery flip-flops? Forget it. A girl after her own heart.

Without hesitation, she ambled right up to Ti and extended a hand. "Hi, I'm Maddie." She twisted a sparkly turtle stud in her ear, scoped out Ti's outfit, and burst into rays of smiles. "I like your earrings. And those boots are *so* sweet."

Ti made it a point never to give in to the love-at-first-sight junk Hollywood fed hopeless romantics. But that rule obviously didn't apply to Maddie. This cutie had Ti hooked and sunk.

Drew rubbed Maddie's head. "All right, sweetie. Let's give Ti some space. She has …" He sent a loaded grin her way. "*Work* to be doing."

Yeah, starting with tucking her heart back down where it belonged.

Drew kissed Maddie's cheek and shot his brother a keep-my-girl-safe look of warning.

Nodding, Cooper slung an arm around Maddie's shoulders. "Ready to find some turtles?"

The silent squeals lighting Maddie's face tumbled out. She closed one eye in an impressive pirate expression and pointed ahead. "To the sea!"

Cooper jogged out with her while Ti stood there, caught up in laughter of her own.

Chloe pinned an *Anderson's Soundside Treasures* name tag on her shirt and flicked her chin at Drew. "Seen much traffic from the festival yet?"

And just like that, the lingering afterglow of Maddie's presence vanished. Drew adjusted his shirt collar. "Not as much as we need."

Ti slipped her hat back on. "Considering ten whopping people came through your doors yesterday and none yet this morning, I'd say that's a slight understatement."

Drew sent her a thanks-for-pointing-that-out glare, but Ti didn't let it faze her. She motioned to Chloe. "Are you on shift until close?"

"Aside from a break for lunch, yep."

"Perfect." Ti grabbed Drew's hand. "We'll see you later, then."

He dragged his feet. "Where are we going?"

"To save your shop."

The intense reactions Ti finagled out of Drew were messing with his head. How he'd let her talk him into taking a day trip to Cedar Island, he still had no idea. Then again, after the way she turned shopping into an extreme sport, he shouldn't be surprised at what she could accomplish.

Crammed in her tiny smart car, Drew clicked the on button to his cell out of habit. Still dead. Obviously, wishful thinking hadn't magically charged it. He tossed it in the cup holder and unwrapped a piece of taffy while peering at the clock. They hadn't slowed down since the ferry ride hours ago. Surely, she was almost done.

"Worried about turning into a pumpkin?"

He looked in her direction. "What?"

"The clock." Ti motioned to the car stereo. "You've checked it, like, every five minutes over the last hour."

Minutes he was losing. "The Ocrafolk Festival's going on right now. Meaning, I'm missing prime time for business. I should be at the shop, not running around on a scavenger hunt for paint and decorations."

"There's no point in starting backward," she said in a Zen-like tone.

He tore off a bite of taffy to keep from spouting off a few proverbs of his own.

"Relax. Chloe can handle it. And it doesn't matter how many people flock to the island. If you aren't drawing them into the shop, you can't sell them anything, remember?" Ti patted his knee. "Trust me."

She swerved around a pickup, tires screeching. Drew almost choked on the taffy. "It might be easier to trust you, if you knew how to drive. This isn't the BQE."

Her contagious laughter filled the car. "Just 'cause everyone around here moves as slow as midtown traffic doesn't mean I drive too fast. And what do you know about the BQE? You've been to the city?"

"Once." He stared out the window at the passing shoreline. "A long time ago." Cutting off that conversation, he grabbed a bag of trail mix and swallowed the pang of memories better left forgotten.

If Ti caught the undertone in his comment, she didn't press it. Instead, she tapped the steering wheel to the beat of whatever song she was singing. Sunlight streamed onto her long blonde braid draped over one shoulder.

Drew fluttered a glance away from her. "You do that a lot, you know."

"What?"

"Sing to yourself."

She looked him up and down. "Better than listening to you crunch on those nuts."

She didn't like hearing people chew, huh? He leaned toward her and exaggerated the munching sounds. "I'm sorry. What was that?"

Ti took one of the nuts and flicked it at his face. "Careful, *Mr. Anderson*," she said like Agent Smith from *The Matrix*.

"You've been dying to say that, haven't you?"

"Since I first found out your last name." Her amusement overran her cheeks. "We're talking some serious self-control holding it in until now."

Fighting a grin, Drew shook his head and sat back in his seat. "Congratulations."

"Why, thank you. I think this victory warrants an iced coffee." She zipped up to the curb beside a café, killed the engine, and wagged her brows. "You know you want one. I mean, I know caffeine isn't as big of a rush as that red pill, but ignorance has its perks."

He rolled his eyes. "If I go in, will you stop railing *Matrix* jokes?"

"Maybe ... if you actually order a coffee."

What was the point of arguing with her? "At least let me charge my phone first."

Halfway out the door, she shrugged. "I left my charger in my bag back at the trailer."

Of course she did. "Can I borrow your phone, then?" Not being able to check on Maddie was killing him.

"Sure. *After—*"

"Coffee. Got it." With an exhale, he pushed up from the seat. The sooner she got her caffeine fix, the sooner they could touch base with home and hit the road.

Inside, a crowd mingled in front of a live band in the corner.

"Indie music. Sweet." Ti rolled onto the balls of her feet. "And they even cleared a spot for dancing." A look of mischief raced from the corners of her mouth straight to her eyes.

Whatever she was thinking, it couldn't be good. Drew prudently backed away, but Ti caught his shirt. "You know what you need?"

"To get the heck out of here?"

"Practice." Ti plucked her trilby hat off and fit it on his head instead. "You want to show up that Marcus guy and save your shop? You gotta learn to let your hair down, take risks, be spontaneous." She gestured toward the dance floor with her eyes.

That confirmed it. The girl was officially certifiable.

Not backing down, she nudged him in the shoulder. "C'mon, don't be such a stiff. Leave your walker outside, and live it up a little, Gramps."

Drew loosened his tense arms. "I'm not wound as tightly as you think I am."

"You kidding? Even Oprah couldn't get you to open up."

His jaw twitched. "I can have fun."

Ti raised a sassy brow, stole her hat back, and drifted onto the floor. "Prove it."

He started to move but stopped. A backward glance at the fading sunlight outside pulled him in one direction while Ti's unrelenting drive lured him in the other. Releasing a gruff breath, he weaved through the crowd. This woman was going to be the end of him.

He wedged alongside her and cupped a hand to her waist. She dipped her chin. And in a matter of seconds, the dance floor turned into a checkerboard. Each move upped the need to win.

Ti twirled out of reach, drawing him farther onto the floor. He wasn't about to let her slip away. He slid a hand to her back and drew her close.

Her lips grazed his ear. "Live in the moment," she whispered.

The same maxim Dad had taught him stirred from a place inside he'd forgotten existed. Could he go back to living like that?

"You don't even know how to have fun anymore. All you do is smother." The razors in Annie's words clawed down his spine. He dug for another piece of taffy in his pocket, needing a tension releaser.

Ti splayed her arms out, as though asking for his choice.

He took her in under the lights. Could she have known?

With his shoulders squared, he released the wrapper and reached for her hand instead. *Live in the moment, Anderson.*

The band played another song. And another. Dancers came and went, but Drew didn't let Ti go. Every other pressing thought dissolved into an atmosphere brimming with her free-spirited energy.

Time lapsed. In sync with hers, his body came to life. His senses responded—to the music, the adrenaline. He felt every beat, every sway. The lights, the vibrations, the smell of her skin mixed with his. It all pulsed through him until Ti finally planted the hat back on his head as if crowning a victor.

"See, I knew you had that kind of spark inside you. Just took a little uncovering." She winked. "Marcus won't know what's coming for him."

The lights' soft glow clung to her glistening skin. Drew swallowed, searching for his voice. This complicated distraction of a woman knew what he needed more than he did. This excursion wasn't even about paint supplies, was it? She'd dragged him out of his world of stress. Made him forget what he'd lost in the past and what he risked losing now. He'd even forgotten about . . .

A sinking feeling caved into his gut.

The ferry.

CHAPTER FIVE

Assumptions

At the dock, Drew returned to the car and handed Ti her cell. "Chloe isn't answering, but I got through to Cooper."

"Everything good?"

"Aside from missing the last ferry of the night, and every hotel being booked?" He craned his head back. "Yeah, super."

Ti reached over to knead his shoulder. "Just think of it as another helping hand teaching you how to be adventurous."

More like a *strangling* hand. He didn't need to be adventurous. He needed to be home, taking care of his shop and his daughter. Why didn't she get that?

Drew glared at the traitorous clock. "You know that thing's off, right?"

Ti stopped massaging and shrugged. "It'll be right eventually. Next time daylight savings comes around."

"You never reset your clock?"

Another half shrug. "Why bother?"

Drew stared at the headliner. "I knew we should've taken my Jeep."

"Why, 'cause you have an I-missed-the-ferry emergency bag in the back? You do, don't you?"

"No. 'Cause I have a *functional* clock in it."

"Now, how'll you ever learn to roll with life that way?"

He shook his head. The girl was hopeless.

The creak of her door opening turned his head. "Where you going?"

Already outside, Ti ducked back in. "We're stranded at the beach. Might as well enjoy it. Unless you're up for hijacking a ferry." With a feisty smile to match her laid-back logic, she grabbed a blanket from behind her seat and moseyed toward the shore.

Drew stayed put. For all of five seconds. Groaning, he climbed out and met her at the sand. Truthfully, he'd rather be out here than in a hotel, anyway.

He glanced at her heels and smiled in spite of himself. "You might want to buy different shoes to wear around here."

Ti lifted one ankle boot. "These are Kenneth Coles."

Drew blinked at her.

"Kenneth Cole. Nothing, really? Let me see those jeans. Do they have an elastic waistband?"

He held her hands back by the wrists and egged her on with the same phrase she'd used on him the night of the party. "You could guess."

"Wow, Mr. I-have-a-sense-of-humor-after-all. Who knew?"

Keeping a straight face, Drew peered at the water.

She nudged him. "Oh, c'mon. You want to laugh. Admit it."

He pressed his tongue to his cheek to hold it in. Useless. The girl had a serious knack for driving him crazy.

Sobering, Ti rubbed his upper arm. "I'm sorry about the ferry, Drew. Honestly. I know being home is important to you. But can we try to make the best of it?"

Apparently, a half nod sufficed, because she was hauling him down the beach before he got a word out. Though once in front of the indigo sky and peaceful waves, his muscles relaxed on their own. He didn't even notice she'd sat on the blanket until a tug on the bottom of his jeans invited him to join her.

She leaned into his bicep. "So, what's your thing with the ocean?"

He raised a brow.

"I've seen the way you look out at the water."

She had a way of seeing more than she should.

Drew dragged his fingers in the sand alongside the blanket and dodged her blue eyes. If he wasn't careful, he could get lost in them just as easily as in the ocean. "There's no *thing*."

"Right." She stretched back on her hands and crossed her ankles. "Well, whatever romance you've got going on with it, more power to you. I got caught in the undertow once as a kid. Haven't been able to go in the ocean since."

"You don't strike me as the type to get scared."

"You make a lot of assumptions." She nudged him with her foot. "The ocean doesn't terrify you?"

"Should it?"

"It can do a lot of damage."

"All the more reason to challenge it," he barely said aloud. He glanced over to streaks of intuition and something more coloring her eyes.

Wind skimming off the waves blew strands loose from her braid in an image of vulnerability Drew hadn't seen from her until right then.

Not that she'd let it linger. Ti sat up and let her eyes roam over him. "You know what you need?"

Drew tossed his head back. *What now?*

"A salt rock lamp. It'll calm the tension right out of you." She curled her bottom lip under her teeth while scanning behind them to the street. "Wonder if they sell them around here."

"A rock what?" He raised a palm. "On second thought, I don't even want to know."

The roar of a wave breaking against the shore blended into her laughter. Between the melodic sound and the moonlight glistening across her legs, Drew wrestled to look away. He'd lived in Ocracoke all his life. Seen enough vacationers come and go to brush arms with his share of beauty. Still, something about this girl drew him up short. Made him want to pull her close, give pieces of himself away he couldn't afford to.

Dousing the impulse, he faced the wind head-on. With any luck, it would knock his body temperature back down where it belonged.

Apparently, she wasn't having the same reaction. She shivered beside him, stretched the hem of her dress over her legs, and hugged her arms to her chest.

After gripping his knees for a solid minute, Drew yielded to his southern roots. He undid the first few buttons on his shirt, tugged it over his head, and straightened out the white T-shirt underneath. “Here.”

With an expression saying everything she didn’t have to, Ti slipped on his shirt and lay back on the blanket. “Thanks. If I could fall asleep, I’d crash right now.”

“Too cold?”

She gazed at the stars and unrolled his shirtsleeves. “I haven’t been sleeping well lately.”

Drew didn’t know much about her, but restless nights he understood. Deflecting, he slapped on a playful tone. “I hear cutting yourself off after three cups of coffee a day helps with that.”

“Hey, coffee’s a super antioxidant, thank you very much. It protects against all kinds of diseases.” Her mouth slanted. “I read it even decreases the risk of depression. Just sayin’. You might try it.”

“I’m not depressed.”

“Okay, Eeyore.” She propped up on her elbow and stared him down in a silent playoff.

Drew’s eyes reached for the midnight blue sky as he reclined beside her.

“There ya go. See, relaxing isn’t so bad, right?”

“If that’s what you call this,” he mumbled.

“You know what? Forget sleep. We should talk instead.”

“Do you ever not talk?”

Dumb question.

"It'll be fun. Think of it as investing into your shop. I have to get to know the owner, remember?"

Somebody rescue me.

"Oh, stop. I'll make it easy. Tell me five random things about you. I already told you I'm afraid of the ocean. What's *your* greatest fear?"

Drew rolled in the opposite direction, but she lugged him back around. He wasn't getting out of this, was he? He pinched the bridge of his nose. "There's nothing to tell. I'm a boring single dad, content to live in a small town my whole life. End of story."

"Hardly." Arched above him, Ti pried his hand away from his face. "You, Drew Anderson, are an enigma. The fact that you don't even know it proves my point."

He held her pensive gaze. Long strands of hair whirled around her tiered earrings and sloped along her skin to the collar of his shirt. Aw, man. As if the sheen from the essential oil she'd dabbed on her neck earlier in the car wasn't killing him enough.

An inward groan tightened his stomach. He never should've let her wear his clothes.

Drew pulled himself up by the knees and forced his focus on to the tide's rhythmic rise and fall. But even with restricting his vision straight ahead, he sensed her next to him. Could feel the warmth of her arm right beside his. All he'd have to do was turn his head and …

Locked-up memories rippled in with each wave. His pulse joined the sounds of the beach filling the stillness. He breathed in. Out. Closed his eyes.

"Its vastness," he said a few moments later. "My thing with the ocean. The salt, the waves' ebb and flow, the challenge of paddling out in any weather." Conquering the rip current was nothing compared to treading a whirlpool of things he couldn't change.

He drew swirls in the sand with a conch shell. "It's easy to get lost in it." For just a little while.

The silence beside him drew his gaze. No witty remarks or impish grins. Only eyes that understood things left unsaid. "Keep talking. It's soothing."

Drew lay back and wedged an arm under his head. "I'm not good at talking."

"You don't say."

He didn't have to turn to feel her smile.

"Tell me about your dad."

When he tensed, Ti rested a calming hand over his.

He glanced away from the delicate feel of her fingers over his skin and cleared his throat. "Dad first came to Ocracoke with the Coast Guard. He and my mom opened the shop together years later and built a life here. He was a rock for his family in every way. Strong. Faithful. Did what had to be done to provide for us."

Drew scoured the dark heavens, needing the sunrise instead. "He died five years ago. Some tourists were stranded off the coast in a bad storm, and Dad didn't hesitate. Rescue missions were in his blood. We went after them on his old skiff. He saved everyone's life except his own."

The waves played a song of tribute against the shoreline while Ti's thumb caressed the back of his hand in place of words.

"From what I've seen," she whispered a minute later, "it sounds like you're a lot like him."

Drew dropped his gaze back to the unreachable horizon. "He left big shoes to fill." Ones he was failing to honor in every way.

Rather than prying deeper, Ti simply rested beside him. Something about her presence siphoned things out of him before he knew what was happening.

"My mom passed away three years before that. Cancer." A soft breath feathered over his skin. He stiffened at Ti's closeness and the emotions slipping in. "It was a long time ago."

"Doesn't mean it hurts any less." She curled a gentle hand around his arm. "Tell me stories about Maddie."

Now his daughter, he could talk about for hours. Just thinking about her awakened a joy strong enough to crowd out all other thoughts. Each story he shared eased his mind and body and seemed to lull Ti's breathing into a deep, unconscious tempo.

"So, the Energizer Bunny sleeps after all," he whispered while taking in this impulsive, headstrong, hippie girl. A salt rock lamp? He shook his head with amusement until she nestled closer as though curling into a pillow.

Her softness wrecked any possibility he'd be able to sleep. If the hairs caressing his chin in the breeze weren't making him hyperaware of her proximity, the traces of her lavender oil infusing the familiar briny air did him in.

He swallowed hard. Part of him was tempted to relish the feel of this woman beside him. The other part knew that was exactly why he couldn't.

A strand of hair tickled the corner of Ti's nose. She batted it away and reached to yank the covers over her cool body. Instead of blankets, her wrinkly dress and sand-coated skin brushed against her fingertips.

Confusion circled until a slow replay of last night warmed over her with the sun. The way Drew came to life on the dance floor, the vulnerability he shared on the beach. Maybe there was hope for him after all. Even the chance of an actual friendship between them.

Ti pushed her hair off her forehead and fluttered a glance at the empty space beside her. She shot up and looked around.

"It's time to go." Drew's strong bravado matched his tall, determined stance behind her.

The unruly cowlick above his ear wasn't half as turbulent as the look in his eyes. *Alrighty then.* Ti gathered herself and things from the ground. "Had a hard time sleeping?"

He kept his gaze pinned on the ocean. "You could say that."

Unlike her. For the first time in several nights, she'd fallen asleep with ease. No nightmares or restless tossing and turning. Just peace.

They walked in silence toward her car. In the parking lot, her cell lit up with the number from her art studio in Astoria. It wasn't fair for phone calls to rob her of peace so easily.

She cast a tentative glance at Drew before answering. "Hey, Mia. Everything okay?"

When her top employee hesitated, Ti's pulse ratcheted up five notches. The girl rarely ever paused long enough to take a breath. She gripped her keys. "Mia? What is it?"

"I don't know exactly. Maybe nothing. But this man came by the shop yesterday, asking for your cell number. Said you weren't answering your home phone, and he hasn't seen you come in or out of your pad."

He was staking out her house? The panic reeling in Ti's stomach expanded up her throat. Focusing on Drew had been the perfect distraction. Too perfect. She had gotten so caught up in things here, she'd shut out what awaited her at home.

"The guy said he was family. But I don't know, girl. He sort of creeped me out, so I told him I wasn't at liberty to give out personal information until I talked with you first."

Ti exhaled through her mouth. "Don't tell him anything. If he comes around again, call the cops."

"You know the guy? What's going on?"

Ti turned and caught a cutting gaze from Drew—gathering pieces she couldn't afford him to put together. She opened her car door and forced herself to downplay. "Nothing the NYPD isn't used to. It's fine. Listen, I gotta go. I'll touch base in a few days."

Drew didn't say anything after she hung up. At least, not with words. On the drive to the docks, his flexed jaw made it clear he suspected she was hiding something he didn't want her dragging him or Maddie into. Couldn't blame him. But right now, her only choice was to lie low until things blew over back in Queens.

Once aboard the ferry, Ti redirected her energy to figuring out why Drew had woken up as Mr. Stiff again.

A lot of good it did her. He stood off by the rail in one of his brooding trances. Were they back to square one?

It had taken her only a few days on the island to figure out what kind of shop would thrive there. Drew had what it would take to pull it off. She saw it in him last night. They'd made progress. Did she push too hard? What happened?

White water churned along the sides of the ferry like the constant turmoil inside her. She'd escaped it for a few hours last night. Drew's voice had been like a calming lullaby. Maybe it was selfish to want to hold on to that, but he could at least be civil. He had to see the ground they'd gained, whether he wanted to admit it or not.

The drive home from the ferry pulsed with unspoken tension. At the curb in front of his house, Ti cut the ignition and turned. "You wanna tell me—?"

Drew's door squeaked open as he clambered out of his seat.

"O-kay," she said to the empty car. If he wanted to play it tough, fine. Ti yanked the keys out and jogged up the walkway to the screen door swinging behind him.

He might not want her to follow, but they needed to talk.

Inside, he plugged his cell into a charger beside a fish tank brimming with sea glass.

"Drew, can you slow down a sec?"

He trekked into the kitchen without responding.

Alone by the counter in only pajama pants, Cooper turned and lowered a half-eaten bagel from his mouth.

"Where's Maddie?" Drew's single-focused mission ushered him across the room to the back door, where he peeked outside.

"Hi to you, too." Cooper picked up his coffee mug. One glance at Drew's rumpled shirt Ti was still wearing sent his dimples reaching for each other. "Have fun last night?"

Drew's neck twitched. "Maddie. Where is she?"

The slight crease on Cooper's forehead betrayed his steady gaze. "Asleep."

"Still?" Drew's moment of hesitation turned into an advance. "What happened?"

Evading his brother's eyes this time, Cooper took a sip of his coffee.

"Coop."

"She had some trouble with her stomach, but she's fine. Grandma Jo and I took turns checking in on her all night."

Another step closer brought them almost chest to chest. "Why didn't you tell me?"

Cooper broadened his surfer frame. "You couldn't get here. There was no need for you to worry."

"That wasn't your call to make."

"The heck it wasn't."

Ti lanced between them before she had time to think. "Easy, guys. We're all on the same team here."

No one moved. Without a word, Drew finally backed up and trucked for the stairs.

Ti raised an apologetic shoulder at Cooper. "He had a long night."

Cooper let out a terse laugh while picking up his mug. "More like a long decade."

Despite Drew's closed-off exterior, Ti's heart ached for him as it had last night when he'd told her about losing his parents. After losing his wife, too, what did anyone expect?

But whatever the reason, now wasn't the time to get into it. She hurried up the steps after him. In front of a bedroom door, Drew kept his head down and hand on the knob until a father's tenderness gradually superseded all other emotion on his face. Another deliberate breath led him inside.

Ti peered into the room from behind the trim. A gray-haired African American woman sat asleep in a rocking chair across from Maddie's bed, where she lay with a Jack Russell nuzzled against her side and a bottle of Propel within reach on the nightstand.

"Hey, Sea Monkey," Drew whispered as he sat on the mattress.

"Dad!" Maddie rustled without disturbing the dog snoring beside her. "Did you find any sea turtles on Cedar Island yesterday?"

He chuckled. "Not this time. But I did see a school of dolphin early this morning."

"Did they dance for you?"

Those eyes. Even from across the room, their vibrancy reached straight for Ti's heart.

"They sure did." Drew folded the top of her pink comforter down, his face creasing with it. "But it wasn't worth missing getting to tuck you in last night. I'm sorry I wasn't here."

"It's okay. Grandma Jo said good-night prayers with me."

A glance over to the sleeping woman brought him back around with a glint of nostalgia in his eyes. "She's been saying good-night prayers for a long time."

"Yeah, she's a pro. We prayed for you and Miss Ti and Miss Chloe and M—"

"You didn't keep Grandma Jo up half the night, did you?" His teasing tone barely compensated for the audible ache underneath it.

"Only 'cause she had me all excited about making sun catchers today."

"Aw, sweetie." Drew combed her bangs off her forehead. "You sure you're up for that today?"

Maddie clasped two hands around his and faced him with more maturity than girls twice her age. "You don't have to worry about me, Dad."

Ti's grip around the trim constricted at the sight of Drew's Adam's apple bobbing.

He mussed the top of her hair. "How can I not worry about my spunky Sea Monkey? No telling what you talk Grandma Jo into when I'm not here."

Giggling, she batted his hand away. "That's 'cause girls know how to keep secrets."

"Oh, really?" He poked her side. "Now you're gonna have to spill it. What do you say to a dinner date tonight?"

Her eyes sparkled. "Spaghetti and meatballs?"

"You're on." Drew bent down to kiss her forehead.

Maddie pulled her bottom lip in as he stood. "Dad? We could do morning prayers before you go. You know, to make up for missing last night."

The tenderness on Drew's face finished off Ti's heart. She wheeled out of the doorway and leaned against the wall. No wonder he was so stressed about missing the ferry. Who wouldn't be with a precious daughter at home waiting to say bedtime prayers?

Regret for keeping him out collided with something Ti couldn't identify. She only knew she couldn't keep standing there.

She rushed down the stairs and through the door. Outside, she paced along the walkway in front of the house. But before she could sort through her tangled thoughts, Drew strode out with his cell to his ear. His eyes darkened, and Ti's insides twisted even more.

"What's wrong?"

"A message from Chloe." He pocketed his phone. "She got sick yesterday. Said she had to close up a little before one."

Heated silence churned. Drew didn't have to say what he was thinking. Ti could feel the slow burn from here.

He dug his fingers through his hair, turned away, and swore. "I have to get to the shop. I can't afford to miss any more sales."

"Drew, wait." She caught his arm. "I'm sorry. I didn't mean for us to miss the ferry. You were so relaxed at the café—"

"No, I was caught up in whatever spell you were wielding." He rubbed his temples. "That wasn't me. I never should've gone and wasted the day like that."

His estimation of their time together practically slapped her in the face, but a flare of irritation overrode the sting. "I realize fun might be a foreign concept to you, but that's what you were having last night."

"You don't get it. I'm not a wanderlust-hungry adventurer constantly looking for a good time. I have obligations. Bills to pay, people who count on me."

"And I don't?"

He released a hard breath. "Not all of us have easy lives."

Ti clenched her fingers. "You don't know a thing about my life."

"A hopeful artist, running away from whatever mess she got herself caught up in." A piercing gaze darted to the phone sticking out of her pocket. "I know the type."

"And now I know yours." She cut off the tears mounting her throat. "Glad we cleared that up."

Behind his anger, a flash of something broken tugged at his eyes, but Ti didn't stick around to wait for a response. He wanted to see her run away? *Watch me.*

CHAPTER SIX

Currents

Still fuming, Drew rammed through the shop's door and flicked on the lights. Ti shouldn't be upset. She was the one who'd waltzed in here three days ago like some artsy day-dreamer eager to change everything. Including him. What did she think was going to happen?

Frustration propelled him toward the staircase and the need to prove she was wrong about him, but his feet stopped at the barrier he knew better than to cross.

Two breaths. Three. The angry heartbeats assaulting his rib cage slowed as the fight replayed in his head. His death grip around the banister didn't come close to the one drilling guilt into his chest. This wasn't just about Ti, and he knew it.

He sank onto the third step, propped his elbows on his knees, and rubbed the heels of his palms in his eye sockets. *I know the type? Way to be a world-class jerk, Anderson.* With a labored exhale, his fatigued body almost withered into the hardwoods.

Stress and exhaustion weren't an excuse. He couldn't fault Ti for striking pressure points she didn't even know about.

At least it was over now. After the way he'd just treated her, she had every right to pack her bags. She'd go on to her next adventure, and he'd get back to taking care of his family the way Dad would've. It was better that way. For everyone.

He pulled himself up by the rail and headed to the back workroom. Only one way to move. Forward.

As Drew made his tea, the unused furnace in the far corner practically smirked at him with taunting reminders of the role art had played in his life once. He stirred a spoonful of sugar in his mug and fixed his gaze on the electric teakettle, but the pull didn't relent.

It wanted to mock his past, too? Fine. He tossed the spoon on the counter and crossed the room, ready to tell the worthless furnace where to stick it. Yet the regrets that surfaced weren't the ones he expected. He dropped his fist to the edge and traced his hand along the cold, unyielding metal. Remorse didn't change the fact that some fires were meant to go out.

Mug in hand, Drew plodded over to the computer. Time to press on.

Within the hour, Ti's bright yellow smart car cruised up along the curb. Mixed feelings tensed his muscles all over again. She was probably dropping off the things they'd bought yesterday. Or she was stopping on her way out to give him the earful he had coming. But instead of doing either, Ti toted supplies to the front of the shop and started mixing paint.

Drew cautiously eased through the door. "You didn't leave?"

"I changed my mind." In jean shorts and a yellow tank top as bright as her car, Ti tied a matching bandana under her hair and kept right on working. "I'm from Queens, Drew. Your attitude doesn't intimidate me."

Too bad he couldn't say the same. Everything about this girl intimidated him. More than it should.

The magnitude of what a jerk he'd been since she came to town sank another blow. "Ti ..."

"I told you I'm here to help. So, you're just gonna have to get over yourself and get used to it." She jimmied open a paint can and plunked a stir stick in it.

Smiling at her obstinacy, he started toward her. "Ti—"

"And I warned you, I call things like I see them." A woman on a mission, she stirred with enough vigor to power a speedboat. "You're not gonna scare me away. I—"

"Ti!" He cut off her incessant buzzing and waited for her to meet the sincerity in his eyes. "I'm sorry." He let each word fall between them with the weight they carried. "I was way out of line back there. It's not an excuse, but Maddie ... she's ..."

"Your whole world." Her voice grew solemn. "I don't blame you for being protective. I understand."

And was far more forgiving than he deserved. "Still, I'm sorry for what I said."

Ti tucked a wayward wisp of hair under her bandana. "Apology accepted. Now, you ready to get to work, or what?"

She didn't let much get to her, did she?

Drew rolled up his sleeves. "Yeah. I'm ready."

He hoped.

"Good." She handed him a brush and tray. "Here. Painting makes everything better."

Drew took one look at the turquoise paint and shook his head. He still had no idea what this had to do with business, but he wasn't about to start another argument.

Ti quickly fixed her own tray and started on the shutters closest to her, all while singing to herself. Of course.

Barefoot, she swayed with as much radiance as the studs in her ears catching the sunlight. Stubborn and brazen, yet faithful and forgiving—despite his arrogance. She'd called him an enigma, but Ti Russo was a mystery of her own. One capable of tearing through walls he shouldn't be lowering.

Looking away, he loaded his brush and fanned a coat of paint over the top edge of the weathered shutter. Why couldn't life's blunders be as easy to cover?

"Falling short," he said after a few silent minutes.

Ti turned. "What?"

"Last night, you asked me my greatest fear. I'm afraid of letting Maddie down. Of her realizing I'm not everything she needs me to be."

"That'll never happen. You're the kind of dad little girls dream of." Her hand stilled above the shutter, but she didn't peel her gaze off it. "You take good care of her."

"More like the other way around." Maddie had been the brave one, comforting him when his faith faltered. Drew brushed along the grains. "She got real sick last year. Almost like her body started working against itself. Doctors couldn't explain it. We saw specialists. Made ER visits. We were at the end of our rope when a GI doc finally diagnosed her with an autoimmune disease."

Images of his little girl in the ER shuddered over him.

Ti curled her fingers around his. Consoling.

"It's mostly been controlled with medications these last few months, but flare-ups can strike anytime." He lowered his brush and his chin. "Without insurance, the medical bills … If she ever needs to go to the ER again, and I can't afford to …" Thick layers of unsolicited emotion clogged his voice without warning.

"The shop's going to make it, Drew. I promise. Single parenting is anything but easy. This situation isn't your fault. You're doing the best you can." Ti's blue eyes teemed with an assurance he wanted so much to grasp onto, believe. It rooted straight into the torment of doubt he kept hidden from everyone but this girl who seemed to see right inside him.

A palpable energy stirred between them—her fingers still grazing his, seconds passing in breaths and heartbeats.

The rapid movements in her chest said she felt the magnetized pull, too. With a forced blink away from him, she slipped back to her paint station. "You should let Maddie help out around here. I could use a hand with some of the projects," she rambled quickly, a waver short-circuiting her usual flow. "And you'd be surprised how much art can do for the soul."

And how easily it could break it.

"You could make your own artwork, too, you know. Turn this shop into anything you want. No limits." Ti fanned a stroke across the shutter. "Find that source of passion, and you'll find a lot more than a successful business."

Her reverence for art whispered a familiar craving through his soul, an echo without an answer.

He didn't respond. Couldn't. But even the quiet kept an electric current surging through the unspoken waves between them. The flutter on her neck almost cut off all logic telling his treacherous legs not to move a muscle.

Curbing the connection, Drew stayed put and focused on painting instead. Better to follow her lead and keep things light. Easy. He rubbed his chin while eying the turquoise glaring at him in the sun. "You sure about this color? I mean, don't you think it's a little …?"

"Eye-catching? That's the idea, Grasshopper."

Of course it was. Bright and feisty like the artist who chose it. Their sideways glances intersected long enough for two half smiles to mirror each other. "You give nicknames to everyone you know, or am I just special?"

"Oh, you're definitely *special,* Mr. Anderson."

One day, he'd stop walking smack into these things. "Bet your parents had fun with that sense of humor of yours."

She snorted. "More like I was stuck with a joke for parents." Her spine turned rigid, her brushstroke frozen in place.

"You all right?"

"Yeah." Head down, Ti adjusted her bandana and avoided his eyes. "I'm gonna grab a coffee. You want a coffee?"

He wanted her to be honest with him. Wanted to put her at ease.

He scrunched his face in mock disgust, and whatever had her so tense passed with a breeze blowing her hair along her neckline. Her usual impish grin re-emerged. "Right. The grass drinker. For a second there, I forgot I was in an alternate universe where people can survive without coffee."

"And yet the dramatic continues to thrive."

"Always." Ti curtseyed and spun toward the front door.

If he figured out even half of what went through that girl's head before the summer ended, he'd be the one bowing for an award. If they could survive working with each other, maybe they'd both win.

Ti returned a few minutes later, all traces of unease hidden under the bliss of her mojo. She had the skill of deflection down even better than him. He'd give her that.

Remnants of their earlier fight waned a little more with each dip of the sun. Aside from having to stop intermittently to take care of a few customers and check in on Maddie and Grandma Jo, Drew labored alongside Ti most of the day.

Parched and beat, he raised the bottom of his T-shirt to wipe the sweat from his face and took in the reward of their hard work. The giant sand dollar stepping-stones and decorative multicolored rocks lining the walkway to the front door weren't half bad. And he had to admit the freshly painted shutters "popped" from the background, as Ti had promised.

He got the feeling he would be eating his words about this not making any difference.

Drew joined Ti around the side of the shop, where she was rinsing out the brushes and trays.

The girl owned the patent on turning a five-second glance into a gloating fest. “Come to tell me I was right?”

He ran his tongue along the corner of his mouth. “We'll see.”

With her brow raised in challenge, she pushed her hair off her forehead with her wrist. “We sure will.”

Man, she was seriously going to demolish his pride before it was all said and done.

His laughter slowly transitioned to a pang of sobriety. “I'm really sorry for earlier. For these last few days, actually. I haven't been fair to you.”

“Don't worry about it. You were shooting it straight, just like I asked.”

A trail of self-consciousness crawled up his cheeks. He'd been far from straight with her. Or with himself, for that matter. His heart rate elevated.

He trained his gaze on the wall, like he'd morphed into a building code inspector. What was he, twelve? What was his problem? Swallowing, he faced her again. “Ti, I—”

“There you guys are.” Cooper rounded the corner in flip-flops, a pair of board shorts, and an O'Neill T-shirt. “Figured you'd be ready for a night out after working all day. Beach party starts at nine, so that leaves us ...” He checked his phone. “Four hours to hit up the festival first. You game?”

Ti had to be tired after the hard work she'd put in today, but her eyes couldn't hide the lure of a party. “As long as I can shower first.”

Cooper's dimples sank around his smile. “I'm sure we can make that happen.”

Oh, brother. That was Drew's cue to leave. Restraining an eye roll, he backed away. "Have fun."

"You're not coming?" Ti looked surprised.

Unlike Cooper. "C'mon, hoss. Have fun for a change, and drop the 'I have business to take care of' excuse."

Better than the business Cooper obviously had planned tonight.

Drew cut off the thought. That wasn't fair. Ti deserved to have a good time, and Coop was the guy to show it to her. Besides, Drew already had a dinner date.

CHAPTER SEVEN

Secrets

Ti met Cooper outside the trailer in an off-the-shoulder blue romper, silver Gladiator sandals, and a matching silver fringe necklace.

His eyes shimmered compliments over her.

She ran a glance down his low-hanging jeans and white T-shirt against his tan body. "Not bad yourself. How many girls you planning to pick up tonight with the casual model look you're rocking?"

Cooper laughed. "Now, what makes you think I'm like that?"

"If you're trying to keep it a secret, you might want to tell those dimples and scruffy jaw to play along."

His boyish grin obviously couldn't be tamed. "I might just be a chivalrous guy, wanting to show the new girl in town around without any ulterior motives." He hooked an arm out for her to hold. "Worth taking a chance, right?"

He had her there. Ti took his arm as he led them around the side of the house.

From the screen door, a Jack Russell barked with the chutzpah of a pit bull.

"Easy, Jasper," Drew said as he approached the door. One catch of Ti's gaze, and he backed out of view with the dog.

For the hundredth time today, the look in his eyes melted over her. The man had more depth than she could uncover. Maybe she shouldn't stay in Ocracoke to try, but fleeing was what had landed her here to begin with. She couldn't keep running away when things got difficult.

"Don't let him get to you."

"Hmm?" Ti faced Cooper as they walked.

"Drew. He doesn't mean to come off as hard as he does sometimes." Cooper ran his fingers through his sandy blond hair the way his brother often did. "He's carting around some hefty baggage."

Ti stared at her sandals and twisted the bangles lining her wrist. "Aren't we all?"

"Some more than others."

If he only knew.

She peered back at the house. Drew deserved a good future, despite what his past held. She'd almost left earlier today. But whether he wanted her around or not, she needed to see this through. For him and Maddie both.

Hollers rang from a few blocks up the road. "If you try that nonsense again, Miss Hensley, you're out. You understand me?"

Ti and Cooper traded a quick glance and hustled over.

A white-haired man in starched dress clothes stood outside the hotel Livy worked at, ranting at her. Must be her landlord-slash-boss, Mr. Fiazza. Didn't matter who he was. The fact that he was giving her friend the third degree was all Ti needed to know.

She charged straight for him, but Grandma Jo beat her to it. Where'd she come from?

"Now you listen, here, Stan." Ms. Spunk marched him backward. "There's no need for you to take your grumpiness out on Livy. Why don't you loosen that tie you bought for prom and go back in to entertain your guests?"

Ti's laugh tumbled past the hand she clamped over her mouth. The old geezer speared a look at her, but a clamor behind them drew all their gazes to the hotel's side door. A staff worker dumped a wooden pallet onto a stack beside the dumpster. He turned, froze at everyone looking at him, and ducked back inside.

Good call.

Stan's dark brown eyes returned to Grandma Jo and challenged her back a step. "You'd do good to mind your own business, Jolene. This is between me and a noncompliant employee."

"Hogwash." She waved off his power trip. "If you weren't wound up so tightly, you'd see your lack of people skills is the problem, not Livy. Never *have* known how to treat a girl," she said with a huff.

Stan shuffled a foot closer, jaw retracting. "And maybe if *you* weren't busy driving me crazy all the time, you'd acknowledge my people skills run a very successful business."

The inch separating them brimmed with a current Ti could feel ten feet away. Those were sparks if she'd ever seen any. The kind that had been charging for years. Decades, even.

Filing that tidbit away for later, Ti gently eased toward Livy and tiptoed away with her.

"Thanks for the intervention." Livy untied her apron. "That man's a total prat."

And yet she kept working for him. Was she that tight on money? It didn't add up. Ti peeked behind her. With his attention still locked on Grandma Jo, Mr. Fiazza didn't even notice they'd left. "He wasn't ranting about me staying with you the other night, was he?"

Ti grabbed her friend's arm when she didn't answer. "Liv?"

She bit her lip. "I told you he'd freak if he found out."

Cooper caught up to them. "It's not your fault. Marcus probably ratted Livy out to his dad because of something he got peeved at Drew over."

"Hold up a sec. Mr. Fiazza is Marcus's dad?" Ti tapped a knuckle to her forehead. Comprehension settled, guilt on its tail. More like Marcus had gotten peeved at *her*. She wouldn't have hurled an insult at him the other day if she'd known it would backfire on Livy. "Um, I think I might've caused this."

"No, trust me." Cooper lounged an arm across Livy's shoulders as they entered the festival. "It's *always* about Drew."

"What's the deal between them?"

"Family rivalry junk." Cooper steered them toward a stand selling cold drinks. "But after Drew out surfed Marcus in every competition growing up, let's just say it got personal. Marcus even opened his own gift shop just to take away from our business."

"Wait, back up. You're telling me Drew's a surfer? The guy who rails me for being spontaneous?" *Seriously?*

Livy shooed away a horsefly. "There's a lot more to Drew than he lets on."

"Tell me about it," Ti mumbled. There was a lot more to this little town, too. Maybe her visit would keep her secrets hidden more easily than she thought.

Or tangle her deeper into new ones.

Cooper handed each of the girls a drink while peering toward an Italian businessman across the crowd. "Excuse me for a moment, ladies."

Livy took a sip of her lemonade. "And there he goes."

"To ask that guy his suit measurements?"

"To mingle with the life he lost." Livy swirled her straw around her cup. "He had a big corporate job in Hatteras. Moved back home about a year ago when he got laid off."

"A year ago, huh?" Ti followed Livy's line of sight toward Cooper talking with Guido, looking as smooth as an executive bagging a deal. *And the curious world of Ocracoke just keeps getting more intriguing.*

Livy nudged Ti with her shoulder. "So . . . ?"

"So, what?"

"You're gonna make me pry it out of you? You and Drew. You two have enough sparks shooting between you to start your own welding company. Give me the deets. Are you two hooking up?"

Sweet tea ran down Ti's chin. "Hook up with Family Man?" She had to be joking. Drew was anything but the hooking up type. "Sorry. I don't date hopeless romantics."

"Who said he was?"

"Are you kidding me? If he stares into the horizon for a long-lost love for much longer, a message in a bottle is going to float to shore."

"It's not like that."

"It doesn't matter. The guy's marriage material."

Livy stopped her by the elbow. "Is that so bad?"

"Not for someone like you. C'mon, Liv. This is me we're talking about here. You do remember Murray, right?"

Her lip curled. "Hard to forget a guy who treats women like used laundry."

"Exactly why we worked."

"Do you even hear yourself right now?"

Ti turned to the closest booth and nearest form of distraction. She fingered through a stack of canvas prints.

Drew had every right to be a hopeless romantic and miss the wife he loved. What man wouldn't? The poor guy's fairy tale had gotten cut short. Ti wasn't about to put him through any more heartache. "Drew's dealing with a lot right now. I don't want to add to his hurts."

"No one said you would."

Now, who wasn't listening to herself?

They passed a guy with a shaved head and black T-shirt leaning against the side of a booth while scoping out the scene. If his tattoo sleeves and unshaven jaw hadn't screamed he was Ti's type from a distance, the suggestive eyebrow he'd just shot her way confirmed it.

Walking backward, Ti resisted the default instinct drawing her to the sultry grin fading in the crowd. She'd been down that same road a hundred times. Same guy, different faces. What if there was more for her?

Livy dragged Ti on by the wrist, as if reading her thoughts.

A little ways down, a fluorescent orange flyer on one of the vendor's stands practically reached out and tripped her. She had to have misread that. She snagged a copy and scanned it over. "A surf competition's coming here? To Ocracoke?"

Livy peeked over Ti's shoulder at the flyer. "Yep. In less than a month, this place will be packed."

That could be great for business. Ideas ignited. It would only give Ti a few weeks to prep, but she could pull it off. If Marcus wanted a fight, she'd bring him one. "You know what? I'm gonna skip the party this time. I have some things I need to work on."

"You sure?"

"Yeah, you go ahead with Cooper." Ti pecked Livy on the cheek. "I'll come another night. Promise." Right now, she had a competition of her own to plan.

Drew propped his surfboard against the back of the house, unhooked the strap from his ankle, and glanced up at a light on in Cooper's trailer. Back already? Then again, he wasn't surprised. Coop never failed at his agenda.

Pangs Drew had no business feeling lurched to the surface. Stomping them back down, he faced the stars and soaked in the night's breeze rushing over his wet skin. He'd needed the ocean tonight. But as usual, he came back empty-handed.

He entered the kitchen through the back door.

Grandma Jo set a mug in the drain rack and offered him the same steady smile he'd leaned on for years. "Conquer any demons this time?"

Drew tugged his ear. "There's always tomorrow." He went to grab some cash from his jacket on the coat rack. He'd only been gone an hour since tucking Maddie in for the night, but Grandma Jo had watched her most of the day.

She stuffed her hands in her pockets. "Are we really going to do this same dance every time I babysit? It's been ten years."

"I don't ever want you to think I take you for granted or assume—"

"That I love that little munchkin like my own grandbaby? That's one assumption you're more than welcome to make, young man."

Drew dipped his chin in concession. "How'd she do to-night?"

"Perfect. The spaghetti dinner you two had must've knocked her out. She hasn't stirred an inch since you left."

"Good." He breathed a sigh on his way to check on her.

"And Drew?"

He peered behind him to a sage-like expression.

"Those answers you go seeking in the waves... You might want to start thinking about what happens when you find them." Grandma Jo slipped outside, leaving him with something else he didn't want to deal with right now.

Better for her to be evasive than to dive into her usual rant about divine providence. If God had a hand in things, He would've offered more than a decade of silence. Drew wasn't looking for the answers she thought he was.

Upstairs in Maddie's bedroom, he swept his girl's bangs to the side and pressed a light kiss to her head. Jasper yawned, stretched his paws in opposite directions, and burrowed under her armpit. One thing was for sure. Maddie never had to question whether she was loved.

What he'd give for that to be enough.

Drew ruffled the dog's ears and turned to leave, but a catalog on the nightstand caught his attention. He flipped to a page flagged with a bright pink sticky note. Boots. Just like the ones she'd seen Ti wearing.

His arm drifted to his side, his heart a mirror of the tangled spool of yarn Grandma Jo must've left behind. How could he expect anything less?

He set the yarn over the catalog, crossed the room, and stopped in the doorway to peer back at Maddie one more time. The steady heartbeat on her neck sent concerns about her illness colliding with the need to protect her.

Drew eased the door shut and lowered his forehead against it. He was supposed to be stronger than this. Strong enough to focus and provide for her. To get himself together and keep Ti from dismantling the safeguards he'd erected for a reason. Maddie didn't need to cling to hope that would disappoint her. Not again.

In the bathroom, he turned the shower all the way to cold, but thoughts of Annie burned from somewhere he couldn't reach. Where embers should have died a long time ago.

Drew balled the washcloth into a wad, hating that he'd allowed old frustrations to resurface. He'd shut them out for good. Moved on. But the tighter he wrung the cloth, the faster locked-up emotions unraveled.

He chucked the washcloth against the shower wall and rinsed the salt and sand from his hair. Water streamed down his skin until unanswered questions drained into a pool of regret for ever giving Annie control of his heart. At least the scar she left behind promised one thing.

He'd never make the same mistake again.

CHAPTER EIGHT

Challenge

In Grandma Jo's backyard, Ti waved away a mosquito with her camera and scooted to the shady end of the picnic bench to block the sun. After being here nearly a week, she should've built up a base layer for a tan by now.

She'd certainly built up a thick skin being around Jekyll and Hyde the last few days. All business, Drew had shut her out again. Probably thought she'd sweet-talked her way into crossing his rigid work boundaries by coming to the cookout. Ha. If Grandma Jo had given her an option, Ti would've gladly passed on being the fifth wheel.

A commotion from behind the picnic table lured Ti around and stole her focus. She zoomed in on a shot of Maddie dribbling a basketball. No surprise, the girl had mad coordination to match her grace and style.

"You got nothing on me, old man." Maddie left her arms up in Cooper's face after swishing a basket.

And trash talking to boot.

Ti bit her lip to squelch a laugh. Bury her heart? Too late.

"Old man?" Cooper spun the ball around his back, checked it with her, and dribbled it between his legs. "You're getting it now, Freckles."

Hiding her smile behind the camera, Ti captured their banter, laughter, and horsing around. Candids had always been her favorite. They told stories most people didn't notice.

"Taking more notes?" Drew set a plastic cup in front of her as he straddled the bench. "Lemonade. Hope that's okay."

"Yeah, fine." Ti tucked her camera in its bag and took a sip. Bittersweet. Kind of like being here right now.

She swirled the base of her cup in mindless circles over the checkered tablecloth, looking everywhere but at the green eyes capable of stirring feelings she didn't understand. At least behind her camera, she could pretend to have a legit reason to crash their family barbeque.

Grandma Jo placed a covered salad on the table in front of Drew. "Is the grill fired up?"

He tipped his cup toward the smoke in the air. "Yes, ma'am."

"No burning my chicken this time, young man." She waved a giant spoon at him. "You hear me?"

"Hey, now. That wasn't my fault last time."

"Mm-hmm." She nudged Ti in the arm with her elbow. "Come help me in the kitchen, sugar. We need to make sure we have something edible."

Drew scrunched his face. "Very funny."

Caught between laughter and panic, Ti tried not to spew her drink. She dabbed her mouth with her sleeve. "I'm the last person you want near the kitchen. Trust me. I don't cook."

"Nonsense." Grandma Jo tugged Ti up by the arm. "My house, my rules."

A flicker of a grin quirked Drew's dimples. "Have fun."

She almost *accidentally* spilled her cup of lemonade down his shirt on her way up. So tempting.

An oversized glass jar full of dark liquid stopped Ti at the back steps. She raised her sunglasses to the top of her head. "Um, Grandma Jo, you want me to bring this in? Looks like you might've left it outside by mistake." Like, a month too long. Did she even want to ask?

Maddie's sweet laugh trickled over from the corner of the yard. "That's sun tea, silly. It's supposed to be outside."

"You're actually gonna drink that?"

Cooper and Drew's amusement joined Maddie's. Well, at least Ti could add comic relief to her purpose in being here.

Cooper spun the basketball on his finger. "Don't worry, Big Apple. We'll have you drinking sun tea and calling soda 'pop' before the summer's over with."

Not in this lifetime. "Don't count on it, Billy Bob."

"I like a challenge." Cooper made a jump shot. The ball rebounded off the backboard and rolled into Ti's feet. "Up for a little two-on-two later? You and me versus Drew and Freckles?"

This time, Drew almost choked on his drink. He scrambled for a napkin. "I doubt she'd want to break a nail."

Glaring, Ti kicked the ball into her hands, lined up her shot, and bent her knees. "I might've walked the runways in London, but I grew up on the streets of Queens." The ball cleared the basket with nothing but net. She hiked a brow and the corner of her mouth at Drew. "The only nails anyone's losing are the ones you'll be chewing off."

"Ohhh!" Cooper palmed the ball at Drew. "Someone get him some ice for that burn."

Grandma Jo rasped a contagious chuckle. "Ooh wee. If there were ever a picture to take, it'd be of Drew sitting there as nervous as a cat on a hot tin roof."

"Okay, okay." Drew sauntered over and stole the ball from Ti. "You and me later, tough girl." If he played as unfairly as his dimples did, she might be the one in trouble.

Refusing to show a hint of being flustered, Ti flaunted a gangster pose. "Bring it."

Grandma Jo stretched an arm across Ti's shoulders. "A girl who can hold her own. Told ya you were already a part of this family."

Not if Drew had a say in it. His smile fell as he jerked his gaze away from her.

Ti's chest caved. Being unwanted wasn't new. Why was she letting it get to her?

Grandma Jo nodded to the back door. "C'mon. Let's take that confidence to the kitchen."

Had to be better than trying to figure out Jekyll and Hyde. The guy seriously needed to pick a personality and stick with it.

Inside, Ti did a double take to make sure the door hadn't been a portal into Cracker Barrel's kitchen. Savory southern aromas raced for her growling stomach. If she wasn't careful, she'd forget she was a vegetarian.

Grandma Jo fanned through a stack of mail. "AARP, life insurance, funeral discounts." She dumped the envelopes in the trash without opening them and kept on trekking to the counter. "I swear, as soon as you hit your sixties, the world's ready to put you in the grave." She waved one hand over her Betty Boop apron like Vanna White and hung the other on her hip. "I've still got some spunk in me, don't I?"

"In spades." After washing her hands, Ti sat on a bar stool behind the breakfast counter. "You'd have to to keep up with Drew and Cooper."

"Don't I know it." She tossed Ti a blue polka dotted apron in the shape of a dress from the fifties. "Let's keep that spunk rolling."

"Um... I really wasn't exaggerating earlier. You don't want me ruining your meal."

Grandma Jo handed Ti a knife and cutting board. "Why don't you let me be the judge of that?" Back at the sink, she rinsed a colander of peeled potatoes. "Your mom never taught you your way around a kitchen?" she called behind her.

"My mom wouldn't even know what to do with utensils unless they were a lighter and a spoon." A terse laugh tailed a confession she'd meant to keep to herself. What were the chances the sound of the running water had drowned it out?

Grandma Jo took the seat opposite Ti while extending half the potatoes and a motherly smile. "You know, Karl and I tried to have kids for ten years. Ten." Shaking her head, she sliced a potato into quarters. "It felt even longer. Doctor's appointments, treatments, expenses we didn't have no money for. Even got pregnant once but miscarried a month later."

Ti pulled her sunglasses from the top of her head and set them aside. "I'm so sorry."

"Don't be, sugar. Those were the years my faith was born." She tossed the cubed potatoes into a bowl. "Oh, I got angry with God, all right. Gave Him a good talking to more than once." Her chuckle slowly gave way to a sobered expression. The kind that had known the deep recesses of loss yet still found hope.

Ti followed her line of sight toward a shelf of picture frames. Beside a few that must've been of Grandma Jo's family, a photo of Drew and a woman holding a redheaded baby skewered Ti right down the middle.

"Can you imagine growing up with seven siblings?"

That would've required parents who actually wanted kids. Regaining her composure, Ti spun around on the stool. "Must've been nice to have a big family."

Grandma Jo huffed.

"Or not?"

"It had its moments." She pushed another pile of potatoes off her cutting board with her knife. "People think being the youngest sibling means you get spoiled, but let me tell you somethin'. It ain't true. Mama was so frazzled trying to keep up with everything, she didn't have much time to tend to us youngins. My middle sister basically raised me."

She peeked over at Ti's much higher pile of unsliced potatoes. "If you can wield a paintbrush across a canvas, you can handle a knife and cutting board. Apprehension is all in your head. Come on, now. We've got hungry boys waitin' on us."

The woman could match Ti's bluntness any day. She refrained from laughing and got to work. "Yes, ma'am."

After finishing her stack, Grandma Jo began chopping an onion and some celery. "When I couldn't get pregnant, I thought I must not've been fit to be a mama. That I'd done something wrong."

Somewhere in the hidden places, Ti's heart winced.

"But God had plans of His own. Had a whole family for me here all along." She blinked away the sheen in her eyes and smoothed out her apron's waistline. "Mind you, it didn't happen when and how I thought it should've, but He's got a way of working out the unexpected. Even when we think He's forgotten us."

Ti swallowed the rise of tears coating her throat out of nowhere. Springing from her seat, she bumped the cutting board into the ceramic bowl. "Sorry. I, um, left my lemonade outside. I should probably go get it before the flies take it over." And before memories confiscated the composure Ti needed to make it through being surrounded by a family she didn't belong in.

"You just worry about taking on Drew, sugar. I'll finish up here."

Without giving Grandma Jo a chance to change her mind, Ti fled through the screen door. A wall of humidity slammed into her body, the sight of Maddie swept up in Drew's arms right behind. Ti slid her sunglasses back on. She shouldn't be here.

"She kick you out already?" Drew asked. Apparently, Jekyll was back.

Partway to the picnic table, Ti stopped to iron out the wrinkles from her forehead and turned. "I warned her I'd ruin things." She evaded the inquisitive look dissecting her words and hooked a thumb over her shoulder. "I just remembered I have a painting I need to finish."

"Can't it wait?" Maddie swung around her dad's waist. "Or you could bring it here. You can work on it before lunch. We have time."

So much for a decoy.

Drew lounged an arm across Maddie's back and cocked his head. "Unless you're trying to back out of our game. Not saying I blame you. Just a little surprised."

When did he get so good at pushing her buttons? That was supposed to be *her* skill. A glance from Drew's taunting eyes to Maddie's hopeful ones did her in. "You wish. I'll be back in five. Actually, make that ten." Coffee reinforcements were definitely in order. With any luck, she'd find some armor for her heart while she was at it.

At the grill, Drew basted the chicken thighs for the fifth time. No way he was letting those suckers dry out. He cut a tiny sliver into one. Juicy perfection.

Too bad he wasn't having as much success keeping his focus. His gaze kept drifting toward Maddie glued to Ti's side at the easel, like the sorcerer's apprentice. Hard to fault her. Ti's paintings were spellbinding—like most everything about her.

Grandma Jo materialized out of nowhere. "You gonna let me taste test those?"

Flinching, Drew juggled the tongs like a devil stick to keep from dropping them. "Jeez. Wanna give someone a warning before sneaking up on them."

"People only flinch like that if they're already on edge."

"I'm not on edge." He turned over the rest of the thighs and added some burgers.

"Mm-hmm." She butted her way into his space. "You go on, now. I'll take it from here."

She couldn't be serious. "You're relieving me of my duties?"

Grandma Jo looked his shocked profile up and down. "Do we need formal papers drawn up?" She gestured for the tongs.

Tight-lipped, he held them out to her but didn't let go. "Don't you be messing up my chicken, now. They're just about perfect."

She gave the tongs a tug. "And don't you be worrying about my lunch, sugar. You have *other things* to concentrate on not messing up." With her usual lack of subtlety, she waved him toward Ti. She must've missed seeing Cooper take her to the festival and flirt with her today. There was nothing to mess up.

"Go on and get before I invite Mrs. Cunningham over."

Both brows shot to his hairline. "You're evil."

She laughed. "Balances out my charm."

Not the trait he was thinking of at the moment.

Drew turned in time to graze arms with Coop, whipping past him to the porch. Drew grabbed his brother's arm. "Hey.

You're not going AWOL on me, are you?" He had a knack for sneaking out at random times.

"Just running to take care of something." He shook his watch forward on his wrist, adjusted his Tar Heels hat, and kept walking. "Save me some chicken." The screen door swung behind him.

Left alone with the women and no task to occupy him. Perfect. Drew took one look at Grandma Jo and strode for Ti and Maddie instead.

"Dad, look. Isn't it cool? It's a picture of the shop." Maddie set a paintbrush on the easel ledge. "Ti let me help paint."

He eyed her paint-smudged fingers. "I see that. How about you go wash up before we eat?"

"Right now?"

Face stern, he dipped his chin at her.

"Yes, sir." She trudged up from the lawn chair and across the patio.

Ti mixed red and blue paint on her palette with her knife. "She's a natural artist."

He wasn't about to tell her art was part of Maddie's DNA. He tapped his shoe against a root and motioned to the camera slung over the chair. "Do you take photos as well as you paint?"

Her brush hiccupped across the canvas. Recovering, she resumed her graceful movement. "They're both just hobbies. Outlets I picked up as a kid."

The slight quiver to her voice hinted to something unspoken. But the more she lost herself in the imagery in front of her, the more her shoulders seemed to relax. "I had this silly dream of opening my own gallery one day."

"Why didn't you?" Drew took Maddie's seat.

"No point chasing childhood daydreams, right?"

"Says the girl insisting I be less practical."

All smiles, Ti threatened to tattoo him with her fan brush.

"Seriously, though. You could open any kind of gallery you wanted. Where'd you learn to paint like that?"

She scrunched her lips together as if debating whether or not to tell him. "Sorry. That's classified."

"Oh, c'mon." He stretched back against the seat, foot propped up on his knee. "I think the owner has the right to know his artist's credentials."

Moaning, she craned her head to the sky and then stabbed the paintbrush in the air at him. "Fine. But no laughing."

Now he was intrigued. "Promise."

"Bob Ross." She returned to painting but peeked a sideways glance at him.

He tried to school his face. "The afro dude on PBS?"

"Don't mock." She poked him with the end of her brush. "The guy was an artistic genius."

"I'm not mocking. Just surprised."

"That I had cable as a kid?"

Eyes rolling, he nudged her back. "That you gleaned so much from a TV show."

Ti added striking definition to the painted shutters with the edge of her knife. "Trust me. I owe the foundation of my technique to him. But it was more than that. He knew how to create these entire worlds you could escape into. So serene and magical."

She switched back to her fan brush. "The first show I saw was of this gorgeous trail winding into a fall forest. Honestly, there wasn't that much to it, but something about the path drew me in. I wanted to go there, you know? To be right in the middle of the trees. Figured if I couldn't be there physically, painting it was the next best thing. Haven't stopped since."

Head angled, Ti took in her own world on the canvas before adding a finishing stroke. "What do you think?"

That she was far more captivating than she realized.

When she turned her blue eyes on him, it took massive restraint not to wish he could escape in the painting, too.

Keep his guard up around her? Right. How many more times did he need to prove that was pointless?

Listening to her open up rendered his muscles useless. Voice, too. Good thing he hadn't lost his ability to swallow. Because he wasn't about to let the lump in his throat show.

Cooper sprang through the screen door with Maddie on his back. "Ready to ball?"

"*After* lunch." Grandma Jo carried a platter of simmering chicken and burgers across the patio. "Last one to the table does the dishes."

A sidelong glance launched them into a sprint to the table and Drew into a prayer of relief for the interruption. If Ti stuck around much longer, he was bound to lose his resolve.

Coop swung a leg over the bench. "What's wrong, hoss? You scared Ti's gonna take you down?"

More like he feared she already had.

CHAPTER NINE

Afterglow

Five days hadn't killed the afterglow of Drew redeeming his grilling skills. Now, if he could figure out how to bring some of that luck to the shop, he'd really be accomplishing something.

At his desk, he swept a page off the printer and glanced between it and the computer screen, certain one of them would belie the other.

He wasn't that lucky. Even if it wasn't much, the past week's sales outranked those from the last several combined. He succumbed to a smile. Ti's outdoor remodeling made an impact, after all.

Man, it killed him to admit that.

A series of laughs out front billowed in through the screen door. Drew set the sales report aside and moseyed over. Leaning an arm into the trim, he took in the same sight that had become a norm around here. Maddie attached to Ti's hip—two rays of sunshine swaying on the old porch swing that Ti had found out back and restored.

Once again, she was right. Getting Maddie involved in projects around the shop seemed to boost her spirits. Or maybe it was just from spending time with Ti.

He never doubted they'd bond. Knew it was inevitable. But seeing Maddie come to life around Ti was terrifyingly beautiful, like a summer storm claiming the ocean at sunset.

Maddie dragged her bare feet along Jasper's back at the base of the swing. Of course the dog had fallen all over himself when he met Ti. Because what would her résumé be without adding Dog Whisperer to the list of credentials?

Jasper rolled over in a shameless request for a belly rub. With his paws in the air and tongue out, he panted his contentment at getting both girls to fall for his charm.

His charisma almost rivaled Ti's. In a white textured tank top, a long flowy skirt, and earrings reaching her shoulders, she filled the space with her larger-than-life presence.

The wind toyed with her hair as she faced the sky. Most people came here to seek out the sun. With Ti, it was like the sun found *her*. It shimmered over her skin and highlighted her laughter, rooting a surge of warmth inside his chest.

When she looked over and caught him watching, an almost coy smile filtered through the strands of hair gliding across her cheeks. He should've looked away but couldn't.

She handed Maddie some rope fishnet and a vintage mason jar the same shade as the Grecian Isle paint she'd used on the shutters.

Grecian Isle? Tell me I didn't just think that.

Ti had him calling the paint colors by name. This was bad. Trying not to laugh at himself, Drew tipped his head back. Man, he was in deeper trouble than he thought.

"Morning." A middle-aged woman wearing an oval pendant necklace strolled up to the girls.

Jasper hopped to attention and went to town sniffing the stranger's ankles.

"Jasper!" At the snap of Maddie's fingers, the dog trotted back to her side.

"Oh, that's okay, sweetie. I don't mind." The woman gestured to the turquoise swing they were on. "That's such a stunning color. I couldn't help noticing it from the road. Do you have any swings for sale?"

Great. Let the eating of his words commence.

Ti slanted a wry smirk his way. "Unfortunately, no, but I'll be sure to suggest that to the owner." She rose and lifted one of the mason jars filled with the shells she and Maddie had collected earlier. "We do have these souvenirs in the same color, though."

"Well, how cute. It'll go perfectly in my sun room." The woman beamed. "I'm redecorating—going for a chic beach theme. Got all kinds of ideas off Pinterest, but I don't really have a knack for crafts. I'd hoped to find some homemade treasures while here this week."

Another telling grin swept in Drew's direction. "You don't say."

He slinked away from the door before the conversation turned into a full-blown I-told-you-so fest, but he only made it a few feet toward his desk when the word "free" brought him to a stop. He hastened back around in time to hear the woman thanking Ti for the gift.

He stretched the screen door open after the customer reached the curb. "What was that?"

"That, my friend, was the power of free advertising." Ignoring his blank expression, Ti returned to her spot on the swing and resumed her artwork. "That tiny investment is going to reap marketing benefits for you. Just watch, ye of little faith."

"Forgive my doubt, oh wise one." He feigned a bow.

Maddie chuckled at his wink.

He reached for his back as he straightened. The surf had been extra choppy this morning.

"You look a little stiff there, cowboy. Too much fun on the mechanical bull last night?"

"Funny."

"Or are you still sore from Coop and I whipping your butt in basketball?"

"Even funnier." Drew unbuttoned his cuffs. "And you owe me a rematch."

Maddie stifled a laugh. "No offense, Dad. But you might want to learn to cut your losses."

Unbelievable. Betrayed by his own daughter. He shook his head. "All right, ladi—"

A fluster of barks from across the street turned Jasper into a reactive spaz. Maddie double-looped his leash around her wrist and dug her heels into the ground. If Jasper had any clue how small he really was, he might not be so quick to throw on his Wonder Dog suit.

Drew's laughter vanished when the growling across the road matched scathing stares from the schnauzer's owners. What were Annie's parents doing on this street? They hadn't spoken to him since the day he and Annie got married.

Her dad's disapproving stare raked over him. Apparently, time hadn't changed anything.

Ti swung her head back and forth between them like a tennis referee. "Making new friends again?"

More like reliving mistakes. "Not today." Drew gripped a piece of taffy in his pocket, refusing to move until the Barretts rounded the corner and meandered out of sight.

"You wanna tell me what that was about?"

"Nope."

As Drew turned to go inside, a sun-bleached blond surfer coasted up to the curb in his golf cart and hopped out. "Sweet. I've been hoping to cross paths with you."

Ti looked behind her and back. "Sorry, do we know each other?"

"Not yet." Surfer Dude extended a hand. "Carter Elliot. I'm visiting from California. You?"

Ti rose to her feet and returned his handshake. "Ti Russo. New York."

"Business or pleasure?"

Her gaze drifted from Maddie to the ground. "Little of both."

"Ahh. Those are the best kind." He called to a woman with a pixie haircut in the golf cart, "Sue, you got any of my business cards on you?"

The cute woman flittered over with a card in hand.

"Thanks, babe." He kissed her cheek. "I own a gallery in San Francisco. I'm always looking for new talent. If you have any work with you, I'd be interested in taking a look."

"Really?" Ti stumbled over the word. "Wait. How'd you know I'm an artist?"

He hurled a glance over the storefront. "Besides transforming this place?"

Drew shoved his sleeves up his arms. There was nothing wrong with his shop. What did Mr. California know about it? He ripped off a bite of taffy. Better than chewing someone out.

"I've seen you taking shots around the island. As a gallery owner, you learn to take notice when you see an artist in love with her work. It's usually a good sign."

"Photography's just a hobby. It's not professional quality."

"I doubt that." Carter smiled with far too much charm.

Ti bent his business card back and forth. Was she blushing?

"You have a portfolio on you?"

"Um, yeah, actually." She pointed to her smart car. "You have a few minutes?"

"I'm all yours."

Feelings Drew had no business having sank into the middle of his chest. A chance for Ti to showcase her photos in a gallery—what she'd always wanted and certainly what she deserved. She would thrive in California or anywhere the wind took her. Girls like her didn't have roots.

Still clutching the taffy wrapper, Drew strode inside to make his usual afternoon tea. He almost snorted at his routine. Nothing like landing the gavel on the defining line between them.

He stopped by the magnets along the wall by the staircase, peeled one off, and sighed.

"*You can turn this shop into whatever you want.*" Ti's infectious words steered his eyes upstairs. Maybe it was time to change his inventory. Finish what he'd once started.

Sunlight flickered over the picture of Dad and him on the wall and refracted across the shop Dad had poured his life into. How could Drew risk letting him down?

He couldn't. Period.

Drew tossed the empty taffy wrapper in the garbage along with the thoughts sidetracking him from the only thing he needed to concentrate on. He returned to his desk with his green tea to sort through which bills he could afford this week. With discipline and focus, he'd see this through on his own.

Several minutes later, the over-the-door bell chimed as a mom and son strolled in behind Ti. The boy ran into the front display and landed his sticky hands against the glass.

Drew bit back the comment he wanted to make and nodded at the woman browsing the back shelf of nightlights. "Let me know if you need any help."

Ti propped an easel against the base of the counter and started rifling through drawers.

Drew strained to ignore her. Right.

Exhaling, he set his pen down. "What are you looking for?" he whispered.

"Your label maker. I know you gotta have one."

Always ready to crack a joke.

"You know, organization can save you a headache. You should try it sometime."

"What do you think coffee's for?"

"Are you on your third cup already?"

"Is that a rhetorical question?" Ti leaned against the counter and studied him with an artsy glint in her eyes.

He shifted in the chair. "Just because I don't have my own portfolios or approach business with your carefree spirit doesn't mean I'm completely anal."

A clamor in the corner drew both their attention to the monster of a boy smearing his hands over another display case.

A few choice words stayed locked in his throat until the mom and kid exited the shop. He reached under the counter for a spray bottle.

Ti looked from the cleaner to Drew and arched a brow. "You were saying, Mr. Clean?"

He sidestepped around her.

"Drew, c'mon, I'm teasing. Business isn't about being free-spirited. It's about knowing what your customers want. Look, I'm the first to admit I never got my MBA, but I know art, and I know people. And you can't sell anything unless you understand your audience."

He spritzed the glass. "And you understand them already?"

"Luckily for you, I actually mingle with people." A thoughtful expression took over. "Families come here on vacation to escape the monotony of everyday life and make new memories. They don't want the same generic souvenirs they can get anywhere. They want something memorable to remind them of what they experienced on this gorgeous island."

Sometimes, all Drew could do was beg his face not to show how much her passion and insights took him aback. Despite his keeping things all business with Ti these last few days, she hadn't pulled away. Hadn't let his distance damper her energy or her commitment to helping the shop turn a profit. She'd never stop surprising him.

As usual, his smile betrayed him.

Ti picked up her easel and headed across the floor.

"Where are you going?"

"To get to work," she said on her way past him.

"You call painting work?"

"I usually call it joy. But at the moment, I call it saving your butt."

He followed her into the back room, where she set a half-finished canvas on her easel. "Hand paintings of the island? I doubt that's very cost effective."

"Paint once, digitalize for endless options. Prints, magnets, note cards, coasters, tote bags. Possibilities, my friend." An appraising glance around the room ended in a look he knew better than to encourage. "You know what you should do?"

Hightail it out of here?

"Offer art classes for kids. This space is perfect for it. Just get rid of that giant furnace or kiln or whatever that is over there. What is that for, anyway? Oh!" She tapped her fingertips together. "You could totally have a pottery class. That'd be awesome, actually."

Drew rubbed his neck. She wasn't supposed to be in this part of the shop.

"It'd be a great way to bring in extra revenue. Families will eat it up. I'm telling ya. It'll give them a fun activity to do when they need a break from the beach."

Did her mind ever slow down? He grinned in spite of himself. But any humor quickly gave way to the reality always lingering in the forefront. "I'm sure you'd enjoy teaching art classes while you're here, but I won't be able to keep that up when you leave."

"Sure you could. I'm a great teacher." She lifted a smock and sauntered over.

He backed away. "Not happening."

"Who said I was talking about teaching *you*?" Her gaze strayed past him as the over-the-door bell dinged.

Maddie ran straight into his legs. She swung around him, eyes alight as she took in the painting. "Wow, is that the harbor?"

"Yep." Ti ran her fingers along the side of the canvas. "Well, the start of it, anyway. I still need a few more pictures to capture the heart of it. Speaking of which ..." There was that dangerous look in her eyes again. "Is Chloe on shift this evening?"

"Yeahhh." This couldn't be good. "Why?"

"'Cause you, Drew Anderson, are taking Maddie and me out on the water tonight."

He coughed. "Excuse me?"

Maddie squeezed his hand in both of hers, excitement already bubbling over. "We can take her to the inlet. Uncle Coop and I cleaned up the skiff this morning."

"I don't think that's a good idea."

Ti mussed his hair. "I know staying here with the diffuser I got you and a barrel of taffy would be relaxing, too, but this will be better. Promise."

Relaxing was definitely off the docket.

Evading her dangerous ocean-colored eyes might've helped if her herbal shampoo weren't messing with his head. "I … I thought you were afraid of the water."

"Of being *in* it, not on it." She crossed her arms. "Besides, I have a song to help with that. I'll teach it to you."

"Negative."

"Aw, c'mon, I can't sing alone."

"Never stopped you before."

"Don't make me start now." Humming, Ti clapped his shoulder. "I'll bring the food. You bring the drinks. It'll be fun. A little spontaneity's good for you, remember?"

When he didn't relent, she lifted her cell to her mouth. "Owner would rather use his label maker than hang out with two of the coolest chicks on the island."

He tried to steal the stupid phone, but she jumped back and circled an arm around Maddie. *Cheater.*

"Please, Dad?"

Drew looked from one expectant face to the other.

Like there was ever a chance of him saying no.

CHAPTER TEN

Sinking

A low-hanging sun and lazy breeze welcomed them to the harbor. Carrying her flip-flops and camera, Ti stepped onto the pier's warm wooden planks and drank in the beauty of the expansive horizon intersecting the quaint docks.

She could get lost here. Could forget what kind of girl she was and stop running for good.

A twinge of guilt snuck in. To be fair, she hadn't fully lied about her reason for coming to visit. Establishing her own art studio this last year had depleted her well of inspiration. She needed to replenish. And she was being useful here, right? Couldn't she stay a little longer?

Maddie let go of Drew's hand and darted for a shallow, flat-bottomed boat tied up to the dock. Jasper barked at the rope as Maddie wrestled the knot. Everything about the precious scene opposed the unrest inside Ti. She needed to pull herself together.

"Don't untie it quite yet." Ti crisscrossed a pair of paddles over the boat's sides, placed the thermos and picnic basket they brought on one of the seats, and knelt on the pier to square off the right angle.

She positioned the boat in the right-hand side of the frame to leave room for adding text to the image. Creativity surged with each take until questions about returning to Astoria gradually subsided.

"Okay, you and Maddie get in." She motioned Drew toward the boat. "Hold her on your lap."

Unlike Jasper, who leapt in without any prodding, Drew angled his chin in hesitation. Ti waved him on. Exhaling, he pulled a life jacket over Maddie, got situated, and helped her in. "You're not putting our faces on postcards, are you?"

"Why? You don't want to be famous?" Ti laughed at the taut expression he gave her. "Relax. With the sun where it is, you'll look more like silhouettes. No one will make you out. Promise. You're just in it for effect."

Ti twisted the lens to focus on the backdrop, capturing a soft image of a dad and daughter creating a memory together. Jasper added a scoring bonus. Families were going to love these prints.

"Now, do something funny. We need a few candid ones."

With Maddie, Drew didn't seem to need much prompting to lower his guard. A tickling fest brought priceless moments to life on camera. Even if all the shots didn't turn out to work for souvenirs, they'd be treasures for the two of them to keep.

Ti's throat tightened at how tender he was with his little girl and how much she made Drew come alive.

"All good?" he asked.

Ti scrolled through the stills. More than good. "Perfect."

"Now, it's your turn." Maddie climbed out of the boat, Jasper her shadow, and extended a hand in front of Ti.

"Maddie." Drew's low tenor rumbled behind her.

Ti gripped the camera. "Um, no. That's okay, love. I'll stay behind the lens."

Head tipped, arms crossed, Miss Obstinacy tapped her foot. "A lot of people come here as couples. Don't you think *they'd* want a few souvenirs, too?"

Dang, she was clever.

A quick glance at Drew caught him sitting as rigidly as if he had one of those oars staked to his spine. At least Ti wasn't the only one uncomfortable with the idea. But Maddie's unrelenting hazel eyes shot down their rebuttals before they could get them out.

Ti shook it off. What was the big deal? They could fake romance for two minutes for the sake of the shop.

She stole a moment to make sure the camera settings were good and slipped the strap over Maddie's head. After giving a quick set of instructions, she stepped into the skiff.

Cautious strides led her across the rocking boat to the seat Drew was still glued to. She fidgeted above him in search of a non-awkward way to join him until he finally gave in to a smile and reached a hand out to steady her.

Fat chance any steadying was happening.

She gave up hiding her amusement and let him take her into his lap. The boat swayed with the movement, stirring up her fears more than expected. She circled her arms around Drew's neck without thinking.

"Don't worry. The sound's much calmer than the ocean, especially in the harbor." His husky voice echoed the security of his hand pressed against her lower back.

Ti averted her gaze from the white foam beside the boat back to his eyes. Like drowning in those green beauties was any safer than going down in the water. She'd look away if they'd let her. They held on instead, driving up her pulse.

If his dimples were any indication, he must've felt her heart rate beating through her wrist onto his neck. "So, how do we do this?" he asked.

Breathe? No clue. And what happened to that breeze?

"Come on, guys," Maddie called. "Look romancy or whatever."

Ti pinched her lips together. Romancy. Right. She loosened her hold on Drew's neck and tried to shove enough fog from her brain to picture which romantic poses would work best for prints.

Another glance around the setting made the choice for her. She stretched her fingers behind his ear, leaned back so her hair dangled over the boat's edge, and angled her feet in the air. Borderless, carefree, picture-perfect romance. It would sell, all right. Even she was buying it.

Camera snaps sounded in the background. "Gorgeous," Maddie complimented like a professional photographer working a shoot.

Drew and Ti both laughed as he pulled her up. But once face to face again, the same intensity from a moment ago crippled her. He brushed a strand of hair off her cheek, his eyes never leaving hers. Being this close to him felt good, real. Too real.

"How we doing?" he asked through a grin that was about to demolish her resistance.

"I think that's probably good." She shot up from his lap. The boat rocked, but nowhere near as forcefully as the waves inside her stomach.

Ti held in a breath as Maddie crawled into the boat with the camera.

"Did they come out okay?" Maddie asked.

Ti secured the camera away from the water. Not that it helped relax her nerves. Her heart sank without explanation as she scrolled through the shots. "They're perfect." Almost enough to believe she and Drew hadn't been pretending.

The scene's irresistible charm must've been getting to her. Even though Drew was intriguing, it wasn't like things between them could go anywhere. A stable family man like him and a tainted wanderer like her? Yeah, right.

Ti curled an arm around Maddie's shoulders and closed out reactions she didn't need to be feeling. She was here to help them. That was all. "I think you have a photographer inside you, missy."

"Really?" Maddie looked to Drew, who smiled his agreement without needing to see the proof. Once he secured her in the boat, he undid the rope and started the motor—all while avoiding Ti's gaze. For once, she was thankful.

"What's with the oars?" she asked him.

"Backup."

As deeply as Ti gulped, Drew must've heard her. "Don't worry. This skiff's been in my family for generations. My dad taught me everything I need to know about helming this boat."

"And Dad taught me."

Ti stared at Maddie. "*You* can drive this thing?"

"Sure."

Of course she could. Ti averted her attention back to her camera.

A ways out on the sound, she shot several takes of the sunset's rich pinks and oranges cascading over the harbor and melting into the horizon like watercolors running off a canvas. She clung to the beauty as the view behind Drew unleashed another reminder of why she was here. They were about to give every other store on the island a run for their money. Her future might not change, but at least Drew and Maddie's could.

Before retiring the camera to her waterproof bag, Ti snapped a few photos with their feet hanging over the side of the boat. Ankles crossed, dog paws perched on the edge, nothing but endless blue hues in the background. She couldn't have framed better shots if she'd had props.

Drew hitched a grin at her flip-flops. "Took my advice, huh?"

"Just 'cause I found a pair of cute shoes that *happened* to be comfy doesn't mean my other ones weren't working just fine around here."

He coughed into his hand. "Liar."

She splashed water at him, but he laughed even harder. *Punk.*

"Did you know Blackbeard died here?" Maddie said out of nowhere as they approached a small inlet.

Ti looked from her to Drew and back. "Really?"

"Yep, the island was his favorite spot. And since he was a pirate and all, that must mean Ocracoke's a little piece of treasure."

In case Maddie's cuteness didn't cause Ti's heart to swell enough, the love in Drew's expression overran every space inside her until there was no room left to breathe.

"You know," Ti said. "I think you might be on to something." Ocracoke had more treasures than she'd ever expected to find.

A splash on the opposite side of the boat whipped all their heads toward Jasper doggy paddling the rest of the way to the inlet. Apparently, someone was a little excited.

Drew hopped out and dragged the boat onto the small, secluded shoreline.

"Ooh!" Maddie sprang to her feet. "Is that why Grandpa named the shop Anderson's Soundside Treasures?"

"You got it." Winking, Drew lifted her from the boat and then helped Ti out.

"Come on." Maddie grabbed Ti's hand as soon as her toes reached the sand. "This is where Dad used to come to—"

"Okay, Sea Monkey. Ti doesn't need a guided tour. Why don't we eat first before it gets dark?" He retrieved the thermos and picnic basket from the bottom of the boat.

Ti dispensed the sandwiches she'd made. "I don't cook. So, you're stuck with peanut butter and jelly. Hope that's okay."

"No worries." Drew peeled open the plastic wrap. "It's hard to go wrong with a PB and J." One bite into it, and his face disagreed. He worked his jaw, looking like someone had lathered sticky putty all over it.

Ti tore off a small piece of her own. Not small enough. The bread stuck to the roof of her mouth in a thick coating. She tried not to laugh while prying it free in a not-so-ladylike manner. "Sorry. It's a little dry."

Drew finally got it down. "No, it's just very, um…" His lips quirked. "Peanut buttery." Muted laughter shook his shoulders.

"Shut up. Jelly has a lot of sugar in it. I didn't want to put too much on." She flicked a shell at him and stretched for the thermos, desperate to wash down the sandwich.

He snagged the thermos before her fingers grazed it. "I'm sorry. Are you thirsty?"

"You think you're funny, don't you?" Ti went for it again, but he scooted out of reach. Swapping it from hand to hand, Drew had her practically tackling him to steal it. She grabbed it. "Better watch out, Houdini, or you'll end up mysteriously lost at sea."

"Not before your phone will."

A glance at her cell on the blanket spurred a dozen comebacks she wanted to record in front of him. Tempting. Almost as much as lingering this close to him was. With his hair damp around his temples from the day's heat and a whimsical slant playing in his eyes, she almost pressed in and lost herself in a moment no camera could give justice to.

And end up complicating things?

The instant shove-back in her thoughts broke Ti away. Eyes averted, she toyed with the thermos instead. "This isn't green tea, is it?"

"Is that a rhetorical question?" He mimicked her tone from earlier.

"I hate when you do that."

"I know." His way-too-amused grin barely got the words out. "You might end up liking the tea, you know."

"On a scale from zero to zero?" She twisted the cap off and fake-glared at him before taking a swig. Darn. It was actually good. She hid her reaction behind the lid. No way she was letting him win this one.

"Did you know June 15 is World Sea Turtle Day?" Maddie chimed in. She tore apart her sandwich a piece at a time, apparently the only one unfazed by its dryness. "Female turtles lay their eggs in the same place every year."

"Is that right?" Ti couldn't help enjoying her enthusiasm.

"Yep. I've seen babies on this inlet before. Hatching usually happens between March and October, but I like to come by in the summer, anyway, just in case they come back." Maddie left a pile of crust on her napkin for Jasper and flitted off to the far tip of the inlet.

Drew admired his daughter, playing in her element. "She wants to be a marine biologist."

Given her love of turtles, Ti couldn't picture any better career for her. "I'm sure she'll make a great one."

"Someday." He kept his focus ahead, but Ti didn't miss the audible concern for the future tussling with his words.

Rather than press, she excused herself to give Drew some space and joined Maddie at the shoreline, where she was sifting through sand for pieces of sea glass.

"That's a pretty one."

Maddie examined the contours while spinning it around in the remaining sunlight. "Yep, I think it passes the sparkle test. I'll keep it."

"The sparkle test, huh?" Ti repressed a chuckle.

"Shine quality. We only keep the best. It has to be special. At least, that's what Dad says Mama used to say."

A bracelet around Maddie's ankle glistened in the light. "Did your mama make that?"

Maddie straightened the glass pendant above her foot. "One of the few. She left most of them unfinished. Dad says that's what artists do. Something about unrest ... I don't remember now. But one day, I'm gonna learn how to make pretty jewelry, too."

Comprehension poured in with the soft waves banking against the shore. Ti peered back at Drew, staring out to sea like a sailor waiting for the tide to wash away all traces of heartache. White foam clung to her ankles, reality not letting her go.

No wonder Drew had been resisting any connection with her. His guarded disposition wasn't because he disliked or misunderstood art. It was because he'd loved and lost an artist.

CHAPTER ELEVEN

Void

Ahead, moonlight draped over Maddie's strawberry blonde curls while she sorted through her newly acquired treasures. Jasper trotted alongside. Both still full of the same joy that had been buoying them all evening.

Unlike Drew.

Ti peeked at him beside her. The walk from the harbor carried about as few words as the boat ride from the inlet had. Maddie had managed to pull him out of his reverie earlier. Had even gotten him to laugh and horse around with them for a while. But every time he caught himself having fun, he'd retreat.

What was going through his head? He had to know Ti wasn't trying to—couldn't begin to—compete with his late wife. But helping out had become more than just a distraction tactic. She couldn't walk away now. Maybe if she could put him at ease...

While walking, she gently nudged Drew with her shoulder. "Sorry for keeping you out later than planned."

"Again." He stayed face forward, but the shadow of a grin fell on her.

"Hey, at least no one contemplated hijacking a ferry this time."

A soft laugh drifted over her. "Speak for yourself," he half-whispered.

Ti ran a finger along her hoop earring, thoughts circling in the silence. "Drew, I want you to know I think you're a good businessman. I haven't meant to overstep—"

"Anderson." A shaggy-haired guy about Drew's age jogged up from the opposite direction with a surfboard in hand. "Are you seriously selling your Monsta 3?"

Maddie whipped around. "Your competition board? Why would you sell that?"

Because he'd make any sacrifice to provide for her. Ti's already-tense heart compressed even more as she ushered Maddie forward.

Drew scratched the back of his neck. "Yeah, why don't we hook up later, Palmer. Tomorrow morning at Eduardo's?"

The dude clasped Drew's hand. "You got it, bro."

Once the guy jogged on, Maddie shimmied out of Ti's hold and marched right up to her dad. "How can you get rid of your shortboard?"

He ruffled her bangs. "It's complicated, Sea Monkey."

"No, it's not. You—"

"Oh, good. You saved us a trip." Of all people, Marcus strutted up with the same brunette from the party the other night. Wearing a button-down this time might've helped Ti's gag reflex if he didn't have the top four buttons open.

Jasper released a low growl when Marcus and the girl stopped in front of them under a streetlight. "We were just on our way—"

"To a *Miami Vice* reunion?" Ti tipped her head to the side. "Let me guess. You're hoping to borrow a clean V-neck, since all of yours must be dirty, right? Sorry, but Drew tends to go for the manlier look."

Marcus skewered her with a glare until a slow leer burned with enough heat to singe those chest hairs of his. "It's a good thing your girlfriend thinks she's funny. Maybe her stand-up act can support you after I buy your shop at the auction and put you out of business."

He roped an arm around the brunette and flaunted an envelope at Drew. "We told Mr. Parsons we'd save him a stamp and hand-deliver your foreclosure notice ourselves."

Auction? Foreclosure? Why hadn't Drew told her things were this bad?

Drew yanked the envelope from him and tore it open. "Mr. Parsons was supposed to give me more time. I . . ." With a sharp glower at Marcus's smug look, Drew crumpled the page.

"Don't beat yourself up, Anderson. Not everyone can be in the ninety-eight percent of Americans who actually make good on their loans." He tapped Drew's shoulder. "But hey, we can still have one last shop-to-shop showdown during the surf competition, huh? For old times' sake."

Still clutching the paper in a death grip, Drew barreled into Marcus's face.

Ti squeezed between them and braced a hand to Drew's heaving chest. "Not here." She motioned with her eyes toward Maddie.

Drew slowly backed down but didn't unclench his fists. Ti pried the notice free, looped her arm around his, and urged him forward. Despite how much she wanted to pluck Marcus's curls out one by one and shove them down his throat right now, this wasn't the time or place.

"Hope I didn't ruin your night," Marcus called in a singsong voice from behind them.

Drew's veins bulged against Ti's grip on his arm.

She tugged him forward. "Keep walking."

A cool gust of wind met them around the corner like a godsend.

"Dad, what's he talking about?"

With the same tenderness Ti had seen Drew offer Maddie again and again, he wiped all traces of frustration from his face and took her hand. "Nothing I can't take care of, sweetie." He kissed the top of her head. "It's gonna be fine."

Cooper and Livy waved at them from across the street. "Right on time, guys." Cooper tossed a football at Drew. "Ready to hit the beach for a few?"

Ti slid the notice in her pocket and gathered Maddie's hair off her shoulders. "We should probably get to bed—"

"Only if you're ready to take a beating." Drew spiraled the football back at his brother.

Ti gaped at Drew.

"What?"

"*You* want to stay out later?" She edged closer and lowered her voice. "After what just happened?"

Drew swooped Maddie up on his shoulders and jogged backward. "What's life without spontaneity, right?" With a visibly forced smile, he turned and caught up to Cooper.

What in the world?

Livy pressed an arm into Ti's. "Did you guys have fun tonight?"

Ti peered behind her toward Marcus's trailing silhouette. "Um, sort of."

"I'm impressed you even got Drew out there."

"Why?"

Livy twisted the drawstrings on her shorts and kept her head down. "Just 'cause." She cupped her hands around her mouth. "Hey, guys, wait up." She waved Ti forward. "Come on."

Okay, apparently everyone on the island was trying to compete for Ti's Queen of Deflection title tonight. Shaking her head, she jogged onto the beach with the rest of the group.

Talk about being dethroned. Marcus's bombshell grated on Ti's nerves the longer she sat watching Drew act like the run-in didn't happen. No one could blame him for not wanting to think about losing the shop right now, but something more was bothering him. It had been all night. Was she a painful reminder of what he'd lost?

"They're great with her, aren't they?" Livy popped the tab on her soda can and jarred Ti from her thoughts.

A few feet off the shore, Drew and Cooper threw the football above Maddie and Jasper, playing monkey in the middle. The stars glittered above them like her sparkly flip-flops.

"Maddie couldn't ask for more." Other than a mom. Ti traced the prong between her toes. "Did you and Drew ever date?"

Liv almost snorted out her drink. "Do you have to ask?"

"What? You'd be good for him." Liv might've had a rough stint in London, but she was the kind of girl guys like Drew went for.

"He's like a big brother. End of story."

"Okay, fine. What about Cooper? You're telling me you two never hooked up?"

"This is Coop we're talking about. Of course we did." Livy dug her toes in the sand. "But it didn't take long to figure out we make better friends." She leaned her palms on the blanket. "Besides, his heart's already taken. He won't admit it, but it's there."

Ti brushed the sand off her hands. "Ocracoke's infamous ladies' man fell in love, huh? So, why go chasing after second place?"

"Same reason we all do."

To fill a void. Story of Ti's life.

Livy gazed at the Andersons. "I'm just glad they took me in as a friend when I first got here. I would've been lost without them. They're good guys."

Yeah. The kind who sacrificed to take care of the people in their lives. The kind women dreamed of marrying and building a future with. Both guys deserved the whole Pleasantville-life that came with this adorable town.

Once again, she ached over knowing Drew'd had that once. Wind tangled knots through her hair, brokenness through her heart. No one could expect him to settle for anything less now.

Drops of water sprinkled onto Ti from behind. She spun around and peered up at Cooper's mischievous dimples. He snagged a towel from the blanket and rubbed it over his hair. "Drew and I think we should teach you to surf before the competition. You know, to make sure you feel a part."

"I think you mean feel humiliated."

"Not possible."

"Mm-hmm." She stole his balled-up towel and chucked it at his face.

"Hey, you're always talking about needing the full Ocracoke experience to help with your art, right? There's no better way than to dive right in."

"Not gonna happen, buddy. But I'll give you bonus points for the smooth try."

"Well, if you're gonna play hardball, then I'm sorry."

"For what?"

"This." Without warning, Cooper scooped her up and hauled her to the water.

Drew flopped down on the blanket beside Livy while Cooper threatened to toss Ti in the shallow waves. Maddie hung from Coop's arm, coming to Ti's rescue. Laughs and squeals erupted in the familiar song of bonding they'd shared all week.

Drew would have better luck shaking every last grain of sand from his hair than shaking off the images of Ti spending the evening with them like a part of their family. Why'd he agree to bring her to such a personal place today?

Jasper's barks joined Maddie's laughter as she fought to take Cooper down from behind. Ti flailed, her hair an untamable force in the wind.

"That could be you, you know?" Livy nodded at the shore.

Drew sat up. "I don't do that."

"Have fun?"

"Flirt." Unless he wanted to make an idiot of himself. Like he needed another reminder of the charisma and impulse he lacked. Besides, what was the point in starting something that had a time-ticking expiration date on it?

Livy's gentle touch to his arm mirrored the intuition in her eyes, despite his attempt to avoid it. "I know Ti shares similarities with Annie. And believe me, I don't want anyone to get hurt, but I've seen the way you are around her, Drew." She raised a shoulder. "You like her."

"Like her?" He looked at Ti as she fought to keep her feet from skimming the waves. "The girl drives me nuts. If her New York accent didn't irk my nerves enough, her matching no-filter issue is gonna give me an ulcer one of these days. Don't get me started on that phone of hers. And a fear of the water? C'mon. Who doesn't love the ocean? That's just not natural."

He brushed a shell off the blanket, unable to tear his gaze from Ti's aggravatingly contagious smile. "A coffee-addicted, nonstop-talking vegetarian, who always has jokes. She's—"

"Drew." Livy squeezed his arm to cut him off. "Exactly."

"Exactly what?"

"My point." She picked up her drink. "You're really daft sometimes, you know that? You're good for each other. Don't be afraid to give it a go."

He managed to shut his jaw before a horsefly could zip inside. "You're crazy."

"No, I'm observant. A trait I picked up from *the girl* you can't take your eyes off of."

He fumbled for a response, inadvertently adding a thousand exclamation points to Livy's comment.

She fixed him with another perceptive gaze. "It's been nine years. No one expects scars to disappear magically. And I'm not saying you have to make some big commitment. I just want to see you remember how to have fun again."

"You're barking up the wrong tree, Livy." He shifted on the blanket, the concave dips and mounds in the sand a reflection of his thoughts.

With a gentle smile saying what he knew was coming, Livy set her drink aside. "It's time to move on, Drew. Annie's not coming back."

He exhaled without looking at her. "And in a few short weeks, Ti will be gone, too."

The thought of facing Maddie's disappointment when that happened burned him. Coming to the beach was a mistake. This whole day was. As much as he couldn't stand Marcus, at least his sucker punches reminded Drew what was at stake this summer.

He rose and called Maddie over.

Livy scurried up to her feet. "Drew, don't be mad."

"I'm not. It's late, that's all. I need to get Maddie in bed." And himself back on target. Starting with a call it would kill him to make.

CHAPTER TWELVE

Release

Busting his butt at work all day kept Drew's mind off his talk with Livy about as well as failing to sleep had. Thankfully, Ti hadn't been around much today. He could only tackle one challenge at a time.

Behind the counter at the shop, Drew slouched in his chair. The foreclosure notice in his lap could've dragged him through the floorboards with its gravity, but he had to do whatever it took. Selling his shortboard this morning had already gutted him. Might as well keep the blows coming.

He switched ears and held the phone with his shoulder while background music looped through its third sequence.

"Hello."

Drew scrambled up in the seat. "Mr. Parsons. Thanks for taking my call this late in the day. I'm sure you're trying to get out the door."

"It's no problem. I assume this is about the notice."

The one about to cost him everything? *Yeah, you could say that.*

Drew set the paper on the counter and resituated positions. Twice. Ten minutes of being on hold should've given him enough time to prepare at least one compelling sentence.

"This is just as awkward for me, Drew. I've known you all your life. Your father was a good friend. But I can only bend the rules so much."

"I know. And I can't tell you how much I hate putting you in this position, but I thought I had a little more time to work this out. Things are picking up here. If we can hold off until a week after the surf competition, I promise I'll make good on what I owe." No matter what he had to do.

Drew tapped the stapler to his forehead, grateful Dad wasn't around to hear him grovel. He looked away from the photo of them on the wall. "Four more weeks, Mr. Parsons. Please."

His pause stretched. "I'll see what I can do."

Drew's shoulders caved with a breath of relief. "Thank you." He closed his eyes after hanging up. *Please be enough time.*

A *clank* in front of him jerked his head up. From behind Ti's cute little *accessory* glasses, headstrong eyes met his with a look he was beginning to know by heart. He peered from her to the fish tank full of sea glass she had just heaved onto the counter.

She gripped the sides and leaned over it. "Sea glass."

"Um, yeahhh. I see that." Drew rose and circled toward her. "What is it doing out of my living room?"

"Possibilities. Remember?" Ti dug her fingers into the massive collection. "What tourist wouldn't love a souvenir from Ocracoke's shores?"

He unburied her hands and motioned to the displays behind her. "That's why I sell shells. You sure you're okay? You didn't skip your third cup of coffee today, did you?"

"No, you don't understand." She withdrew a bracelet from her pocket and laid it beside the tank. "I'm not talking about premade shipments from China you can get anywhere. I'm talking about authentic jewelry handmade with local glass collected on the very island the tourist visited."

A slow simmer built from the base of his stomach.

Ti dipped her head under his. "It's the perfect merchandise. Valuable. Worth a higher price. Customers will love it. I'm telling—"

"These aren't for sale." Releasing his balled-up hands didn't stop his veins from throbbing. He grabbed a fistful of taffy.

"What do you mean they're not for sale?"

He skated around her. "Drop it, Ti."

She stalked after him. "What's your problem? This could be the prime inventory to highlight during the competition. At least finish hearing me out."

"Don't have to. The answer's no."

"Drew." She caught his sleeve. "Why are you being like this? I know the glass might have sentimental value, but we're talking about—"

"You don't know a thing about it."

Her hold on his arm faltered. Instead of zinging an obstinate comeback, she blanched as if backhanded.

Remorse coiled around the anger already twisting in his chest. He didn't mean to be short with her. Didn't want to hurt her. But she didn't know how far back the glass collection stretched. What selling it would mean.

Ti lifted her lashes toward him, determined stance reestablished. "Maybe not. But I know you need this."

Currents of grace and conviction streamed from her blue eyes.

The over-the-door bell chimed, but he didn't release her gaze. Not when Cooper strode in carting a folding table. Or when Livy moseyed up to give Ti a hello kiss on the cheek. Not when the bell rang a second time. Or when Grandma Jo's voice sounded in the background. Drew didn't blink, let alone breathe, until Maddie's arms curled around his waist.

"I can't believe I finally get to make my own jewelry," she practically squealed. "This is the coolest!"

Drew stuffed the taffy in his pocket, whirled her up into a hug, and set her back down with a kiss to the head. He took in each face looking back at him from around the shop. "What are you guys all doing here?"

Grandma Jo flaunted a no-brainer look. "We're here to help."

"Sorry we're a little late." Livy tossed Cooper a teasing glare. "*Someone* got tied up figuring out which way to part his hair."

"Real funny. I had a time-sensitive matter to take care of."

"The hair," Livy mouthed from behind him while patting the top of her head.

Cooper sauntered toward Drew, dimples sinking in. "But I wouldn't miss helping out my bro." He planted a hand on Drew's shoulder. "'Cause nothing says brotherhood like stringing bracelets together."

Ti turned in the opposite direction but couldn't hide the laughter bobbing her shoulders.

Drew fake-punched Coop in the ribs. "Get outta here."

Laughing, Cooper stumbled over to finish setting up the worktable. Maddie dove right in getting everyone squared away with materials, while Livy and Grandma Jo brought in chairs from the back room.

Moved by his friends' and family's willingness to help him fight for the shop, Drew wrestled with apprehension until Livy's words from last night finally broke through.

"It's time to move on."

He thought he had. Annie certainly didn't give him much of a choice. Forward. That had always been the goal. No living in the past. But it took only one peek at the tank behind him to admit he'd been clinging to parts he was still afraid to let go of.

Ti twisted her earring while staring at the floor. Here she was, caring enough to push him beyond his borders. Again. And he'd gotten defensive like a jerk. Again.

Cooper tossed a wad of hemp string at him. "Don't think you're getting out of this, hoss."

"C'mon, Dad," Maddie seconded.

Ti grabbed Drew's hand. "Actually, will you excuse us for a sec?" She steered him to the back room and started to pace. "I'm really sorry to broadside you like this. The idea for the jewelry came to me last night. I got so excited thinking about the difference it could make in sales, I sort of ran with it."

Sort of? She didn't know any other mode. He blocked her path to the furnace. At least this project distracted her from pressing about her pottery idea.

"I know other stores sell jewelry but not like this. I honestly believe it'll be a good thing for the shop, but I should've asked you first. I should've—"

"Ti." He intercepted one of her strides past him. "It's okay."

"Really?"

He peered back at the glass and released an exhale along with his hold on things he couldn't change. "Yeah, really. Sorry I snapped at you earlier."

Her smile out-sparkled any sea glass he'd ever found. In classic Ti-style, she sprang her arms around his neck with her bubbling-over enthusiasm. "It's gonna be great, Drew. Promise."

His muscles constricted against her curves, the need to let go clashing with the fear of what that would cost him. A breath at a time, his fingertips traced her waistline till they grazed the warm skin along her lower back.

An ache seized the center of his chest. Not just from the craving for physical contact. Something more. Deeper. A yearning for release to hope again.

His arms tightened around her. *I hope you're right.*

Two hours of banging out the jewelry had sounded better in theory. Ti tied a knot in the anklet she was working on and rubbed her sore fingers.

Cooper plopped his last piece on the stack in front of him. "Ten. Tell me that meets my quota."

Maddie set a cute turquoise bracelet on top of a pile twice the size of his and grinned. "Amateur."

"Oh, yeah?" The screech of Cooper's chair blended into Maddie's squeals as she bounded away from him across the display room.

"Should we call it a night?" Livy hauled a box up from the floor.

A quick survey of all they'd accomplished ended with a nod. Ti scooped up her pieces and set them in the box. "I think we made enough for now. Thanks for pitching in, guys." She cupped a hand over Grandma Jo's. "Seriously. It was a huge help."

"As long as we get to keep one, we'll call it even." Grandma Jo fingered an eye-catching necklace and winked.

Ti laughed. "Gotta appreciate a woman with style." She cut a glance Drew's way. "Maybe you can rub some off on *this* one."

He stretched his arms behind him in a yawn. "There's nothing wrong with my style."

"Says the button-down poster child." All right, fine. So, he pulled off the loose-fitting shirt, rolled-up sleeves, sexy look pretty darn well, but still. The guy needed variety in his life.

Drew pushed on the table to stand, slid a bracelet on his wrist with extra flair, and waved it at her. "How's this?"

"Fetching."

A glimpse of an eye roll circled over her as he turned.

"C'mon. At least let me buy you a Henley or something."

Without taking the bait, he kept striding for the register.

Cooper finally lowered Maddie's feet to the floor.

Still breathless from laughter, she gave him a good shove and scurried over to Grandma Jo and the chance to pick out her own handmade treasure.

"You're coming out tonight, right, hoss?" Cooper leaned in front of the register. "Don't try to tell me you're gonna pass up a drink after two hours of bedazzling."

Head angled, Drew pushed his sleeves up higher. But before he could get out a response, Cooper wheeled around. "That's what I thought. Ladies, drinks at Dajio's?"

Livy perched a hand on her hip. "You buying?"

His dimples answered for him.

Grandma Jo traipsed over with an arm around Maddie's back and nodded at Drew. "I'll take her home. You stay out a while."

"Aw, I don't know. I should—"

"It wasn't a question." Shutting down any rebuttal, Grandma Jo led Maddie outside.

Ti curled a strand of hair between her lips to keep from laughing. She liked Ms. Spunk more and more each day.

Livy slid the box of jewelry on the counter. "Need help cleaning up the rest of this?"

"I got it." Drew tapped some papers into a stack. "You guys go ahead."

Cooper held the door open, while Ti waved Livy on.

Drew had said he was fine with letting go of the glass collection. And truthfully, he'd been a good sport making the jewelry. But he'd stayed quiet most of the evening. A shade of torment still colored his eyes, but it had turned even more complex. Should she risk asking?

Ti folded her arms over the counter as he finished closing out the register. She tapped a paperclip against the wood. "I'm really sorry about overstepping my boundaries on this. I honestly didn't mean to push."

"Thought we settled this already."

"So did I. But you've seemed sort of—I don't know—off."

"Nope." He rounded the edge, strode for the table, and folded the first chair. "Just have some things on my mind."

She followed. "Thinking about the foreclosure notice?"

Drew's hand idled over the next chair but only for a moment. "Among other things," he mumbled.

With her fingers laced behind her, she raised her shoulders. "You want to talk about it?"

He cut a not-happening glance her way.

"Right. Not good at talking. Got it. But if you wanted to—"

"Ti…"

"Okay." She raised her palms. "I just want to make sure you know you're not alone in all this."

Without looking up, he slowly propped a third folded chair against the others.

Ti bit her lip. There she went, crossing boundaries again. What was wrong with her?

But instead of retreating, Drew approached her. "You really care about helping us, don't you?"

"Of course I do."

Deep green eyes backed her up a step. "Why?"

"I ... just do."

He edged closer. In a matter of seconds, his presence filled the entire room. His aftershave, the hint of green tea on his lips, the unruly section of hair screaming for her fingers. She shuffled another inch backward.

Drew's chin dipped slightly, taking his gaze with it. "What you did today ... getting everyone involved like that. It was sweet." The corner of his mouth crept to the left as he found her eyes again. "Presumptuous, maybe. But sweet."

Despite his playful smile, something deeper lingered. Something she couldn't read.

"Drew." Ti set a palm on his chest. His very *solid* chest. Dumb move. She whipped her hand away as if she'd just touched the fired-up furnace in the back. Smooth.

She tucked her fingers safely under her arms and oscillated her weight from one leg to the other. Antsy much? Jeez, she needed to get a grip.

He angled his head, green eyes claiming her. The heat of his skin this close drove her senseless. And with one heartbeat, antsy turned to downright paralyzed.

CHAPTER THIRTEEN

Connection

Ti dislodged the breath trapped in her rib cage and straightened. But once caught up in Drew's gaze again, logic melted to the floor. He could say he was fine all he wanted. Could use any diversion tactic available. But nothing could mask the hint of uncertainty shadowing his eyes. It gripped her now as much as it had the night she first saw him. Even more so.

"There's something you're not saying." Her insubordinate hand reached for his cowlick. "Something hidden in this unsearchable mind of yours." Did it have to do with his late wife? With Ti? It made sense for him to fear getting hurt all over again.

When he lowered his gaze, the furrow in his brow squeezed around Ti's heart. She would be lying if she denied the connection between them. It surged with such intensity right now, her pulse nearly beat through her skin. But they couldn't go there.

Could they?

A slow blink lifted his eyes to hers and hedged her back another step until there was nowhere else to go.

"You always call it like you see it." He flexed a palm to the wall pressing into her back. "So, tell me what you see?"

She'd have to remember how to breathe first. Words stayed buried under her diaphragm. One swallow. Two.

"Brokenness," she finally said. So much, the pain could've been her own.

His Adam's apple bobbed. "And you think you can fix me."

What? "No, I—"

"Then why do you make me want to …?" His focus grazed her lips. "Why do you have to be so …?"

Her heart hammered against reason. "So what?"

The inches between them confiscated each breath. She balled her fingers to keep from grabbing his shirt. But what if—?

"So complicated." With a hard exhale, Drew hung his head. He relented to the hint of a smile, as if pondering an inside joke, but the flicker of amusement faded as quickly as it came. He pushed off the wall and ran a hand under his collar. "We should probably go."

Sure. As soon as her legs solidified again. Or at least once her brain regained control of the rest of her. Had she seriously almost kissed him? How reckless was she?

Ti wandered around the shop—the part of him he would risk everything for. She wouldn't jeopardize that. Wouldn't let herself hurt him. Or Maddie.

After he finished putting up the table, he met her at the door. Not much rivaled the humidity's thickness around here, but the awkward silence trailing them outside might've had it beat.

Drew cast a glance in her direction as they walked. "You must've thought the jewelry thing wasn't going to go over well."

"What makes you say that?"

"Your earrings."

She stopped, head tilted. "I'm sorry, do you have a jacket I can borrow? 'Cause it just got a little windy out here in left field."

He laughed. "You wear those big hoops or long dangly things when you're in a good mood and studs when you're upset about something." He lifted a hand to her teardrop earrings. "So, I figured these medium ones were a cautious middle."

She breathed in at the touch of his fingertips skimming her ear. "I … don't coordinate my earrings with my mood."

His grin disagreed. "If you say so." He pushed his rolled-up sleeves above his elbows, his countenance drifting in the opposite direction. "But you know the jewelry isn't enough, right? The foreclosure … I only have four weeks …"

"The jewelry's just a start. I have more ideas. Some good ones."

A soft smile landed over her. "I'm sure you do."

He might not believe those ideas could help, but they had to. It was all she had to give him.

A few minutes down the road, Drew's attention gravitated toward his house.

Ti leaned an arm into his. "You can take your drink to go, if you want."

"You really do have mind reading on your résumé, don't you?" His chuckle drifted down the street and into a chorus of crickets.

The southern live oaks bordering the road bowed their branches to the wind while their leaves entertained the breeze.

A gray and white Shih Tzu vaulted off a woman's lap on a nearby tree swing and raced to the edge of the property as they passed.

Drew gave the dog's head a good rub. "No coming in the street, Rufus."

Of course he knew the dog's name. Small-town charm at its finest. One of its many perks. Ti toyed with her bracelet. "Grandma Jo seems like a real blessing."

"More than I deserve. The woman's been watching over our family for decades."

"Was she a friend of your parents'?"

He nodded. "She lost her husband early. Since she doesn't have children of her own, we sort of adopted her into the family. Even more so after my mom died."

The streetlight streamed over the pavement. "That must be nice."

"Becoming a widow early?"

She shoved him. "Having a group of people who love you like that. A family you know you can always count on." A traitorous knot seized her throat.

"You didn't have that growing up?"

Ti's balance snagged on his question.

Drew caught her arm. "You okay?"

Anything but.

Eyes of genuine concern searched hers, and the panic commandeering her spine turned into guilt. Here she was, smack in the middle of his life. He had every right to inquire about hers. But how could she let him see where she came from? Her heart thrummed like the wings of a dozen horse-flies.

"Ti?"

Startling, she jutted a thumb behind her. "I actually have something I need to work on tonight. Will you tell Livy and Cooper I'm sorry I can't make it?"

"Um ..." He raised his shoulders, confusion marching across his face. "Sure."

"Thanks." She turned before his expression cut any deeper.

Halfway back to the house, Ti stopped with her hands on her knees and inhaled slowly. The briny air that had once burned her lungs now soothed them. Not good. She was getting too comfortable, letting feelings that were off-limits side-track her.

She raked her bangs off her forehead with her glasses, drove her attraction to Drew out of reach where it belonged, and waited for some semblance of concentration to break through.

The surf competition. That was the only thing she needed to focus on right now. She turned in a circle, wheels spinning. They needed to make the most of the crowd being there. The shop was on track to handle it. They just had to get customers in the door without interference.

She shot her head up. *Got it.*

Her one-mission path directed her straight to Mr. Fiazza's. In case there was any question which house was his, the cut-out yard sign with a big *X* over a dog going to the bathroom on the grass eliminated any doubt.

Ti knocked on the door, slipped her hands in her back pockets, and smiled at the dragonflies dancing around the porch light. "You guys should leave while you can. Trust me."

A bustle stirred behind the door. An even crotchetier version of Mr. Fiazza than she remembered emerged. "Who in the—?"

"Mr. Fiazza, we need to talk."

"Not at this hour, we don't." While mumbling under his breath, he tucked one side of his white bathrobe tighter into the other and doubled the knot on his belt straps. "You have some gall coming here like this."

"You haven't known me long. You'll get used to it." She peeked around his unhinged jaw toward a fifty-five-inch flat screen mounted on a wood paneled wall opposite a corduroy couch. Apparently, electronic upgrades trumped all others. "Nice digs."

His five-foot-six frame grew an extra inch in an attempt to block her view.

"Listen, this'll only take a minute. Then you can get back to the Double Jeopardy round you're missing right now." She stopped the door with her hand as he swung it. "I know you have a thing for Jolene."

He gaped at her. "What did you just say?"

"Relax, Romeo. Your secret's safe with me. I just thought you might want a chance at winning the woman you love."

Turning a memorable shade of maroon, Mr. Fiazza strode onto the porch. "This is absurd."

"No, letting pride rob you of the things you've always wanted is absurd." Ti folded and unfolded the arms of her glasses, back and forth. "You've loved her since, when? High school? She married someone else. You got bitter. But by the time she was widowed, you'd caused too much of a rift between you to ever think things could change."

Mr. Fiazza matched his son's scathing stare. "How do you know all this? You some kind of reporter?"

"Just observant. And I don't need to dig up details when you just confirmed them."

He opened his mouth but snapped it shut. She had him, and he knew it.

"So, what do you want?"

"I want to coach you how to be around Jolene."

The corner of his eye twitched. "In exchange for ...?"

"The pallets from your hotel."

"You want my trash?"

"I'm going to make art pieces out of them."

"Uh-huh." He studied her like she was the one who needed a white robe—the kind with arms that buckled across the back for restraint.

Ti blew off her offense over his lack of artistic vision. The real reason she came was more important. "Plus," she added, "I want you to get Marcus to back off Drew for a while."

Mr. Fiazza scoffed. "My son has a mind of his own."

"One that's greatly influenced by what his father thinks, I'm sure." Ti crossed her arms, not backing down. "Traffic from the upcoming surf competition will bring enough business for everyone. Just talk him into not interfering with what we're doing at the Anderson shop. That's all I'm asking."

He heaved a sigh. "Fine."

"Thank you." Ti fluttered her fingertips together. "This is gonna be fun."

With an almost imperceptible nod, Mr. Fiazza reopened his front door. "Good night, Miss Reporter."

"I'll meet you here tomorrow at seven." Ti leaned around the door as it closed. "First item on the to-do list is to get you pants that actually reach your shoes. Then we'll tackle manners," she slipped in right before the door slammed.

With her shoulders to her ears, Ti let out a small squeal. Even living a *Grumpy Old Men* remake couldn't dampen her spirits. She was going to save Drew's shop if it killed her.

Back at the trailer, she changed into boxers and an off-the-shoulder T-shirt, curled up at Cooper's desk with a bag of kale chips and a notepad, and started sketching some designs for the pallets.

Almost an hour later, a soft knock at the door interrupted the silence. She cracked it open. "Drew?"

"Your light was on. I thought you might still be up. But if it's a bad time, I can … What is *that*?" He motioned to the bag in her hand.

She flung it behind her back. "Nothing," she mumbled through a mouthful of kale.

There were those stinking dimples again. He poked his head inside the trailer. "Crunching all by yourself where no one can hear you, huh?"

"No." She bit down as quietly as possible.

"You know I'm gonna give you flak for this."

"Whatever, Alfalfa."

He danced from under her hand reaching for his cowlick. Why did he have to be so adorable sometimes?

Ditching the bag of chips, Ti leaned against the trim. "Listen, I'm sorry about dipping out earlier. I had some business to take care of."

"You don't have to apologize for coming and going as you like."

"I know."

"Okay."

"Okay." She grazed her toes along the back of her calf.

An awkward shuffle ensued until Drew lifted a to-go coffee cup and the corners of his mouth. "Penance."

She arched a brow.

"For that thermos stunt I pulled at the inlet. Among other mess-ups," he added softly.

"You brought me coffee at ten o'clock at night?"

He feigned shock. "Sorry, I must've confused you with the girl who usually carts a caffeine IV around with her. You have special timeframes for drinking coffee?"

"Only when I'm breathing."

"That's what I thought."

Conceding, she took a sip and fluttered her lashes. Pure heavenly perfection. "How'd you know how I like it?"

Deferring to a lopsided smile, he backed up and turned. "Night, Ti." The afterglow of his presence spread through her to places hot coffee couldn't touch.

"Night," she whispered back.

Even after he disappeared inside, Ti stayed in the doorway with her cup in hand and heart jumbled in her ribs. She faced the Prussian blue sky and clutched her arms over her chest. She'd learned to fool a lot of people over the years. Maybe even herself. But pretending she wasn't falling for Drew Anderson was one act no amount of deflection could mask.

Hope tingled from the ashes of buried dreams. What if he felt the same?

CHAPTER FOURTEEN

Yielded

The sunrise warmed Drew's back on his way home from the beach. In the backyard, he propped his longboard against the house and rinsed off under the outdoor shower. Salt residue ran down his skin and into the sand at his feet. It would be nice if his stupid nerves would drain as easily.

He flicked a glance at the trailer.

"I just want to see you remember how to have fun again."

Debating with himself all morning hadn't shaken Livy's words from his thoughts. Maybe she was right. He could be the carefree guy he used to be. Have fun without giving his heart away. Cooper did it all the time. What was a date or two? No strings attached.

Apprehension sparked. Drew lowered his head under the cold jets of water trying to lodge sense into his thick skull. What was he doing even thinking about asking Ti out? Even if she weren't out of his league, marrying his first and only girlfriend right out of high school didn't exactly make him a dating guru.

Ti had been an international model, for Pete's sake. Who knew how many smoother, more experienced guys had already offered her all she wanted. What could he possibly add? Smothering affection? Small-town chains? Extra baggage? He'd been down that road once. Knew where it led. This was stupid. He shouldn't even be thi—

"That's it!" Ti flung open the door to the trailer. In the same wide-neck shirt and boxers from last night, she stumbled onto the patio, waving a high heel in the air at a seagull. "You and me, buddy. Let's finish this."

Drew slowly turned off the water. He pinched his lips together to hold in a laugh and eased toward Ti from behind to disarm her. "Easy there, killer. No one needs to get hurt."

She whirled around, hair a hot tangled mess. "That seagull needs to die."

Man, she made keeping a straight face impossible.

He turned the shoe over. "I hear death by stiletto may be considered malicious intent. Wouldn't want you to add any more time to your sentence."

With one side of her shirt drooped off her shoulder, hair blowing in the wind, and a frenzied look in her eyes, Ti failed miserably at looking dignified while staring him down. "It's not funny."

"Oh, no, trust me. It's *very* funny."

She stole her heel back and whacked him with it, but he only laughed harder. "You're lucky I don't have my phone on me right now."

"You're the lucky one. 'Cause this ..." He waved a hand over her frazzled pose. "Is definitely picture-worthy."

"Shut up." Her mouth quirked.

Drew dipped his head, waiting. Three, two, one ...

Pent-up laughter tumbled out on cue. Ti shoved his shoulder. "That stupid bird shouldn't be allowed near anyone's window this early. The blasted ferry horn is bad enough. I hardly got any sleep last night."

"Maybe you shouldn't drink coffee so late."

Ti mirrored his impish expression. "And maybe a knight in shining armor shouldn't have brought a girl penance she couldn't refuse."

"Touché." He rubbed the back of his neck.

Her gaze slanted past him to his board. "So, that's where you run off to every morning. To exercise at the crack of dawn. On purpose." She tipped her chin. "You need help."

Drew angled his chin right back at her. "Says the rabid-looking girl flailing a high heel at an innocent seagull."

"Glad I can bring out your sense of humor."

"Your specialty."

Barefoot and unfairly adorable first thing in the morning, Ti chewed on her bottom lip. Sunlight glistened over her skin, and all he could do was stare. *Words, Anderson.* Maybe if he punched himself in the jaw, it would actually remember how to work.

"I should probably get ready." She hooked a thumb toward the trailer.

"Yeah. Yeah." Drew gestured behind him. "And I should ..." *Go get a life. Or at least a shred of manhood instead of standing here like a preteen with no clue how to talk to girls.*

"So, I guess I'll see you at the shop."

"Yep. Ready to sell things." *Ready to sell things? Really?* He conquered the ocean every morning, and here he was drowning on dry land.

"Right," she said slowly. "Glad we clarified that."

Someone needed to put him out of his misery now before it got worse.

Once Ti turned to go back inside the trailer, he squeezed the bridge of his nose. Good thing Cooper wasn't around to see this. The jokes would never end.

Drew trudged over to the shower to finish rinsing off his board. It was probably better he hadn't asked her out. What would they do all night? Play *Whose Line Is It Anyway* until he actually came up with one?

He turned off the water, but images of Ti's bare shoulder catching the sunlight kept pouring in. He banged his forehead against his board.

"You all right?"

Drew flinched backward and pivoted toward Ti standing on the patio. *Tell me she didn't see that.* "Uh, yeah. I was just ... checking the board. You know, making sure everything's nice and sturdy." He patted the solid foam. "Yep. All good."

Ti nodded, the corner of her lips climbing her cheek. "Mm-hmm. Well, I forgot to mention I have something I need to do this morning, so I'll be at the shop a little late."

"Oh. Okay. Yeah, sure. No problem." Drew backed up. "I have some things to take care of first, too. So, I should get a move on." He stumbled into his board, turned, and batted it between his hands like a gyroscopic juggler. Once he stabilized the stupid thing, he breathed in and turned once more.

If the amused look on her face was any clue, a career in the circus might not be a bad idea. He passed off a casual nod and made a beeline around the side of the house before he could open himself up for any more blunders.

Halfway to the front, he forced his feet to stop and waited for his brain to catch up. This was ridiculous. So, he could tattoo World's Rustiest Dater on his head. So what? If anyone would be able to laugh about it with him, it would be Ti.

With at least a meager grasp on confidence, Drew jogged back to the patio. "Ti," he called as she was about to shut her door. He latched on to her crippling blue eyes. "I was actually wondering if I can take you somewhere tonight." He picked at a mosquito bite on his arm. "Unless you already have plans with Cooper."

"Cooper?" A slow grin built behind her eyes. Her lashes dipped and lifted slowly. "Not unless we're all hanging out together."

"Not tonight." He leveled his shoulders. "Chloe's coming in at four, so that should give us enough time."

"For what?"

"A surprise."

Eyes squinting, she studied him. "All right, Mr. Evasive. Four o'clock it is. But I'm gonna be wearing stud earrings if you don't give me a clue how to dress before we go."

He laughed. "Point taken."

Drew rounded the corner of the house again and relaxed his muscles. Now that the asking part was out of the way, he just had to make it through the actual date part. A flicker of sunlight filtering through the trees drew his gaze to the sky.

Little help here wouldn't hurt. If he were going to pull this off, he'd need all the help he could get.

The wind fanning through the Jeep windows felt more like someone had a hairdryer trained on them. Seeing the wild ponies had been totally worth slumming it in the heat, though. Ti had never seen Spanish mustangs before. Such a unique breed. Their carefree roaming was almost liberating. As if that same peaceful freedom was within reach for her, too.

The way Drew's face had lit up watching her, it was like he could see inside her. Knew what she craved, needed. More than that, it was almost like seeing her reaction had brought *him* joy.

Ti warded off the ball of emotions always hovering near-by, stuck her hand out the window to wave ride the wind, and redirected her thoughts. "I know it sounds weird, but the terrain through this stretch reminds me of Africa."

Drew's foot slipped off the gas pedal. "You've been to Afri-ca?"

"Once. On a safari photo shoot."

"Right." The clipped word kept him face forward.

"It's nothing like being here," she ribbed. "I still can't be-lieve we went somewhere today we actually had to drive to." She stretched across the console to poke him in the arm.

A sidelong glance careened into her from the driver's seat. "We're not done yet. You haven't experienced Ocracoke until you've explored its full sixteen miles."

"From a bona fide highway, no less. I'm impressed."

"Forget the highway, City Girl. Wait till I show you what going off-road really means."

Both brows reached for her bangs. "I knew it. That ten p.m. noise ordinance in the village is just a ruse, isn't it? You're all really a bunch of bad boys up to no good."

His husky laugh curled around her with the wind. "You figured me out."

Not even close.

She raised her feet to the dashboard and crossed her arms over her knees as sand dunes passed beside them. Whatever had gotten into Drew today, she had to admit she liked it. Maybe things could work between them after all. Was it insane to hope?

The wheels crunched over sand as he slowed the Jeep to a stop beside what looked like a trailhead. He opened his door. "Ready?"

"You promise you're not trying to coerce me into the water, right?"

His dimples sank into his cheeks. "Wouldn't dream of it."

"Mm-hmm." When Ti bent behind her for her hat and bag, a magazine tumbled onto the floorboard. She raised her sunglasses to her head and did a double take. *Oh. My. Word.* She snatched it up and rushed outside. "Is this what I think it is?"

"What?" Drew met her around the passenger side. Face dropping, he grabbed for it. "It's nothing."

Ti backed up, waving it out of reach. "A J. Crew catalog? You were scoping out the Henleys, weren't you?"

"No." He stretched an arm behind her, but she skirted around the bumper.

Whipping her head up, she jabbed a finger at a dog-eared page. "Ha! You were so thinking about getting one."

"And you're *so* gonna get a good swat with that thing if you don't give it to me."

She handed it over but held on, looking him up and down.

His eyes circled to the sky. "What are you doing?"

"Picturing you in a Henley. Very attractive." Oh, she loved turning his cheeks that crimson color.

He yanked the catalog back, tossed it inside the Jeep, and concentrated on untying his surfboard from the roof rack. "I rescind my earlier comment, by the way." He cut her a mischievous glance. "You better run when we get to the beach."

"Good thing for me, I get a head start." With that, she tore off down the trail past a sign for Springer's Point. It would take him at least another minute to get his board down. *Sucker.*

A canopy of live oaks shrouded a sandy path leading her deeper into what could've been a Bob Ross painting. Undeveloped, tranquil beauty enveloped her the farther she jogged. Past a gravesite, past an old brick cistern until she finally wandered onto Pamlico Sound's quiet shoreline unfolding before her.

Drew came up from behind. "You're lucky I have a longboard slowing me down."

She turned, unable to curb the setting's effect. "It's gorgeous, Drew."

"I had a feeling you'd like it." The same joy that had overtaken his expression when they were with the ponies replaced his playfulness now. "Thought it'd be a good spot for some inspiration."

He'd picked this place out for her artwork? She looked down and dug her camera out of her beach bag. "That's really sweet."

"You have an incredible talent, Ti. It deserves a stage." Thoughtful eyes angled under hers. "Don't ever doubt that."

The only thing she doubted right now was her ability to breathe when he looked into her soul like that—made her feel treasured, whole. Spoken with such sincerity and encouragement, his words wove inside her and fanned the kind of belief she'd always grappled to make her own. Her mouth turned drier than the sand burning her feet.

As usual, he seemed to read between the lines and didn't press. Instead, he staked his board in the sand, tugged his shirt off, and motioned to the water. "Sure you don't want to go in?"

Ti forced her eyes off his defined abs and lifted her camera. "I'll enjoy it from here."

"This isn't the ocean. You can walk out a good fifty feet before the water reaches your waist."

"It's all you, Surf Champion."

He nodded in concession. "Fair enough."

Nothing was fair about him or this island she was beginning to wish more and more were her home.

"Settle down? You ain't that kinda girl, Russo. Do yourself and every guy you're with a favor. Remember who you are."

Memories from her last fight with Murray before leaving London squelched any hope of his being wrong.

"You all right?"

Ti blinked toward Drew, thankful for the reminder to avoid making a mistake. "Fine. Yeah." She raised her camera and focused on what she was here to do. Create art. Nothing more. "You go on. We're losing daylight."

With visible reluctance, Drew headed into the water.

She took multiple shots of him paddling out, sun glistening over him. They'd make perfect prints for what she had planned. The more she gave herself to her creative drive, the more she became one with it. No dark memories. No tainted thoughts. Just life and joy that the escape of art always provided. Minutes lapsed, but she wasn't ready to let go.

Seated on her blanket, she scrolled through the frames until a shadow brought the guy she'd met at Drew's shop the other day into view above her.

"Sorry. Didn't mean to sneak up on you." Carter staked his board in the sand as Drew had done earlier. "How's that painting we talked about coming along?"

"It's getting there. You sure you want to buy it?"

"No question."

Out on a paddleboard, the same woman with him the day they met waved to shore. Carter nodded. "My wife, Sue, and I loved what we saw in your portfolio. Hang tight, and we might have more to offer than just a bid on a painting." His eyes glinted with intrigue as he tipped his head. Instead of expounding, he grabbed his board and turned to jog to the other end of the beach.

Drew trekked out of the water, gaze locked down the shoreline. "New friend?"

"That was the gallery owner from Cali. Remember?"

He mumbled something that sounded like, "Unfortunately." Evading her eyes, Drew raked his wet hair off his forehead. "He make you an offer?"

"Not exactly."

His jaw flexed in and out. Yet rather than say anything, he traded his board for a towel and dragged it over his face and hair.

Apparently, that conversation was over. Even if Drew hadn't ended it, Ti wouldn't have been able to carry it on. Or any form of intelligent communication, for that matter. Not with his muscles, sculpted by years of mastering the waves, rippling in front of her. The way he filled out his button-downs had given her enough to imagine as it was. She didn't need real-life visuals stoking the fire.

She looked away. "I, um, got some takes that should appeal to the competition clientele." And a few she wouldn't mind keeping for herself.

"Good." He took a swig from his water bottle while plunking onto the blanket beside her.

Live currents filled the almost-nonexistent space between their arms. She curled in her bottom lip, wishing for his lips instead.

Stop. Just stop.

Damp wind blew off the endless stretch of water onto her flushed cheeks. He, on the other hand, probably wasn't hot at all. Her eyes followed the water droplets carving paths down his tanned skin.

After one ridiculously long minute of silence, Ti elbowed him. They needed levity. Fast. "You know, you could throw on a Henley right now if you had one." She tugged him down when he started to stand. "All right. I'm dropping it. I do think you'd make a good J. Crew model, though."

He made it all the way up this time.

Ti clambered to her feet and caught his hand a few paces down the shore before he got away. "Okay, okay. I'm done. I swear."

An incoming wave lapped over her ankles and lured her gaze across the water. She planted her hands on her hips, tilted her head, and stared at the horizon with the best existential expression she could assemble.

A sigh from beside her joined the wind. "What are you doing?"

"Shh." She waved a hand at him. "Don't make me break character. I'm being you right now."

"What?"

"Your romance with the water ... I'm testing it out."

He shook his head at her. "I do *not* pose like that."

"You don't see yourself doing it. How do you know?"

"Because life pondering doesn't look like a teenage girl waiting for her boyfriend to come back." From behind, Drew straightened her head, took her arms in his, and crossed them in front of her.

"Excuse me, Siddhartha. I didn't realize *life pondering* had to be so manly. Is this better for you?"

With his bare chest secured against her back and bulky arms over hers, he brushed his cheek to her temple. "Getting there."

Any more so, and his masculinity would override everything around her. Even the beach's salty aroma couldn't match the traces of his aftershave mixing with the earthy scent of his skin. He smelled like summer. One she didn't want to expire.

Ti stared across the vast expanse of water. No beginning or end. No answers. Just mysteries. But in Drew's arms, she could almost believe life had a plan. That it could be safe, forgiving. Maybe even paint her into this dream permanently.

The setting sun doused the ocean's canvas with watercolors no brush could replicate. She soaked it in. "Are you sure your sunrises beat this? 'Cause these colors are pretty amazing."

"They're a worthy opponent." Though he kept his tone light, it held an unmistakable reverence.

"Well, this view is definitely on my top ten list."

A stilted laugh rustled her hair. "No way this can compete with the places you've seen. You've been all around the world."

Ti yielded to the urge to nestle deeper into his embrace and whispered, "But never right here." In arms of strength and tenderness. No one had ever held her like this before.

She'd encountered a lot of things she'd never expected while traveling the world, but none more than wanting to stay on this shore. With him.

In the stillness, dragonflies zipped around them, as if dancing to music. Ti closed her eyes and listened along. The water's gentle lull against the shore, Drew's steady heartbeat, the wind's sigh through the trees.

She wasn't supposed to fall for this place, this life. It was temporary. With no more rumblings from Queens, she couldn't justify staying much longer.

The thought of leaving dragged her heart out with the tide. This was exactly why she kept her heart off limits. Better to keep things light and uncomplicated. For everyone.

"Tell me something." She turned on a mischievous tone. "How does a surfer become a business owner?"

"How does a model become a business owner?"

Her tight lips caved to a smile. "At least one of us got a sense of style out of it. You could use that in all areas of life, you know. I mean, look at your fellow surfers." She motioned to another guy on a longboard.

"The dude with the man-bun?" Drew snorted. "If you ask me to wear skinny jeans next, this friendship is over."

She laughed. "Hey, there are going to be lots of beach bunnies hopping around here soon. Don't you want to be in the running?"

He released her from his arms. "Oh, I'll be running, all right. In the opposite direction."

She turned and cocked her head at him. "You're telling me you have no interest in finding a relationship?"

"One based on how I wear my hair? Not particularly." He pulled his T-shirt on. "Relationships are nothing but infatuation, anyway." Intense green eyes roamed over her. "Physical desire. It's intoxicating."

He had no idea. Heat waves rippling off the sand commandeered her body a cell at a time when he looked at her like that.

He blinked away. "But it eventually fades like everything else."

Ti hid the unfair reactions he ignited. "Yeah, sorry, James Dean. I'm not buying it."

"Nothing to buy. I'm just being real." A wry look tinted his eyes. "This outspoken girl I know taught me to call things like I see them."

"Oh, really?" Ti hedged him backward like he normally did to her. "And you're honestly trying to tell me you don't believe in love?"

Her stomach pinched at the question. At the hope of his saying he still did. That this man—who'd made room for his wayward brother in his home, who would give his daughter the sun and moon, who'd honored a widow by welcoming her into the center of his family—might open his heart to her, too. If she found the courage to tell him how she felt... If she were honest with them both, maybe he'd—

"Not anymore." His voice barely crested the waves.

Ti's feet sank deeper into the sand, his words into her chest.

Was there no chance she could change his mind?

CHAPTER FIFTEEN

Circumvent

On the front porch, Drew pulled his keys from his pocket. "Are you as hungry as I am?"

Ti slipped off her wide-brim beach hat. "Hungrier. You're used to the sun zapping all the energy out of you."

"Nothing a little coffee can't remedy." He winked while pushing the door open.

She followed. "You said the magic word."

He flipped on the lights in the kitchen, dropped his keys on the sideboard, and headed for the cabinets. Cooper had to keep coffee in here somewhere.

As he rummaged around, Ti flopped on a chair and scrolled through the pictures on her camera. "I feel like I got the inside scoop of the island tonight. These shots are exactly what I've been looking for. I should probably be the one making you dinner in return, but, uh …" She made a clucking sound with her tongue. "Need I remind you of the peanut butter incident?"

He ducked into a bottom cabinet to confine his laughter. Obviously, not far enough.

Something nailed him in the back. "Keep laughing, buddy. If you cook me something that doesn't include saltwater taffy, I'll be impressed. By the way, you gonna tell me what the story is with that, or what?"

Drew bumped his head on his way up. The girl never missed anything.

He dusted off his knees, words spewing out before he even realized it. "It used to be my thing with my dad. Every Saturday, we'd buy a pack from the Community Store and eat it while we worked the shop. When he died—I don't know—I guess carrying on the tradition made it feel like I wasn't letting go of him."

He scrubbed a hand down his face. Was he seriously telling her this right now? She'd basically said back at the beach that she thought he was a hopeless small-town romantic. Admitting a codependency on a stupid piece of candy wasn't exactly proving her wrong. Nice.

He twisted a dish towel in opposite directions and cut himself off from spouting out the rest. They needed a subject change.

A red container behind a loaf of bread on the counter beamed at him. Coffee. Finally. He pulled out the coffee maker and an impish tone. "You know, you could think of cooking as making coffee with a few extra steps."

"A few steps too many."

"I thought all women could multitask."

"I'm not *all* women."

She could say that again. Ti wasn't like anyone he'd ever met.

The thought almost capsized him. Did he really believe that? He scavenged for a tablespoon and his voice. "How many scoops?"

She spun around. One look at him holding the canister shot her up from the chair. "Uh, no. Hand it over. I've tasted your coffee before. Trust me. You need to promise mankind you'll stay far away from all coffee makers forever."

"Anyone ever tell you you're overly dramatic?"

She bowed. "Why thank you."

Shaking his head, Drew made his tea while Ti got her caffeine fix going. The fridge's steady hum filled the room as he leaned back against the counter. "It's weird when it's this quiet."

"Where's Maddie?"

He took a sip from his mug. "At a friend's house. Two very convincing little girls cornered me in the shop this morning."

"Pushover."

He nudged her in the shoulder.

"Ow." Ti looked from her pink-tinged skin to the apparently useless hat on the table and grimaced. "How could I get sunburned that late in the day?" She twisted her head in an attempt to survey the damage. "I can't see. Is it bad?"

Considering the sun looked incredibly sexy on her skin, yeah, it was bad. At least, for him. Light shades of pink peeked through the blonde hair dangling down her back.

Inhaling deeply, Drew curled her hair to one side and gently skimmed a thumb across her bare shoulder. Heat worse than anything sun-induced radiated through him. "You just need a little aloe," he said, raspier than he meant to. He cleared his throat and retried. "You won't even notice it tomorrow."

"Really?" She turned and peered up at him with an adorable naiveté in her eyes.

As if that kaleidoscope of blues didn't have him drowning enough normally.

Thankfully, his feet ignored the disjointed rhythm pounding in his chest and backed him a cautious step away.

A hint of sass shifted her demeanor. "Wait a sec. Aloe? This is a beach guy's smooth come-on tactic, isn't it? Sucker a girl into allowing you to rub lotion over her back?"

And once again, Ti Russo took home the World's Most Straightforward award. He laughed. "More like a beach *girl's* tactic."

"You're kidding. Girls really use that line?"

"What? You don't think girls come on to me?"

Her gaze traveled over him. "Oh, no. I'm positive they do. I'm just surprised they use such cheesy lines."

"You have better ways?" He shouldn't enjoy baiting her this much.

A slow blink fanned her long lashes toward him. "You just act naturally."

Who needed tactics when a single look incapacitated him? He managed another step backward. "I'm gonna go grab that aloe." And maybe take a cold shower while he was at it.

In the upstairs bathroom, Drew splashed water over his face and stared at his reflection. "Fun. That's all this is. Two single adults flirting. Don't complicate it." He retrieved the aloe from under the sink and faced the mirror one more time before trekking back downstairs. "Just be smooth. You got this, Anderson."

As soon as he rounded the corner, Ti jumped away from the counter and hid something behind her back. He appraised the room. The only thing it could be was …

Unable to suppress a grin, Drew started toward her. "Is that my tea?"

"No." She slinked along the counter while sheltering the contraband behind her.

"You're actually starting to like green tea, aren't you?"

She shook her head and slid farther away.

"Then what are you hiding?"

"Nothing."

"Oh, really?" Drew set the aloe on the table and closed in on her. "So, you won't mind if I take a peek behind—"

Ti squealed and made a run for it, but he caught her at the waist and spun her around. A flash of his mug she hid behind her slid into his periphery, but nothing was pulling him away from the flustered look in her eyes.

Backed into the corner, Ti braced both hands against him. "Okay, fine. Your grass tea is halfway drinkable. Happy?"

Drew clutched the counter on either side of her. "Is that an official concession?"

"Don't push it."

"Only fair, considering you push every border I have."

She raised a brow.

Under the ceiling vent, loose strands of blonde hair spilled down her neck and rocketed Drew's temperature in the opposite direction.

He edged even closer. "You know, you do the no-tactic thing pretty well."

Her smile pulled to the side, his eyes following every move. "I'm not flirting."

"No?" His gaze lingered over her lips. "Then why do I want to kiss you right now?"

Her lashes dipped. "Green tea withdrawals?"

Hints of his favorite drink on her breath ushered him another inch forward. "I think I know a way to remedy that."

She lifted those ocean-blue eyes to his, and the current pulled him under. Shutting out every other thought, he leaned in until his lips barely brushed hers. Soft, silky. The proximity alone ignited a hunger he'd almost forgotten how to feel. He raised both hands to her cheeks. "Ti …"

The creak of the back door opening sent Drew flinching a solid foot backward.

Cooper made it only two steps inside before freezing. His all-too-observant glance between Drew and Ti merged into an obnoxious grin.

Drew stared at the tiles while raking his fingers through his hair. "Thought you were watching a movie tonight."

"Well, you know, some people say you find the best entertainment right in your own home."

The amused lilt in his tone was two seconds away from getting him hurled back out the door.

Cooper opened the fridge. "Sorry for interrupting. I only stopped in for a sec to grab something." He waved a six-pack in the air as corroborating evidence. His smirk followed him all the way to the door. "Just pretend I wasn't here."

Like that was happening.

A thick silence hovered in the kitchen once the door shut.

Drew tugged on his ear. "Good thing we're all pros at acting naturally." The churn of the air conditioner absorbed his attempt at a lighthearted laugh. He tapped his thighs. "So, I guess we should probably scrounge up something for dinner." Or anything to circumvent the awkward vibe taking over the room.

"Good idea." Ti reclined against the back of the chair closest to her.

While setting a couple of take-out containers on the counter, he glanced her way. "I'm sorry. I'm not very good at the dating scene."

Ti picked up her hat and folded the brim back and forth. "You want to date me?"

The softest uncertainty in her words tightened across his chest with reminders of how she viewed him. Of course she wouldn't want to date him. He backpedaled. "Nothing serious. I mean, I know you're not sticking around. And I understand if working together takes this off the table. I just thought we could have a good time this summer. You know, keep it light. Unattached."

She nodded without looking up from the tiles. "Unattached. Yeah." Swallowing something unspoken, she tucked her hat under her arm and grabbed her camera. "Listen, I think the sun took more out of me than I thought." She strode for the door. "I'm gonna turn in for the night."

"You sure?" He lifted a container. "It'll just take a minute to heat up this Thai food."

"No, it's cool. I'm pretty wiped." She already had her foot on the first step outside. "Thanks for today, Drew. It was really nice ... all of it." Her momentum drove her right past the hitch in her voice.

The door closed and ushered another round of weighted silence over Drew, but this time a sense of loss closed in with it. What just happened? A moment's hesitation spurred him into a jog. He hit the bottom of the stairs before she reached the trailer.

"Ti, hold on." He turned her around. "I'm sorry if I crossed a line in there."

"You didn't do anything wrong."

"Are you sure? 'Cause I don't ever want to make you uncomfortable." He squeezed his shoulder blade. "I really like hanging out with you, and I don't want to ruin that by overcomplicating things."

She kept her gaze fastened on the hat she was still fidgeting with. "Summer dating's hard to complicate. Like you said, it's just unattached fun. And if you're lucky, you walk away with half-decent memories to add to your collection. Everyone wins."

"Um ... I'm not sure that's what I—"

"Don't worry. I'm known for a good time. It's actually the only noteworthy quality I have on that résumé you're always talking about."

He ran a knuckle across his brow. "Okay, can we start over here? 'Cause I think something got lost in translation." Wasn't this what she wanted?

A long breath finally lifted tragically beautiful eyes toward his. "The only thing lost is me. I shouldn't have stayed here this long."

She didn't want to be here. Pangs of rejection quaked through him like muscle memory. "No, I shouldn't have thought—"

Her cell phone's ring struck the space between them.

Turning, Ti took the call. "Hey, Mia, can I call you …?" She strode a few steps away. "Wait, slow down and start from the beginning."

The concern in her voice ratcheted Drew's already-raised pulse. He circled around to survey the look on her face.

Her sunburned skin paled. "He *what?*"

CHAPTER SIXTEEN

Illusions

Ti ended the call and started to pace. How could he break into her art studio? And what did he expect to find? A safe chock full of hundred dollar bills? This wasn't a John Wayne movie.

She pressed both sets of fingertips to her forehead. Figures he'd gotten out of there without leaving any evidence behind. Must've wised up some in prison these last eleven years.

Images of him violating her space crawled up her skin, repressed memories shuddering back. If any of the neighborhood kids had been in the studio when he'd snuck in, Ti wouldn't have forgiven herself.

Shame burrowed into her with the nails digging into her palms. She should be there, protecting the ground she'd fought to gain. Not hiding like the powerless girl she used to be.

Drew interrupted one of her back-and-forth strides. "Are you okay?"

The genuine concern in his eyes wrapped around her like arms of assurance. The very ones she wanted to hold her right now. Could she tell him the truth? "Drew, I…"

Another ringtone butted into the silence. This time, from Drew's cell. He swiped the screen. "Maddie?"

Ti's heart rate kicked up a notch.

Drew looked from the ground to Ti, forehead creased. "Yeah, she's right here." He held out the phone. "She wants to talk to you."

Ti stole a minute to iron out the tremble in her voice. "Hey, beautiful."

"Hey. If my dad's standing right there, just play it cool."

Ti met Drew's curious gaze, tried not to give anything away, and turned to mosey in the opposite direction. "Cloak-and-dagger. Got it. So, what's up?"

"Winnie and I were talking about birthday parties, and it got me thinking. Dad's birthday's coming up. He *never* makes a big deal out of it. But I want to do something special this year. Maybe a big party. I don't know. Just something where he can have fun and stop worrying so much for a change."

Only ten years old, and the girl caught on to more subtext than most adults.

Ti's heart pinched as she looked behind her toward Drew's broad shoulders under the porch light. "I think he'll really like that."

"Me too, but it has to be a surprise. Winnie's older sister helped us come up with a whole undercover plan. Starting with this call. She said to tell Dad I was asking about shaving my legs. That should make him squirm enough to drop it."

Ti covered her mouth too late to rein in a laugh.

"I think we should have the party at our friend Jacob's. I'll call him tomorrow from here so Dad doesn't overhear. We'll need to go shopping and work on the gift, so I'll tell Dad you're helping me with a school project. That way we'll have an excuse for not working on it at home."

Who knew someone so cute could be so cunning. "Sounds like you have a pretty good plan in place."

"But it'll only work if you help. Please?"

Two phone calls. Two parts of her pulling in opposite directions. She couldn't forsake the life she'd built in Queens. But what about the one she was falling in love with here? How could she let down people counting on her in both places?

Another glance at Drew confirmed she couldn't leave. Not yet. "Consider it done."

Squeals erupted through the phone. "I'm so glad you're here, Ti."

"Me too, love." She cleared her throat. "Now, stop conspiring and go play Girl Talk or something."

"What's that?"

Nothing like a reminder of how old Ti was getting. "Never mind. Just have fun."

"Okay. See you tomorrow?"

Ti peered toward the trailer she'd just been on the verge of packing up to leave. "Tomorrow." Two and a half more weeks. The competition would be over then. She could stick it out that long before going home.

She ambled back over to Drew, surrendered his cell, and lightened her tone. "Girl stuff. She thinks she's ready to shave her legs."

Maddie had called it. Drew played hot potato with his phone, a look of horror shooting down his face. "She what!"

"Don't worry. I'll talk her into waiting a few more years."

Avoiding her gaze, he slid his phone in his pocket and hardened his tall frame. "I appreciate that, but you don't have to stay, you know. You obviously have things at home to take care of." A slow blink lifted green eyes full of regret toward hers. "There are no obligations holding you here."

Obligations. That's how he viewed things? She swallowed the sting. "I know."

"Good." His line of sight rebounded around the patio. With his thumbs in his pockets, he tapped the front of his thighs. "So, we should probably get some sleep. I'll tell Maddie you had to go."

He wanted her to leave? Ti didn't respond. *Couldn't* respond. She simply held her arms across her torso and prayed they'd keep her insides together until Drew disappeared in his house.

As soon as the door closed, she fled into the trailer. She chucked her earrings on the desk and clenched the back of the chair. *Unattached.* The word seared into her like a branding iron.

The ceiling fan swooshed above her. Unbidden, dark images funneled to mind. Deep voices rumbling against her chest. Musty perspiration stinging her nostrils. One after the other, tainted memories shivered down her skin. "*She's not worth it.*"

Ti stared at the blades circling overhead and sang to herself until the song she and Cass wrote together as kids finally shut out the words repeating in her head. But the deeper she strove to escape into the song, the deeper the yearning collided with the security she'd felt with Drew earlier today. The kind she wanted to be real.

Stupid. Her knuckles whitened over the top of the chair with relentless flashes of things she'd done and who she'd been all her life. Did she really think Drew would see her differently than any other guy did? She knew better. Knew her past branded her. Always would.

She shoved the chair into the desk, grabbed her Mandala coloring book, and curled up on the bed. Halfway through the page, Ti tossed her colored pencils aside. It wasn't helping. She grabbed her camera instead and headed to the ocean.

A cool breeze whispered through her hair as she ran her toes through the warm sand. The view of the stars out here almost rivaled the one from the Catskill Mountains. Her pulse gradually mimicked the wave's rhythmic flow the more she lost herself in taking shots of the moonlight glimmering over the water.

Near the empty lifeguard tower, Ti lowered the camera and waited for the beauty around her to paint over the darkness.

"It's enticing, isn't it?"

Ti whirled toward a voice coming from under the wooden tower. Cooper came into view, sitting alone in the sand. She released a breath. "What is?"

"The beach, the moonlight, the whole *charming* island." He fanned a beer bottle around the shore. "It's a romantic notion. Traveling here for a summer getaway. Leaving the pressures and demands of life behind. You have to admit its lure is hard to deny."

Ti joined him in the sand, leaning back against the opposite post. "Sometimes escaping is all we can do."

Cooper raised his drink in a toast. "To escaping."

She set her flip-flops aside and let the wind extract the remaining tension in her muscles. Better to focus on Cooper instead. "So, who's the girl?"

"What girl?"

"The one who has you hoping she'll come back some day. A summer fling, I take it?"

"You don't miss much." He laughed softly. "It was more like the summer of a lifetime."

"What happened?"

Cooper swished his bottle around, eyes saying what he didn't have to. "We can't escape forever. She went back to her real life. Like everyone does."

Like Ti was getting ready to do.

She traced the suntan lines left on her feet from the flip-flops Drew had talked her into buying when she first got here.

The summer of a lifetime. Did it have to end? She boxed out the thought. "I think it's sweet, you know. What you're doing here."

"And what exactly am I doing here?"

"Pretending you got laid off when, really, you gave up your corporate life to move home and help Drew and Maddie out. Nice ruse."

"I may not be as altruistic as you think."

"But more than you're admitting. Don't worry, Don Juan. I won't blow your cover. How's day trading going, by the way?"

Two pronounced dimples hedged in an impressed smile. "You have a knack for reading between the lines."

"I didn't really think all your time-sensitive appointments were spent doing your hair. Can't miss the right time to sell a stock." She shrugged one shoulder. "And it's not hard to miss things when you're living in someone's space."

Wiping the sand off her hands, she twisted toward him. "Speaking of which. I want you to know how grateful I am for you letting me crash at your pad this last month."

Cooper held her gaze. Instead of words, hazel eyes searched hers for unspoken meaning he obviously already knew.

Ti blinked and rubbed her arms. "It's been really great." So much so, she almost let herself believe it could be more than it was.

"Ahh . . ."

She looked from the sand to a telling grin. "Ahh, what?"

"Time to run already?"

"I have responsibilities at home."

He raised a brow. "Says my brother's dutiful understudy."

Ti folded her arms over her knees while watching sandpipers test the waves' reach up the shore. "Drew might have more things figured out than you think."

Cooper laughed. "Of that I have no doubt." He polished off his brew. "Too bad for all of us, love will always be an unsolvable mystery."

"Nothing mysterious about an illusion. Drew said it himself. Love fades like anything else. Makes you wonder why we keep grasping for something we can't keep, doesn't it?"

A wave raced up the sand and splashed white foam along the tower's front two posts.

Cooper returned his bottle to the empty slot in the cardboard carrier, rose to his feet, and extended Ti a hand. "Maybe we were made to hope."

She scoffed. "And be disappointed."

"Or surprised."

No doubt he knew what she was thinking, but he gestured toward the street instead of pressing. "Come on. I'll walk you back."

"Actually, I need to make a call. You go ahead."

Cooper dipped his chin and started up the beach. "You know, Ti." He turned and shuffled backward. "My dad used to say we'll never find where we belong until we're willing to admit we're lost." He nodded with his eyes. "Just something to think about."

But what if being lost was all there was?

The wave's calming lull drew her focus back to the shoreline and away from what she didn't want to think about. She had to release the ache of wanting to belong here. Daydreams might vie for her heart, but reality never lost.

Drew was right. Obligations didn't tie her here. They tied her to Astoria. She'd head back after the surf competition ended, regardless of what waited for her. Because honestly, what she might return to didn't scare her half as much as what she might be leaving behind.

The feeling of Drew's lips barely touching hers quivered through her again. Stifling it, Ti withdrew her cell and scrolled for the number to her friend in the NYPD. A six hundred-mile stretch didn't erode responsibility.

Josh's voice mail clicked on after the fifth ring. "D'Angelo. Talk to me."

"Josh, hey. It's Ti Russo. Listen, I need a favor. Call me when you have a sec, 'kay? It's um ..." She exhaled through her mouth. "It's important. I'll fill you in later. Thanks."

Near the ramp to the parking lot, the guy she'd blown off at the festival stumbled down the beach with two other guys and a couple of girls on their arms. The one with the shaved head spotted Ti and popped his buddy in the arm. "Looks like we can start the party now."

He shoved a six-pack into his friend's chest and jogged through the sand. With a smile she'd seen a hundred times from different guys, he strutted up beside her. "What do you say to another invitation?" He looked behind him to his friends. "Just a few of us hanging out on the beach. No harm, no foul."

The alcohol on his breath hinted at both. Ti knew his type. Knew this scene. No use resisting the fact that she belonged in it. Even Drew saw through her. "No strings attached?"

His gaze roamed over her spaghetti strap dress. "I knew you were my kind of girl."

Waves in the background washed away the island's temporary illusion from the permanent truth of her identity. "Then what are we waiting for?"

CHAPTER SEVENTEEN

Marks

Moonlight filtered through the shop's back door with the remnants of a day Drew would give anything to start over. Be smooth? Have fun? He steadied his arm in front of the furnace. With any luck, he'd burn off all reminders of how stupid he must've looked to Ti tonight.

Fatigue joined the waves of heat billowing across his face as he removed a blowpipe from the fire. Against a thick sheet of steel, he rolled the molten glass into a smooth shape he could work with. *Careful.*

He put his lips to the pipe, evened his breathing, and blew slowly until a small air bubble expanded inside the glass. Sweat formed across his forehead and raced in rivulets down his temple. *Easy, now.*

But even the glowing orange glass couldn't diminish the images from earlier replaying through his mind. The way Ti's back had fit securely against his chest at the beach. The surge the slightest graze of her lips had sent through him. The ease of spending the day with her.

Why did he have to want things he couldn't keep?

He glanced at the mark of abandonment that had replaced his wedding band nine years ago. Familiar weights of rejection lugged him into the memory of the night Annie left. *"I can't stay with you, Drew. Here, on this suffocating island with your small-town dreams smothering my future. I'm not like you, okay? I need more."*

More. How was he supposed to offer what he didn't have? No spontaneity. No way to compete with the city's bright lights or an artist's wanderlust. He couldn't expect Ti to see him any differently than Annie had. Shouldn't try to *be* any different.

A *clink* jolted him back to the present as a crack in the glass zigzagged down the frail edge he'd let stretch too thin to withstand the pressure.

Like him.

The pipe shook in his hand. Drew bolted up and smashed the ruined glass to the floor, the stool wobbling behind him. He stalked to the front counter, where he seized a piece of taffy and ripped into the wrapper.

Headlights from a passing car streamed through the windows onto the auction sign on the counter and the words Marcus had scribbled over the back of it. *Get used to seeing this.*

Drew lowered the taffy, veins throbbing. With one look at the picture of Dad and him on the wall, he chucked the useless candy into the garbage. He gripped the base of his hair and paced, needing to get out of there and away from the failure he'd walked right into. Dad was counting on him to man up.

The back door slammed behind him on his way out.

He jogged into the wind. Each strike against the pavement hardened the resolve he never should've lost sight of. His breathing didn't slow until he reached his buddy Jacob's. At the pier, he climbed into Dad's skiff and the one place where Drew could still sense his presence.

The movement jutted small ripples across the dark sheet of liquid glass beneath him. Echoes. Consequences. Waves he needed to conquer more than ever.

A gust of misty wind swirled into the harbor and rushed over his heated skin with reminders of Ti's words. "*You could make your own artwork, you know. Turn this shop into anything you want. No limits.*"

Except for the ones that defined him.

The wooden seat's grooves burrowed into his palms with the ache of knowing what he needed to do.

He scrolled to Lenny's number on his cell and hovered a thumb above it. A breath at a time, he squashed each reservation holding him back.

"You've reached Lenny's phone. I'm either out fishing or ain't in the mood to answer. Leave a message or meet me at the docks. Peace."

The beep shuddered with a prompt to surrender what Drew had held on to for so long. "Len—" He cleared his throat. "Lenny, it's Drew Anderson. You still interested in buying my dad's skiff? Give me a call when you get this message. We'll talk figures."

The urge to change his mind pulsed in the thirty seconds it took for Drew to finally hang up. He ran his fingers along the skiff's ragged edges and closed his eyes. "I'm sorry for letting you down, Dad. I hope you understand."

In the bathroom of the motel she'd crashed at last night, Ti turned down the volume on her cell and listened to Josh's message.

"Russo, long time, no hear. I have a feeling I know what you're calling about. Mia gave me a heads-up. I'm all over this one. If the perp goes anywhere near your house or studio again, he'll be in cuffs so fast, he'll be seeing cinderblocks before I ever throw his butt in jail. Oh, and hey. Bree's gonna get on me if we all don't do coffee soon, so no busting my chops on it. Call me with a date, and do me a favor. Watch your back, eh? Later."

Ti set her phone on the sink counter with a sigh of relief. No surprise Mia had already contacted Josh. She'd been Ti's wingman from the day Ti opened the studio. Knew how to take care of and run the shop as if it were her own. And Josh's boys in the 105th precinct were topnotch. Leaving it in their capable hands was the best thing she could do.

Still, just the idea of someone lurking in her neighborhood and searching for her sent shivers down her spine and hot tears up her throat. Being in this dive of a motel wasn't helping.

Ti glanced around the bathroom doorway to Jamie and his friends sprawled across the room, passed out from who-knew-what kind of pills they'd taken last night.

She finished dabbing cover-up over the bruise Jamie had left on her arm when she wouldn't take the drugs with him. Thankfully, he'd crashed before he could force her into what he really wanted from her.

She thought she could do it. Thought she could be with him. But after experiencing what it was like to be in Drew's arms yesterday...

Before she could stop herself, she brushed a thumb over her mouth, reliving the tenderness of Drew's touch compared to the familiar roughhousing of every Jamie she'd ever been with. Her lashes swept together. She shouldn't have let herself hope for more.

Ti cut off the tears, crammed her lip gloss in her purse, and faced the mirror. She flicked a glance from the purplish bruise on her arm to the reflection of her dad embedded deep behind her eyes. "Don't worry. Your marks run deeper. I know who I am."

Like Cooper said, Ocracoke was a getaway. Real life eventually caught up to everyone.

Carrying her flip-flops, she tiptoed across the motel room's prickly carpet and inched the door shut. Her cell buzzed as she turned toward the elevator.

"Hello?" she whispered.

"Ti, it's Maddie. Did I wake you?"

The guilt of letting Maddie down swarmed with the stench of mothballs filling a hallway that could've been part of *The Shining* set. Ti jabbed the elevator button a dozen times. "No, love, I'm awake. What's up?"

"Jacob's down for hosting the party. I talked to him this morning."

Ti lifted the phone from her ear and did a double take at the time. What was with people around here getting up before sunrise? "That's great."

"I'm so excited. Dad's gonna *flip* when he finds out."

About more than just the party.

Guilt took another stab. That was what Ti got for making a mess out of everything. What had started out as a fun distraction turned into a challenge and then became so much more. Instead of playing consultant, she'd gotten her heart jumbled in a web of emotions and dragged Maddie's in, too.

Her promises to Drew and Maddie pressed in. Ti combed her bangs off her face. She had to figure this out and make it right somehow. She needed time to think. Space.

The elevator dinged open. Ti darted inside and pressed the button for the ground floor. With her camera bag clutched to her chest, she huddled in the corner.

"Ti? You still there?"

Part of her always would be. "Yeah, sweetie. We'll talk in a few days."

"Days? Where are you . . . ?"

Reception cut off as the doors closed. Probably better that way. She couldn't handle the questions she didn't have answers for.

The motel's exit opened to dark, taunting clouds. Perfect. Ti tucked her camera bag under her shirt and jogged down the steps. Regret poured with the rain, piercing and unrelenting. By the time Livy's apartment building came into view, the rain had rinsed off the makeup from her bruise. Too bad it couldn't wash away mistakes, too.

From a bench on the porch, Carter set a newspaper aside and rose to his feet. In slacks and a collared shirt, he made casual appear sleek and expensive. "Got caught in the rain?"

Ti climbed the steps. She wiped the rain and tears from her face, grateful one masked the other. "Among other things."

If she read his compassionate smile right, her eyes must've offered a replay of everything that happened last night. Thankfully, he didn't inquire. "I came to extend an invitation." He withdrew his billfold and took out a plane ticket. "Sue and I will be flying back to San Francisco at the end of the surf competition. We'd like you to join us."

Ti's wet arms came uncrossed. "Wait, what?"

"I have a feeling if I don't get you to board that plane with us before we leave, I'll never get you to California. It'd be our loss." He stuffed his wallet into his back pocket and picked up an umbrella from the bench. "If we're going to take our gallery to the next level, we could use someone like you. There's an apartment above the studio you're welcome to use until you get settled."

Ti blinked in hopes the repetitive movement would somehow loosen her jaw.

"You don't have to answer right now. I know it's a big decision. Just promise me you won't rule it out until you think it over." He dipped his head on his way down the stairs.

"Carter, wait."

He stopped on the third step.

Questions joined the raindrops playing percussion over his umbrella. "Why me? There are dozens of artists around here. Take one look inside Down Creek Gallery. The talent level ..."

Understanding tinged his confident expression. "I've been in this industry a long time, Ti. It takes more than raw talent to thrive. Those who can create something life-giving from great heartache—they're the ones who make it as artists." With a definitive nod to match the assurance in his eyes, Carter jogged down the last two steps and over to his rental car.

Could any good really come from heartache? Ti turned the plane ticket around in her hands. Two and half more weeks, and then ...

She winced at the thought of leaving after the competition, but Drew had already made it clear that nothing tied her here. She clutched the ticket to California. Mia could run the studio in Astoria. If six hundred miles weren't far enough away, maybe three thousand would be. It might be her only chance to find out.

CHAPTER EIGHTEEN

Hollowed

In the shop's back room, Drew stirred creamer in a cup of coffee. The spoon's high-pitched clinking infiltrated the stark sound he'd been trying to avoid for the last four days.

Silence.

It used to be a familiar friend. A relief he'd learned to rely on. Now the stillness hollowed out the space with a reminder of Ti's absence. No incessant talking or digs about his clothes. No singing to herself or waving her cell phone around with annoying voice recordings.

His chuckle petered into a sigh. He could say she drove him crazy all he wanted. Could hide behind barriers of self-preservation guarding him from feeling anything for her at all. But the truth was, he missed her. He'd known it the moment he left her to pack up the trailer.

Shoot, he'd practically packed her stuff for her, tossed them out with the words he wanted to take back now. Pride had kept him from turning around that night. What was new?

She was gone, and it was his fault—again.

Now, here he was drinking coffee, of all things. Alone. He looked over at the broken glass he hadn't brought himself to clean up from the floor yet. Maybe that was how it should be.

He jimmied his cell from his pocket. No messages. Why hadn't he heard back from Lenny yet? The guy had been bugging him for months to buy Dad's skiff. And now, Drew couldn't even get a returned call from him. Was he out of town or something?

Drew tapped the phone to the counter. He'd swing by Lenny's after he closed up. One way or another, he had to get the money he needed.

His stomach reeled at fresh images of Maddie in the doctor's office this morning. He clenched them back and called home. "How's my girl doing?"

"You mean since you checked on me half an hour ago? You don't have to hover, Dad. It was just a doctor's appointment. You should be a pro at these by now."

She deserved that title, not him. Having to stand in an exam room, watching his baby girl get steroid shots, never got easier. Especially today.

"Sorry. I'm officially un-hovering. But call me if you need anything."

"You know I will. And Dad? Love you."

Not hovering was one thing. Not being completely head over heels for his daughter would always be off the table. "Love you, too, Sea Monkey."

After hanging up, he gave his mug another stir. This coffee had better be as therapeutic as Ti had made it sound.

The over-the-door bell rang. Drew peeked around the frame toward a brunette in a slouch beanie and blue sunglasses, setting a box on the counter. "Be right with you." He took a sip of the coffee and almost spit it back out. Therapeutic? More like disgusting. How did people drink this stuff without dumping a box of sugar in it?

Mug still in hand, he froze and then leaned backward around the doorway again. A large cardboard box sat alone on the counter. Where'd she go?

She materialized right in front of him. "Hi."

"Jeez." Hot coffee streamed over his fingers. He set the mug down, scrambled for a handful of napkins, and hurried around the corner. But once he caught sight of her by the counter again, his feet slowed. "Ti?"

"They came in." She pulled apart the box's flaps. "Postcards, magnets, matted prints—pick your size. We have tons of options. Aren't they great?"

With his voice gone AWOL, he blinked as if resorting to Morse code. He worked his jaw until it agreed to function. "What are you...? Your hair is... Where have you...?" Okay, make that a *half*-functioning jaw.

The slanted grin he'd called to mind dozens of times these last few days crawled into place. "Don't worry. I'm sure what little caffeine didn't end up on your hands will be kicking in any sec now. If it were coffee, you'd have a better chance."

He ran a knuckle across his brow. "Actually, it *is* coffee."

"I'm sorry, what was that?"

She shouldn't be allowed to be so attractive when she gloated.

Drew played it off, falling right into ease with their normal banter. "This rude New Yorker told me I sucked at making coffee, so I figured I better prove her wrong."

"Mm ... You should probably hire a taste tester. Just be sure she's a connoisseur. No posers."

"Might be hard to find."

"Not for an experienced résumé scrutinizer."

"Touché."

Her smile gradually withered as she dragged her hands along her arms. Pretending nothing had changed could only last so long.

A deep, finger-shaped bruise discolored her bicep. She clamped a hand over it and angled away from him.

A hesitant step led him closer. "Do you wanna—?"

"Answer your questions. Right." She pointed to the strands of brown hair framing her face. "It was time for a change. But..." She slipped off her beanie, shook out her hair, and ran her fingers down to bright blonde tips. "I always keep *some* blonde."

"You do this often?"

"Which part?"

"The hair."

"What about the hair?"

Drew let out a breath. "Never mind." Obviously, things hadn't changed enough to deter her from exasperating him. But she still hadn't answered the question that mattered most.

Ti propped an elbow over the box on the counter. "The rest should be here in a few."

"The rest of...?" he prompted.

"The souvenirs I've been working on. It took enough arm-twisting to get Stan to let me crash with Livy. He'll get his pants all in a bunch if I don't get those boxes out of her place."

"Hold on. You've been staying with Livy?" Confusion sputtered into mixed feelings he wasn't sure how to decipher.

"Stan isn't as tough as he seems, and I can be rather charming."

That was the understatement of the year.

"That's not what I meant. You didn't leave?"

"Not yet. Well, I did go to Hatteras for a couple of days to track down a surprise for the surf competition. I have autographed photos of… wait for it… Brett Barley. Sweet, right?" She tapped a finger to her arm when he didn't answer, uncertainty encroaching on her excitement. "Or not."

"How did you find him?"

"I'm a New Yorker, remember? I know people. Ooh, speaking of connections. Remember that gallery owner from Cali? You won't believe the price he's offering for the painting of the harbor I'm working on. Seriously. The guy's either certifiable or desperate. I haven't decided which."

Or he knew when something was too valuable to lose. Unlike Drew.

Autographs and paintings didn't mean anything right now. Not when his heart was pulsating with things left unsaid. "Ti, about the other night at my house."

"Already forgotten."

Maybe for her. He hadn't stopped thinking about it, wishing for a do-over. Or at least a chance to apologize.

He fidgeted with the button on his shirt cuff. "I was trying to be someone I'm not. It was stupid. The whole thing. Not that I didn't want to kiss you. But, you know, you're … and I'm …" *A complete idiot. Clearly.* "I should … probably start over."

His self-conscious laugh met a blank stare. Instead of unfathomable depths, an ocean-blue wall barricaded her eyes. Man, he'd really messed this up.

A long exhale lowered his shoulders but didn't come close to slowing his pulse. "I'm sorry for walking away that night. It wasn't your fault. I thought …" Why couldn't he finish a single stinking sentence around her? He shook his head. "It doesn't matter. But I don't want you to think—"

"You don't owe me an explanation, Drew. Or an apology. It's fine. You have a lot going on here."

"It's more than stuff with the shop." How could he tell her? "I—"

The front door opened. A young guy in a waiter uniform wheeled in a dolly with three more boxes piled on it.

Ti flitted over to him and heaved the first box up. Drew grabbed the other side and shouldered the weight as they slid it onto the counter.

She pulled open the flaps and unveiled handcrafted souvenirs, one after the other. Wall décor made from driftwood, sea glass mosaics, rustic shelves made out of what looked like old pallets. All of it unique, fashioned with Ti's artistic creativity.

She retrieved a sign with *Memories are made in flip-flops* painted on it and half blushed while tracing a finger over the words. "This one's for me."

Awe swelled in his chest. "How'd you have time to make all this? They're amazing."

"That's just the little stuff." Her brows followed the peak of intrigue in her voice. She opened the largest of the three boxes and withdrew an old window with distressed white trim that she'd turned into a shadow box with droplights.

"Wow."

"That's not the best one." Beaming, she pulled out a rustic multi-colored sea turtle pallet painting and held it to her chest. "Think Maddie will like it?"

Not as much as she loved Ti. The lump in his throat doubled.

"Is that a yes?"

"I can't believe you put all this together. That you'd do something like this for us, despite what a jerk I've been." He released his shirt cuff and looked at her in earnest. "Thank you."

She fluttered a glance away from him while rolling the edge of her beanie around her finger. "You're not a jerk, Drew. And don't worry about it. It's nothing."

It was something to him.

"Please let me put all your work on consignment for you. The talent ... you deserve to get paid for this. I can't just accept—"

"A gift? Yes. You can." Her eyes warmed. "I told you from the beginning, I have money saved from modeling. And Mia's running the studio in Astoria, so income's still coming in. I'm more than fine, Drew. I *want* to give these to you. Let me help where I can."

She really didn't know how much she'd already done, did she?

He grazed a thumb along the edge of the pallet beside him. He couldn't rely on Ti to turn the shop around any more than he could rely on someone else. Owning his responsibility in this for Dad and Maddie's sake hadn't changed. But honestly, his feelings for Ti hadn't either. Four days without her had made that piercingly clear. If there was anything left to salvage, he had to try.

Drew picked at a splinter in the wood until it kindled a spark of courage. "Why'd you stay?" he all but whispered.

Ti clutched the beanie in her fingers but kept her tone light. "You don't really need me to sing the *Gilmore Girls* theme song again, do you?" Her usual playfulness didn't compensate for the wariness tugging at the corners of her mouth.

Drew inched closer and dipped his head to catch her gaze. "Why'd you stay?" he asked again.

The quiet words hung between them, weighing her chin farther to her chest. "I know you told me to leave, but I couldn't bail on you guys. It's more than an obligation to me."

The realization of how she took what he'd said that night backed him up a step.

"I promised I'd help turn the shop around before the end of summer." She peeked up from the floorboards. The uncertainty furrowing her brows begged for a response. "Let me see this through. I'll leave right after the competition. I can even—"

"Ti." Drew caught her hand, his voice finally working. "You're welcome here as long as you like."

"But that night, you said ..."

"A lot of stupid things. Yeah, I'm pretty good at that, apparently." Edging close again, he steadied her gaze with as much repentance and reassurance as he could. "I want you to stay. Not just with Livy, but here at the shop." With him. Beyond the competition.

A hint of mischief simmered on her lips. "You're really desperate for that coffee connoisseur, aren't you?"

More than he fully understood.

"Stay." Drew searched her face. "Please."

Unreadable waves shook the calm in her eyes. Was it too late?

He lifted a hand to her neck, taking in the feel of her hair against his fingers. Maybe it was the ache of missing her or the warmth in his chest from seeing how much she cared for them. But whatever the reason, it stirred up a boldness. Enough to hope the vein fluttering under his palm meant she felt it, too.

The sheen on her lips drew him closer, her fragrant essential oils clouding every shred of logic telling him to let go. Fear collided with desire until the last barrier gave way.

The front door flew open again. Ti jumped back as some skinhead strutted into the shop.

A hazy gaze landed on Ti and darkened. "Jeez, dollface. You just walk out and disappear for four days? I've been looking all over for you. We weren't finished—"

"Get out of here, Jamie." Shoulders back, Ti laced her arms over her chest as though forming a barricade. "We hung out one night. No strings attached, remember?"

No strings. Drew's stomach soured. And here, he'd almost kissed her. Kicking himself, he clenched his teeth. How many times did he have to make a fool of himself in front of her?

The dude's heavy boots clanked over the hardwoods. He grabbed her wrist. "You leave when I say you leave. You owe me."

Two seconds. Drew didn't breathe, didn't think. He pounced on instinct. "Back off." He shoved Skinhead back and swept Ti behind him. "The lady said to leave."

"Lady?" he jeered. "You got the wrong broad." Glaring at Drew up and down, Jamie adjusted his belt. "And who are you, anyway, her pimp or something?"

That did it. Drew grabbed the guy by his black T-shirt, hauled him out of the shop, and nailed a right cross dead to his cheek.

Jamie stumbled backward down the walkway. Straightening, he spat blood on the pavement through a dark laugh. His gaze slanted past him to Ti on the porch. "Oh, this is good. You actually want to be with this yuppie, don't you? Sorry to break it to you, sweetheart, but he ain't gonna go for a girl like you."

Drew broadened his shoulders. "I think you've said enough."

The guy kept sneering and finally raised his palms. "You want a crack at her, bro? Have at it. But from one guy to another, she ain't worth the drama." He smeared the blood on his lip over his shirtsleeve and flicked his chin at Ti while swaggering off.

The creep's car pulled away, leaving a cloud of exhaust and insinuations Drew wasn't ready to face. Adrenaline-fueled breaths stretched his shirt across his chest.

"I'm sorry." A shell of Ti's confident voice faltered behind him. "I shouldn't have stayed with him. He wanted me to do some kind of pills. When I didn't, he got angry. Now he's sulking because I didn't sleep with—"

"Not my business." Drew turned around, fingers still balled, but the bruise on her arm pummeled into his gut with a fist of its own. The idea of that punk hurting her burned to his bones, while knowing she'd turned to someone like that cut through the marrow.

Ti hesitated only a moment before jogging down the steps to him. "Drew." Eyes harboring the damage left from dozens of Jamie lookalikes peered up at him with such vulnerability, his anger wavered.

Unattached. The end of their date replayed in his head—the things Drew had said, the way she'd misinterpreted. Did she really think he was just interested in fooling around with her? The thought gutted him.

"I understand if you want me to go, but please let me help set up the shop first. I have an idea for the back display. It could almost be like our own gallery." She fiddled with her sunglasses, but her speed talking failed to mask the quiver in her voice.

For the first time, the brokenness she hid inside shined through like sunlight through a prism. Layers and angles speared into his own hidden places until deep-seated empathy took over.

"Ti . . ."

She pushed her bangs off her lashes. "With some rearranging, we can really expand the floor plan. It'll still be a little tight, but I can—"

"Ti." He found her eyes. "Come here." The minute Drew brought her close, her tough New York exterior crumbled in his arms, and his heart ached for her even more. He rested his cheek over her head and whispered a truth he never should've given her any reason to doubt, "You're more than a good time."

Silent tears soaked into his shirt as he held her with the tenderness she'd deserved from him all along. "I know this isn't home, but you're safe here. With me." *Please, let it be enough.*

A slow nod brushed against his chest, and he cradled her tighter while he still had the chance.

CHAPTER NINETEEN

Romeo

Ti skipped the bottom step of Stan's front porch and rapped a knuckle over the door. Surprisingly, coming over these last three days had been almost therapeutic. Not that working with Drew at the shop had been stressful. The exact opposite.

Which was the problem.

It didn't make sense for them to be closer now than before. All the work she'd invested into the shop must've earned her a spot in Drew's life a little longer. Or he was even more amazing than she wanted to admit.

She couldn't go there. Head down, heart unattached. With the expiration date on her visit fast approaching, there wasn't another option.

"Stan?" Ti strode inside, tossed her hemp purse onto the recliner, and cued the record player. "Sorry I'm late."

"I thought I might've lucked out this time." Stan shuffled in from the kitchen, wearing a white short-sleeved button-down and high water dress pants that showed off his sock tan line. He lowered a coffee mug and mimicked her blank stare. "What?"

"What? Are you kidding me?" Ti waved at his outfit. "*That's* what."

He huffed. "What does it matter?"

"Oh, trust me. It matters." She prodded him down the hall to his bedroom and set the outfit she'd bought him to wear to the party on the bed.

He hiked up his waistline. "These are my lucky pants."

"The only thing lucky about those babies is no one's ever going to see you in them again. Hand them over when you change. Those bad boys are going to Neverland."

"Anyone ever tell you you're pushy?"

With her fingers on the doorknob, Ti winked. "All for Jolene."

Grumblings trailed the door as she closed it. He made her work too much fun.

A few minutes later, Stan emerged in stylish slacks, a gray dress shirt, and a sleek bowtie.

Ti let out a low whistle. "Stan the man. You're rocking it." She caught his arm as he wheeled around. "Not a chance, mister. We need to get another rehearsal in."

Still huffing, Stan joined her on their makeshift dance floor.

In character, Ti appraised Stan as she imagined Grandma Jo would when she saw him at the party. She adjusted his tie. "My, my, Stan," she said with a southern drawl. "Don't you look dashing tonight. You here with someone?"

He dropped his arms to his sides, turning a complementing shade of pink to set off his gray shirt. "Is this really necessary?"

Ti popped him on the back.

An exaggerated sigh merged into a compliant smile. "I was hoping for a dance with the only woman I came to see."

Ti fanned her face until his not-so-subtle grunt reminded her to act like Jolene instead of a southern belle. Ms. Spunk. Right. Ti hung a hand on her hip and flicked her chin at him. "You gonna ruin the dance by running that mouth of yours?"

His cheek's pink dusting deepened to a boiling red. If he didn't unlock his tight jaw, he might pop a gasket. "Now, you look here—"

"Uh-uh-uh. That attitude isn't gonna win over Jolene." Ti took his hands and shook out his arms. "Try again. Like we practiced."

Stan craned his neck to the ceiling. When he returned her gaze, his dark brown eyes had found their calm. "I can hardly talk when you keep taking my breath away."

"Oh, Stan. Who knew such a romantic lived under that hard shell of yours?"

"All right. All right. Can we just get the dance over with?"

"You can't rush love, Romeo." Ti placed his left hand on her hip and clasped the other in a dancing frame. "Now, remember. *Feel* the music." She motioned to his feet with her eyes. "Back, to the side. One, two, three. There you go."

Stan lowered his arms again, a sheen of worry glistening his brow. "What if they don't play this song?"

"Relax. I'm taking care of it. Everything's going to be perfect."

He resumed his frame but kept a penetrating stare on her. "Drew's really important to you, isn't he?"

Ti stepped on his foot, tripping more over the truth. She swept her hair to one shoulder, twisted the back of her earring, and straightened her bangles. As if stalling would change the answer. "Yes. Can we get back to focusing on why we're here?"

He dipped his head with a grin that knew more than it should. "I think we just did."

A nudge to his shoulder ended in a hearty laugh. The kind she'd imagined hearing from a grandpa.

Stan whisked her around the carpet with impressive skill now that he'd relaxed. After twirling her out and in again, he slowed their steps. "Your father's pretty lucky."

Unease climbed her spine. "Excuse me?"

"To have such a stellar dance partner. I assume he taught you how to dance." The honesty in his expression spoke an innocent compliment, but the simple words triggered reactions she'd lost control of ever since her jarring phone message.

The paralysis taking over her legs weaseled up her throat.

"Ti?"

"Sorry. I just realized the time. I have to work on a painting for a customer. Tight deadline." She urged her body to move. On the other side of the room, she turned off the record player. "We're done practicing. You've got everything down."

"You sure?"

Ti steeled herself before turning and summoned the confident expression she'd learned to wear on runways and photo shoots. The good thing about plastic? It wasn't breakable.

"You're going to do great. Just remember your ABCs—aftershave, breath mints, and charm." Offering another assuring wink, Ti nabbed her purse from the chair and reached for the door right as someone pushed it open.

From the porch, Marcus glared down her profile. "What are you doing here?"

"Playing fairy godmother." And if he knew what was good for him, he'd stay out of her way, or he might end up with her wand stuck up his—

"Ti?" Livy waved from the sidewalk.

Ti flaunted a tight smile at Marcus while grazing past him. "Gotta run."

She joined Livy on what looked like an after-shift walk according to the frizzy curls refusing to stay in her ponytail. "Long morning?"

Livy untied a black apron dotted with stains and balled it up. "Don't ask." She leaned a questioning shoulder into Ti's. "I know I'm busy, but I must really stink as a friend if you're having to hang out with Mr. Fiazza instead. Is that why he's let up on me lately?"

Ti draped an arm across Livy's back, sniffed, and wrinkled her nose. "Either that, or he bolts the other way when you reek of bacon. Please tell me that's from working in the kitchen and not a new bodywash."

"And the Queen of Deflection strikes again."

Livy wasn't so bad at that skill herself.

Speaking of that... Several sidewalk dividers passed before Ti looked up from the ground. "I don't get it, Liv."

"What?"

"Why you're stuck at a job you hate just to pay the bills. I mean, I get wanting to leave modeling. Believe me. But you didn't have any money left over?"

Livy stopped three feet back with her gaze adhered to the concrete.

Ti inched up the sidewalk and angled her head beneath her friend's. "You know you can talk to me, right?"

"Yeah." Nodding with too much effort, Livy evaded Ti's eyes. "I need to get back to my flat to shower. Don't want this bacon scent to turn off anyone else."

"Liv—"

"I'll catch up with you later." She veered to the right, down a side street.

Ti didn't have to memorize every road on the island to know Livy was taking the long route home. With as many detours as Ti had taken herself in life, the long route was the only home she knew.

The gardens and screened-in porches lining the street practically laughed at her for wanting the map to end here. She'd almost kept driving when she went to Hatteras. Maybe she should have.

"Drew's important to you, isn't he?" Important enough to guard both of their hearts.

One more week. You can keep your heart intact for one more week. She faced the warm sunlight weaving through the leaves above her. "Little help would be nice."

Drew's Jeep coasted alongside the curb. He stretched over the passenger seat and lowered his sunglasses. "Going for a run?"

Sending a smirk to the sky, Ti shook her head and approached the Jeep. She folded her arms over the door panel toward the green eyes that kept her anchored here. "Apparently, not today."

CHAPTER TWENTY

Glow

Drew slid a thumb across his cell. Still no messages. Last time Mrs. Cunningham had come in, she'd eagerly caught him up on why Lenny wasn't around. A death in the family brought on a lot of repercussions. He knew from experience. What if Lenny ended up leaving Ocracoke for good? Would he still want the skiff now? If Drew couldn't sell it…

He shoved his phone and the taunting questions into his pocket. One trial at a time.

With a deep exhale, he peeked over his shoulder at Ti hanging the last 8x11 frame on a gallery display she'd created on the back wall. Nine white matted frames showcased stunning takes of the harbor. The sunrise in the middle had held him captive for a solid half hour earlier this morning. Even now, he had a hard time looking away from the image.

Until a flutter of Ti's hair drew his focus to her instead.

After thirty-two years of living in the sun, it had taken less than a month with this outspoken, contagiously energetic, talented woman to show him how dim his world had been without her.

The caliber of her paintings, photographs, and jewelry had transformed his shop. No question. But new inventory wasn't what made the place glow. It was the girl behind the art.

Maybe it was time Drew took a risk on creating his own art again. Would seeing him try change Ti's mind about him?

He looked away from her and added the last of the decorative mason jars to a shelf in the middle of the store. The distraction of gearing up for the surf competition starting tomorrow had kept her inevitable departure date in the background. But now that they'd run out of things to keep them preoccupied, it hung in the air with a thickness even her essential oils couldn't remedy.

The glowing diffuser Ti had coerced him into setting up in the corner sent puffs of mist into the air like they were about to have some sort of spa-slash-yoga session.

Thankfully, she hadn't tried to talk him into selling aromatherapy paraphernalia. Unable to say no to her, he'd have ended up walking around the shop with one of those diffuser pendants tied to his neck while grinding up herbs in a stone mortar.

Laughing it off, he ducked behind the counter and grabbed one of her pallet art pieces to hang. The fake auction sign Marcus had stashed in Drew's yard last week brushed against his knee with a reminder of what was at stake.

He kicked it aside as he rose. The combination of small and big-ticket items should give them a shot at coming up with enough back payments during the competition to appease Mr. Parsons for a while.

His arm drifted to his side. It would work out, wouldn't it?

"It's gonna be fine." Ti strolled up beside him, obviously reading his thoughts. As usual. "All those calluses left from threading the necklaces are totally going to be worth it."

Better be worth something. Chuckling, Drew put his rough hands to work hanging up a distressed pallet Ti had turned into a decorative shelf.

Another glance around the room sent him across the floor to pick up an empty box. He stopped at the jewelry display. "Is there enough?"

Ti stole the box, wedged it against her hip, and took his hand. "It's enough, Drew—all of it. Everything's taken care of. You're taking the night off. We'll do dinner. Six o'clock."

"The night off?"

"Don't worry. I promise it'll be edible."

He raised a brow. "You're gonna cook?"

"Yeah, and we can work on the three-word question issue you seem to be stuck on." An impish grin tailed the barb, but the doorbell chimed before he could dish out a comeback.

Mrs. Cunningham strode in, wearing a wrap-around skirt and a low-cut bathing suit failing miserably at covering wrinkled skin no one's eyes should be exposed to.

"Hey, darling." Her heeled sandals flopped against her feet as she sashayed toward him. "Any chance you can sneak away today? My boat's giving me some trouble. And with Roger out of town again, I could sure use a hand."

Drew kept his gaze neck up. Though, the red lipstick on her teeth was almost as bad as the over-tanned skin sagging above her bathing suit.

She leaned closer, pungent old lady perfume nearly choking him. "What do you say?"

Help? "Um … Ti?"

"Hey, can you—" Ti wheeled around the display and jerked to a stop. Visibly caught off guard, she stared at Mrs. Cunningham like a moth in front of a light.

Mrs. Cunningham shifted her weight, producing ripples in places never intended for any. "You like my suit, dear? Got it at Ann Taylor's last season."

Ti simply stood there, transfixed. Drew elbowed her, but she barely blinked. "I'm sorry, what was that?"

Mrs. Cunningham rattled off another round of praise about her flower-patterned suit.

Ti shook her head without looking away. "Yeah, sorry, still missed it."

He had to move to keep from cracking up. He looped an arm around Ti's back and nodded at Mrs. Cunningham. "Will you excuse us for a moment?"

Over by the door, he scrunched his face at Ti. "What was that? You were supposed to come to my rescue over there."

"From being suffocated between the twin peaks?"

"Aw, jeez, thanks a lot for the mental image. I can never un-see that now."

"You gotta admit. They're kind of a showstopper." Ti opened the door.

Trying not to gag, he followed her out. "Where are you going?"

"To get some coffee before I meet up with Maddie."

"You've been sneaking off a lot lately."

"Look who's talking, Mr. I-Get-Up-At-The-Crack-Of-Dawn. And I'm not sneaking. We're working on her school project."

"Mm-hmm."

"You seem a little tense. You sure now's the best time to go cold turkey on your taffy addiction? You might need it in there. Just saying."

It truly never ended, did it?

She started down the walkway with far too much bounce in her step.

"Wait, you can't seriously be leaving me alone. Make coffee here."

"With the twin peaks? No thanks. Having my life flash before me once was enough. I need the strong stuff to recover. Can I get you anything while I'm out? Mountain gear, climbing shoes?"

He groaned. "How about a squeegee?"

Her laughter chased her down the walkway. "You're getting good at this banter thing, Mr. Anderson. I'm sure Mrs. Cunningham would take you on for a few rounds. Might even get a free boat ride out of it."

"I hate you right now, you know that?"

Ti walked backward, the corners of her mouth quirking. "I'll see if I can find the right bathing suit to remedy that."

He let out a breath. Why did he set himself up for these things? "I can't believe you're bailing on me."

"Sorry."

"No, you're not."

"Not in the least." Laughing it up, she spun toward the street. "See you back at your place at six."

Drew leaned against the porch railing as Ti flitted down the street in the larger-than-life style he admired more each day.

As risky as opening himself up to creating glasswork again was, it didn't come close to the danger of messing up what little time he had left with her. His advances had already driven her away once. He needed to keep himself in check.

Mrs. Cunningham opened the door. "You're not hiding from me, are you, honey?"

He squinted at Ti's fading silhouette. It didn't matter how many days they had left. She was definitely getting it for this later.

As long as whatever Ti had planned tonight didn't demolish his self-control first.

A few minutes before six, a mouth-watering Italian aroma welcomed Drew through his front door. He dropped his keys on the sideboard in the entryway. "Hello?"

Maddie soared around the corner. "Upstairs."

"What?"

She blocked the doorway to the kitchen with her arms and legs like Spiderman. "Upstairs to change before dinner."

He peeked around her, but she pushed him toward the steps. "Go."

"All right, I'm going." In his bedroom, a shirt and a sleek pair of dress pants looked back at him from the bed. Okay, he was definitely missing something. "Mad—"

"Trust me." His little fashionista whirled in and went straight for his closet. She turned with two ties in hand and motioned him toward the bathroom. "I can't decide between these two until I see the rest on you. So, hurry up in there."

This just sailed past weird. "I think I can handle getting myself dressed, Sea Monkey."

She laughed like he'd told a joke from a stand-up act. "That's cute, Dad." Stopping in the doorway, she draped the ties over her shoulder. "Holler when you're ready. Oh, and I left some hair gel on the sink."

Hair gel? "Maddie, what's going on?"

Her heart-grabbing smile lit the whole room. "We're celebrating your birthday." As if it were the most normal comment she could make, she swept the door closed behind her.

It took a minute for him to be able to move as the pieces fused together. Italian aromas, dress clothes, hair gel. She wanted tonight to be a date for him and Ti.

He banged the heel of his hand to his forehead. The phone call from Winnie's. That's what this was about. Maddie had asked Ti to stick around for his birthday. His chest constricted at the implication. Ti had stayed because she was doing Maddie a favor. Nothing else.

His heart ached for Maddie as much as for himself. No use denying it. His daughter was attached. And she wasn't alone.

Casual dating didn't work. Lying to himself obviously didn't either. But what choice did he have? Ti planned to leave after the competition. His resolve would have to hold.

"I don't hear any water running in there, mister."

Drew obligingly hopped in the shower. For Maddie's sake, he'd at least enjoy dinner as if the night would last.

Dressed, gelled, and ready to eat, he trotted down the stairs. One step into the kitchen caught him short.

Ti glided across the tiles in an exquisite golden dress flowing against her tanned calves. She added two goblets to the place settings and peered up at him with eyes that made the blown glass he'd worked with this morning seem lackluster. All traces left of his resolve vanished, along with his ability to form words. Wow, she was stunning.

Amusement climbed her cheek. "Mrs. Cunningham isn't joining us? You haven't been sneaking off in the mornings to rendezvous, have you?"

A laugh unlocked his voice. "Cute. You're still in the dog house for earlier, by the way."

"Dinner penance?"

He rubbed his jaw to fight a grin. "I'll let you know."

"Fair enough." She motioned to his seat, but he helped her and Maddie into theirs before taking his own.

Ti picked out a slice of cucumber from the salad. "Did you know cucumbers are ninety percent water? They regulate blood sugar, relieve headaches, and even promote healthy skin."

"I'll remember that the next time I play Trivial Pursuit."

She jabbed the vegetable at him. "You've been hanging out with me too long."

Not long enough. "Guilty," he said instead. The steam rising from a pan of lasagna lured his focus to the center of the table. "You made this yourself?"

Ti swayed her head. "I *might've* used a lifeline to phone a friend. It's Ethan's Nonna's recipe. Well, a meatless version, anyway." She reached for his glass. "And a little red wine for the grown-ups."

She had no idea what she was doing to him right now, did she? "I can't believe you cooked for me."

Her bare shoulder gave a gentle shrug. "It's a special night."

One he'd never forget.

With her silky hair wound in a side bun, only a trace of her herbal shampoo reached him, but it was enough to fuel the craving to breathe in her soft skin.

He forced his eyes closed. He could do this. One night. One *very* long night.

Once they'd finished eating, Maddie sat back in her chair and rubbed her belly as if it hurt.

"You okay, Sea Monkey?"

"Yeah." She wiped the glower off her face. "Just ate too much." Without giving him a chance to interject, she jetted into the living room and returned with a wrapped box.

"You guys didn't have to go to all this trouble." Drew set his wrinkled napkin on his plate.

Maddie made a teenager-worthy face at Ti. "Told you he'd be like this."

"Like what?"

"All don't-make-a-big-deal-out-of-me," she said in a dopy ogre voice.

Great. Two conspirators rubbing off on each other. Just what he needed.

"It's good to be celebrated every now and then." Maddie placed the gift on his lap and fluttered her fingertips together. "Open it."

Drew looked to Ti, but she kept her expression surprisingly serene. He tore into the wrapping. The paper dropped to the floor, his heart right behind it. The photo of his dad and him at the shop beamed behind a thin sheet of glass in a new frame. He traced his fingers along the edging made of blown glass scraps, like a mosaic.

"The colors are gorgeous, aren't they?" Ti scooted her chair closer to his. "I found the broken glass at the shop in the back room. A customer must've knocked something over without telling you. I don't know what it was, but as soon as I saw it, I knew it'd be perfect. Maddie and I stayed up last night piecing it together. What do you think?"

That this amazing woman would leave him undone every day he knew her.

Tears threatened the border of his longstanding defenses.

Ti's uncertain glance intersected with Maddie's. "You can use the frame for something else if you want. We can put the picture back. I didn't mean to—"

"It's perfect." Regaining his composure, Drew stretched a hand to both of them. "Thank you. This is really special."

"Night's not over yet." Maddie bubbled up, snagged the two ties she'd picked out off the back of the empty chair, and held them against his dress shirt.

Ti motioned to the silver one.

"Definitely," Maddie agreed. "Now, you guys go on. Grandma Jo and I will meet you there."

"Meet us where?"

"Another opportunity for adventure." Ti hooked her arm around his and steered him toward the door.

This couldn't be good.

The undercurrent of mixed emotions that had been following him around all evening like Peter Pan's shadow led the way to his friend Jacob's house.

In the glow of candles and globe lights, Jacob's third-floor deck whisked them into a flurry of music, drinks, and friends. Ti drifted into the crowd toward Livy and Cooper.

As people swarmed in with birthday wishes, Drew kept his eyes on the girl who'd put this all together. In her golden yellow dress, she could've been someone from a movie. Blonde, brunette, it didn't make a difference. She was real. She was here. Right now, that was all that mattered.

Ti glided farther onto the dance floor like she had in the café on Cedar Island. "Ready for some fun?"

As long as it included sweeping her into his arms. Ti's claim on his heart was about to finish off his last ounce of resistance.

CHAPTER TWENTY-ONE

Complicated

Ti slid an empty glass onto a tray as a server bustled by her. She'd call the night a success. Well, other than not having a moment alone with Drew since they'd gotten to the party. Probably better that way. This night was for him and the people in his life. The ones who had always been there for him and would continue to be after this week.

Unlike her.

Why didn't she leave the day she got the first call from Mia? Or at least after she'd brought all the items she'd made over to the shop for the competition. Livy could've helped him take care of the rest.

Then Drew had to go and envelope her in the arms of safety and acceptance she longed for more than anything. Any chance of walking away without scars had died right then.

The yearning for what would never be squeezed back the tighter she gripped her camera bag strap.

From across the deck, Drew's gaze connected with hers as it had numerous times throughout the night. He smiled with his eyes in a picture of happiness she didn't need the camera to show her. That was all she cared about. Seeing him happy. This was the best farewell gift she could offer.

Drew wove through the crowd on his way toward her, but Grandma Jo cut him off halfway over. He sent an apologetic glance to Ti while escorting Grandma Jo onto the dance floor. Ti smiled back, lifted her lens, and snapped pictures of them for the album she planned to put together before taking off.

The thought of leaving burrowed into her with the fabric cinched around her waist. *Stop thinking about it.*

Livy came up alongside her with a stem glass in hand. "Still no dance?"

"Hmm?"

"You and Drew. You haven't gotten to dance yet?"

"Oh." Stalling for a response, Ti curved her hair around her ear and tapped her camera. "I'm on photography duty. No slacking on the job."

"Uh-huh." A telling grin snuck around the edge of Livy's glass.

Definitely time to avert that conversation. "Excuse me for a sec."

Ti approached the deejay to cue the song she'd been waiting for all night and turned in time to see Stan tap Drew on the shoulder to cut in. Ti held her breath. When Grandma Jo accepted Stan's hand, Drew looked like he might have a coronary. His gaze flew to Ti, as if he somehow knew she was behind it all.

He made confident strides toward her again, looking determined to turn down any more dance requests. He might've made it this time if the next suitor hadn't been Maddie.

In the adorable pale pink dress she and Ti had picked out together, Maddie curtseyed and reached for Drew's hands. He lifted her so her feet topped his. And in a matter of minutes, they easily secured the ribbon for the most precious father-daughter dance ever.

If the duo Ti had come to love didn't have her heart caught up between them right now, maybe she could've moved.

Thankfully, someone brushed by and jarred her muscles long enough to get a handful of takes of the dance in before emotional paralysis returned.

She batted away a tear she had no business releasing and breathed in the calming lavender essential oil she'd dabbed on her neck earlier. *Just get through the night. You can do this.*

Livy sidled up beside her again. "They're cute, aren't they? Just missing one more member to complete the family." She leaned closer. "Could be you, you know."

And replace a wife and mother? Yeah, right. Ti folded the edge of her camera strap back and forth but couldn't suppress the question getting the best of her. "How long ago did Drew's wife die?"

Livy coughed through a swallow. She set her glass on the deck rail. "Annie didn't die, Ti. She left them."

"What? I assumed ..." Ti peered toward Drew twirling Maddie across the floorboards. Her stomach twisted. It was bad enough his wife had left such an amazing man, but Maddie? "How could a mom walk out on her own child?"

"Not everything's so black and white." Livy's curt tone echoed her abrupt shove off the rail.

"Liv, wait." Ti reached for her friend's hand. "I didn't mean to offend, but Maddie—"

"Has a good home with people who love and take care of her." Still avoiding Ti's eyes, Livy gathered her hair off her shoulder. "Maybe Annie's leaving was the best way she knew how to love her daughter."

"How can you—?"

"It's late. I need to get back to my flat. Tell the guys I said good night." She turned to leave.

"Liv." Ti dropped her arms to her sides. What just happened?

Her cell buzzed. Sighing, she adjusted her camera strap on her shoulder and withdrew her phone. "Hey, Cass."

"How'd dinner turn out? No fires, right? The oven's still intact?"

"Look who's talking. Don't act like Ethan ever lets you anywhere near the kitchen."

"Not if he wants something edible."

"Exactly." Ti returned Cassidy's laugh. Man, she missed her best friend. Especially right now.

"Tell me she didn't skip the meat," Ethan called from the background. "If the lasagna didn't turn out right, that's why."

"Um, hello, this is Ti we're talking about. Do you have to ask?"

Ti folded her arms over the rail and peered across the harbor into memories of the camp Cassidy and Ethan ran in the Catskills. One summer there confirmed the mountains weren't the right place for Ti, but distance never threatened her connection with Ethan and Cass. Same way it wouldn't steal memories she'd created with Drew and Maddie. Would it?

She swallowed the lump terrorizing her throat. "Listen, Cass, I need to run. Tell Ethan that Nonna's recipe was a hit. Even without the meat. Love you, guys."

"Ti, wait. You sure everything's okay? I've been monitoring your bank account like you asked."

Ti turned to make sure no one was nearby. Darting a glance away from the faces of the party back to the docks, she lowered her voice. "No weird withdrawals or anything, right?" She'd been using her credit card for everything while here, just in case.

"Nothing. It's been quiet. When are you gonna tell me what this is about?"

From the last update her NYPD buddy Josh gave her, there'd been no more signs of someone stalking her. Like he'd turned into a ghost. Maybe he'd given up on finding her. Still, she wasn't ready to get into it with Cass.

"Later."

Cass breathed into the line. "You're family, Ti. Like it or not, I'm gonna worry about you. I know you feel like you need to do things on your own, but promise me you'll remember we're here for you."

"I promise. But right now, I gotta run. Love you, girl." Ti ended the call, tapped her cell against the railing, and exhaled.

A grasp on her arm whirled her around and led her into a dark closet off the side of the house. Drew turned on the flashlight app on his phone.

Ti moved a mop handle digging into her rib cage. "Um ... props for spontaneity and all, but I'm not really the hook-up-in-a-closet kind of girl."

"What?" The flashlight illuminated a rosy flush stretching all the way to Drew's hairline. "No, I didn't bring you in here to ..." He bumped into a bucket and scrambled to steady a broom falling between them. Loosening his tie, he cracked a laugh. "I'm really racking up the smooth points here, aren't I?"

"Need me to bust out my essential oils?"

"Tempting." He cleared the junk between them. "Sorry about this. I just wanted to get you alone for a minute to thank you."

"For what?"

A sobered expression brought him a step forward. "For cooking me dinner, helping Maddie make that incredibly thoughtful gift, pulling off this party." He pressed a hand to the shelf above her. "And that's just tonight. Want me to keep going?"

Ti dodged his crippling green eyes and straightened a bottle of cleaner beside them. "You give me more credit than I deserve."

"More like you don't give yourself enough." Drew dipped his head under hers and wrenched up her pulse. When she leaned back, he looked to the shelf, brow furrowing with something she couldn't read. "Maddie asked you to stay for this party, didn't she?"

"She didn't need me as much as she thought."

His countenance seemed to fall. "Is that the only reason you stayed?"

Her heart rate shot up again. "I already told you. I made a promise—"

"I know." He faced her again, eyes calling hers. "I just hoped it might be more."

More. This close, she couldn't ward off how much she wanted it to be more. How much she wanted this to be real. To last.

Memories flashed in the shadows. Her dad, begging his dealer for the drugs he'd just made Ti pay for in bed. His dealer, pulling his musty T-shirt over his head and tossing her dad only half the stash. "*She wasn't worth the rest.*"

"Ti?" Drew's tender voice brought her back to the moment.

She slipped under his arm, needing to get away and keep him from thinking she could be more than what she was. "We should get back."

"Wait." Drew stopped the door from opening all the way. "Let's get out of here for a little bit. We can slip out the back, hang by the docks."

The claws of her past loosened their grip a breath at a time. Freed, she sank into the comfort Drew provided without even knowing it. "It's kinda hard to ditch a party unnoticed when you're the guest of honor."

"Sounds like the kind of challenge Ti Russo would be up for." His wry grin baited her.

"You really want to sneak out? Sure this isn't your sixteenth birthday party?"

"Add some Zimas and Fuzzy Navels, and it might be close."

Ti squelched a laugh.

"What? Not edgy enough for you?"

"Tell me you threw some Jolly Ranchers in the Zimas, and I'm really gonna be scandalized."

"Laugh it up. I had my bad-boy moments." He peeked through the sliver opening to the deck. When a guest swooshed by, Drew swept the door closed.

"How very 007 of you." Ti took his cell.

"What are you doing?"

"Texting Cooper to create a diversion." She handed back the phone, cracked the door open again, and grabbed Drew's hand.

"Anyone ever tell you you're intimidating?"

"Only guys who whisk me into closets without knowing how to escape them."

"And here I thought I was the only smooth one out there."

As soon as Cooper's voice sounded over the PA system, Ti snuck onto the deck and led Drew down the back steps. "And that's how it's done, rookie."

He dipped his head in admiration. "Never cease to impress."

She leaned against a post on Jacob's pier. "We all have our gifts."

"Not as many as you."

"Me?" Hardly. "All the kudos go to the single dad giving everything to take care of his family."

Drew shot down the compliment with his eyes and rolled up his sleeves. "Maybe we should duke this out in a dance."

"Duke it out?"

He extended a hand and winked. "Just pretend that was smooth. My ego's hanging by a thread."

Ti shook her head, his smile winning hers. She put down her camera bag and slipped off her heels in time for him to sweep her into a dancing hold. She tipped her chin. "The owner knows how to lead. Now who's the one who never ceases to impress?"

"My hip dance moves at the coffee shop didn't give that away already?" He let go to pull off a wobbly Michael Jackson spin.

Ti popped him in the arm. "Don't mock. Letting loose on that dance floor was good for you. That's what I've been trying to tell you about art. You get so caught up in it, you come to life without caring who's watching or what people think. No inhibitions holding you back. You can't contain what you feel, so you just ..." Arms outstretched, she raised her head to the star-filled sky and twirled. "Fly."

When she finally stopped spinning, she faced him head-on. "Haven't you ever felt that way about something?"

Eyes full of passion locked onto hers. A step closer, he traced a finger along her cheek to brush back the hair caught on her lashes. "I'm starting to."

Her stomach dipped at his touch, her heart at his words.

He drew her back into a dancing frame. The music from the party joined the cadence of the waves lapping against the docks. Activity brimmed all around them, but nothing overpowered the rhythm of Drew's heart against hers.

She rested her chin over his shoulder and drank in the feel of his hands securing her close to him. Sturdy, soothing. Strong, yet too gentle to ever hit her. Instead of leaving bruises, they embedded marks of hope deep inside her. She closed her eyes. "Do you know how different you are from most guys?"

A soft laugh trickled against her hair. "I tried to warn you I missed dating school."

"It's not that. You make me feel safe," she whispered.

He pressed a cheek to her temple, and she balled the back of his shirt in her fingers when his lips grazed her ear. "You should always feel safe at home."

Ti strained to focus on the moonlight and begged her lungs to keep breathing. He couldn't know how hard he was making this on her.

The music playing from the deck changed tempo, but they continued swaying to a song of their own.

Her conversation with Livy hovered in the forefront. Thinking he'd suffered the loss of his wife had been reason enough to guard his heart. But to know she'd walked out on him? More than ever, Ti needed to leave now before she risked hurting him like that, too.

She closed her eyes. "Drew, I'm sorry about your ex. I had no idea."

His feet stopped, his muscles hardening against hers.

"I can't imagine anyone leaving you two. I just assumed she died."

He resumed dancing, but his body remained tense. "Being a widower might've been easier."

"She went to New York, didn't she?"

"Left for the city like a starry-eyed artist."

"I'm sorry."

"Don't be. It's my fault. Living here, taking over the shop, raising a family. Those were my dreams. Not hers." He scoffed. "Even during her postpartum, I kept smothering. Kept pushing. So sure she'd want this life, too, if she gave it a chance."

"She never came back?"

"Not even when I went after her, begging her to come home, like a pathetic loser."

"You fight for those you love, Drew. Don't mistake honor for weakness."

Minutes passed with nothing more than regrets and unknowns drifting in the wind.

"When you first came, you reminded me of her." He exhaled over her skin. "All those times I was so rude... It wasn't your fault."

"I understand."

He shook his head. "And that's what makes you different from Annie."

"What if I'm not?"

"Trust me."

"You don't know me."

He leaned back. "What are you talking about?"

"I'm a runner, too. It's what I do."

"What are you running from?"

"Who I am. Things I've done." She withdrew and closed her arms across her torso. "You don't want to be with me."

Drew lifted a hand to her face. "Why don't you let me make that call."

She looked away. "You and Maddie deserve someone who belongs here."

"I'm sorry, have you noticed how much my girl adores you? You've been winning people's hearts here since day one." He gestured toward the deck. "You even have Mr. Fiazza and Grandma Jo dancing together, for crying out loud."

Smiling softly, he brought her to him. "Ti, there are a lot of mysteries I don't have figured out yet. But where you belong isn't one of them." A flicker of pain creased his brow. "I know our lighthouse can't compete with Times Square, but—"

"Stop." She backed away. "Don't you dare discount your life here. Ocracoke, your family, the home you've built—do you have any idea what I'd give to be a part of it?"

"You *are*."

Her destructive patterns didn't have a place in his white-picket-fence future. She wouldn't bring that on them. "You're wrong." She turned to the water, but Drew was already at her side, drawing her around.

He held back the hair blowing over her cheeks and searched her face.

Smiling sadly, she lifted her fingers to his cowlick and slid them to the whiskers shadowing his jawline. "Clean-cut business owner turns scruffy MI6 agent. I must be a bad influence on you. You show up in a Henley next, and the world might end."

Drew cupped a hand over hers. "Ti . . ."

"The surf competition starts tomorrow." She let go. "I'm staying to help until that's over. We shouldn't complicate things."

The corner of his mouth hitched. "I think complicated went out the window the day a gorgeous, outspoken New Yorker barged in and deemed herself my new consultant." He rested her palm on his chest. His heart thundered with the same disjointed rhythm as hers. "I've tried to fight it this whole time, but I can't. And I don't want to keep pretending to. Even if you're just here for Maddie, I—"

"Drew, please." Ti lowered her head. "Don't make this any harder."

Exhaling slowly, he released her and backed up like she'd asked.

She made it only a few strides away before stopping and turning around. Drew remained at the end of the pier—hands in his pockets, tie loosened over his dress shirt—looking every ounce the man she was falling in love with.

Heart taking over, she jogged up and curled her arms around his neck. Strong yet gentle hands found the small of her back, and the tears secured behind her lashes tore through. "Happy birthday, Drew." Her lips brushed his cheek.

He held her a moment longer.

But once her heels met the wood again, she turned without looking back this time.

CHAPTER TWENTY-TWO

Layers

Cramped in Ti's passenger seat, Drew banged his knee on the dashboard. He angled toward the window and bumped an elbow into the door panel. For the love of all things good, why did she have to drive a stinking Matchbox car?

Drew curbed a smile before Ti saw. Frankly, he was grateful her car was still here, period. He'd hardly slept last night, worried she'd be gone by morning. Instead, she'd gotten to work early, raring to go. Even the disappointing lack of business so far hadn't slowed her down.

He couldn't blame her for jumping headfirst into preparing for today. Either she blocked out last night, or pretending it didn't happen was her way of coping. If she needed him to play along, he'd do what he could.

For now.

He still had so much to uncover about her. About how to navigate this relationship. When to push, when to give her space. How to make her see what he did when he looked at her. After the way she'd withdrawn last night when he'd tried, he had to tread carefully. Especially when today brought on enough obstacles of its own.

Each time the wipers dragged across the dry windshield, Drew curled the corners of the flyers in his lap a little more. "You know it stopped drizzling five minutes ago, right?"

Ti lifted her phone to her mouth. "Owner's OCD-ness gets cuter every day."

His eyes circled toward the headliner. "I thought we were done with the owner notes."

She snapped off the wipers but turned up her amusement. "As if I could ever plunder the depths of what makes *Mr. Anderson* tick."

And of course they were back to the *Matrix* jokes. Perfect.

At least she still felt comfortable enough to be herself around him. He'd take that ease in any form today.

Ti parked under a tree, closed her door, and moaned. "Aw, poor little guy."

"Who?" Drew joined her on the driver's side, where she motioned to a gnat caught in a raindrop on her door handle.

He looked over the bug with its tiny wings stuck in the dew. "I think he's toast."

"You're so cynical."

And she was insanely adorable, down to the cute wrinkle between her brows furrowed with compassion. She was opposite him in most every way—and exactly who he wanted in his life. It had taken everything in him to let her go last night. Any more time with her, and he wouldn't be as strong.

Ti retrieved a tissue from her purse and tried pointlessly to free the gnat from its misery.

Drew rolled the stack in his hand into a scroll. "Thanks for helping me get these flyers up. It's a big help." He tapped them against his thigh. "I don't know why my ad in the *Observer* didn't run. I submitted it weeks ago."

Ti stared at him as though unraveling layers between his words.

"What?"

She handed over her stapler. "Give me a minute. I'll be right back."

While she jogged into Thai Moon, Drew stapled the last of the flyers advertising the shop's sales onto the neighboring telephone poles.

"That little punk." Ti wheeled through the door, carrying an open *Observer* in her hands. "Seems a little convenient for Marcus to have an ad front and center while yours got cut."

Drew took the local paper from her. Veins bulged on the tops of his hands. He wouldn't put anything past Marcus, but this was ridiculous. No wonder they hadn't gotten much business today.

Ti set soft fingers over his tight ones crumpling either side of the paper. She peered across the street toward a Jeep parked at the old Island Inn. "Hang tight."

After talking with a group of surfers in the Jeep, Ti stormed back over to her smart car, hair as wild as the look in her eyes. "He's a dead man. I can't believe Stan let this happen."

"What are you talking about?"

"Marcus must've found out what we had planned. He's one-upped everything we've done, stealing our business." She banged her door's top trim. "I'm gonna kill him."

Drew stuffed the paper in his back pocket and hurried to his side of the car before she could take off without him. "Slow down."

"You stay." She shot a no-arguing gaze above the hood. "Those guys will give you a ride to the beach. They've got an in with a good-sized crowd. Go mingle with potential customers. Tell them about the shop. I'll be back in a few."

"What are you gonna do?"

Stormy blue eyes met his, saying everything and nothing at the same time. "I'll meet you in twenty minutes." The gravel crunching under her tires shut out any chance to object.

The overcast sky may have dulled the sunrise this morning, but it couldn't overshadow the fire Ti carried in her wherever she went. Drew faced the hazy clouds. What would it take to keep that fire from going out of his life for good?

"You." Ti shouldered past Stan into his pad. "You were supposed to keep your punk son in check."

"Now, wait a minute, missy. I told you my boy doesn't listen to me. I tried."

"Tried?" Marcus came out of the kitchen with a forkful of some kind of restaurant dessert in hand. He flicked a scathing glare over Ti. "*She's* what all those lectures were about, Pop? You got to be kidding me. I knew you'd pick their side."

Side? What were they, five? "It has nothing to do with me or sides or some stupid high school competition title to reclaim. It's about a man, up against the odds, doing everything he can to take care of his family."

Marcus smirked. "Anderson's not as helpless as you think."

Toe to toe, she clenched her fingers to keep from double fisting him in the gut right now. "It's time to stop nursing your pubescent wounds. If you're so jealous of Drew, why don't you try switching places with him?"

She hedged his V-neck-wearing self into the wall, stole the fork, and jutted it in the air at him. "You want to worry every day about whether you can provide for your sick daughter's medication? You want to bury your own father?"

A cold gaze jerked away from the fork prongs. "Better than watching your old man pine his whole life for a woman he was too afraid to ask to marry him."

"Marcus." Stan rose from the recliner.

"Come off it, Pop. I've known since high school. I found the box of love letters you stashed in the garage. Were you just waiting for Mom to get too sick to care?"

"That's enough." Stan lunged forward. "You had no right going through my things."

"No right? I'm your son. Or is that another regret you're too weak-kneed to admit?"

Stan's face turned as stiff as his polyester shirt.

A crack in Marcus's indignation fractured across his eyes. He nodded as though accepting a truth he'd always believed. "I'm sorry I didn't want to take over the hotel business, Pop. And if I can't earn your respect running my own business, fine. I understand I disappointed you." Staring at the carpet, he ran his shoe along a stain, his voice buried in his shirt. "But did you ever love Mom at all?"

Stan looked backhanded. "Of course I loved her."

Marcus raised a bleary gaze to his dad's. "Then why'd you always wish for another family? What made Jolene and Drew better than us?"

Ti's cell buzzed in her pocket, but she didn't move. She stood on the outskirts of this broken family with her heart in a snare she hadn't seen coming. This had never really been about Drew or surf competitions. All this time, they'd both hidden disappointment and insecurities behind anger, never recognizing who they were truly hurting in the process.

So much brokenness. So many years lost. Something winced inside her.

Another shuffle forward brought a father to his son, choices to consequences. "If you honestly believe that, then the only one I'm disappointed in is myself." Stan cupped the back of Marcus's neck with the kind of strength and affection a father should be known for. "You're my boy, Marcus. The only son I have, and the only one I ever wanted."

The simple affirmation broke through the longstanding doubt clouding Marcus's eyes.

Ti dabbed her own as Marcus slowly grasped Stan's opposite shoulder.

When she cleared her throat, the duo separated and downplayed their reactions.

Ti needed to follow suit fast, or the last people on earth she wanted to cry in front of were about to witness the waterworks. She drew her shoulders back and emotions down. "So, we're good here, right? No more interfering with Drew's business."

The slightest shadow of remorse—or at least embarrassment—tinted Marcus's eyes. The damage was already done. They both knew it. But she couldn't give up yet.

She wielded the fork at Marcus again. "We clear?"

Hands raised, he gave a terse nod of concession. "Crystal."

"Good." She backed away from his hideous shirt and started for the door, already itching for a shower. "Now, do the rest of the world a favor, will ya? Burn your wardrobe and start over."

A confused, "What just happened?" trailed her out the door, followed by Stan's gravelly laugh. "Welcome to life with Ti Russo."

Some life.

On the porch, Ti stole a minute to exhale. The fatherly affection had been too much. Same as the unavoidable awareness of letting Drew down. She closed her eyes, but flashes of his empty shop and his fallen countenance throughout the day poured in. She should've seen Marcus's interference coming. Should've tried harder. Now, she was out of time.

She pushed off the banister and headed to what little chance she had left to salvage her promise to help him. She still had the painting Carter was going to buy. That would count for something, wouldn't it?

Her cell buzzed in her pocket again as she started down the sidewalk. Unknown number. Her stomach lurched. Silence from Queens had gone too long. What if he'd found her?

Leaves rustled in the stillness. She peeked backward to a guy in a hoodie crossing the road, eyes trained on her.

She picked up her pace the louder the footsteps echoed. Not looking back, she rifled through her purse for her can of pepper spray. He gained ground behind her. The can slid in her sweaty hand. Clutching it tighter, she inhaled and whipped around.

"Whoa." A grungy guy, probably in his mid-twenties, raised his arms. "What's with the spray? Jamie said you were supposed to be cool."

Jamie? She ground her teeth. "Cool with you creeping up on me like a stalker?"

"It's not like that. I was just waiting for you to be alone."

"And what part of that doesn't scream stalker?"

He shoved his hood off and stuffed his hands in his front pocket, looking around as though someone might catch them out after curfew. "I'm not very good at this stuff, all right?"

"This stuff?"

"You know." He swayed his head. "Hooking up."

Her grasp around the spray can wavered, but the truth about the identity she couldn't shake held on.

She unlocked her jaw. "Since you're apparently up for taking advice from anyone, here's some for free. Next time you want to go out with a girl, try asking instead of treating her like a hooker in a back alley."

The guy looked up from the pavement and shrugged like a dense jock on prom night. "So, you wanna go out?"

Ti pivoted without answering. Unbelievable. Then again, what'd she expect? It was how every guy saw her, treated her.

Except Drew.

The thought stopped her midway into her car. She'd wanted so much to be as good to him as he was to her. Wanted to love him the way he deserved. Maybe she still had one more chance.

CHAPTER TWENTY-THREE

Impassable

Drew set a glass of water on Maddie's nightstand and charged Jasper with keeping vigil. She'd seemed drained since the party. Had he kept her out too late that night? As if she would've let him take her home early. He laughed softly, kissed his stubborn girl on the head, and crossed the room.

Marcus's handiwork today had done its damage. But whatever backlash Ti unleashed on him earlier had at least salvaged a percentage of the sales they'd forecasted for the first day of the surf competition. Things would be okay. He just had to keep pushing hard.

In the doorway, he looked from the text reminding him of Mr. Parsons's deadline back to Maddie's silhouette. Despite how strong Maddie was, Drew had to do a better job at shielding her from his stress level. She didn't need anything else taxing her.

"I promise to take care of things," he whispered. Including finding a way to keep Ti in their life. Maddie needed her as much as he did.

After stopping in the kitchen to reheat his tea, Drew joined Ti in the living room.

She crossed her legs in front of her on the carpet and lowered the remote. "How's our Sea Monkey doing?"

Our Sea Monkey. The word warmed through him. "Sound asleep."

"But you're worried anyway."

He really couldn't hide anything from her, could he? He placed his mug on the end table. "Her color's a little off. I don't know. It's probably nothing. I'll check on her again before I go to bed."

On the floor in front of him, Ti patted his leg. "Never feel guilty for wanting to take care of those you love."

"Says the pot to the kettle. You're still not going to tell me what you did to Marcus, are you?"

She shook her head. "For your own protection."

"Right."

Diverting as usual, Ti flipped through the channels until she found an old *Magnum, PI* episode. "Mm." She lifted a fruity smelling drink away while scooting up against the couch. "Here's what I really want to know. Do you think Tom Selleck was born with a mustache?"

"Okay, I think you've had enough to drink there." Drew went to grab her cup, but she held on.

"It's not like it's a Zima."

"Yeah, that joke never gets old."

"Hey, I'm just choosing to be merry. 'For every minute you remain angry, you give up sixty seconds of peace of mind.'" Ti regained reign of her cup and took a satisfying sip.

Drew tried not to laugh. "Quoting Ralph Waldo Emerson. Should I be scared or impressed?"

"You'd be amazed at the words of wisdom you can find under a Snapple cap." With another tension-releasing laugh, she went back to channel surfing.

He'd let her have the distraction. He could certainly use one himself. More from how hyperaware he was of Ti sitting between his calves than from any aftermath of Marcus's stunts.

Truth be told, Drew didn't expect today's sales to accomplish a miracle. It would take more than topnotch inventory or a flash sale to cover the level of debt he carried. As much as he appreciated Ti's effort, this was something he needed to take care of alone. Still, if he could take away her disappointment, he'd do it in a heartbeat.

Drew risked a hand to her chin and steered her focus to him. "Ti, I want to make sure you know how much you've helped us. Everything you've done—all your artwork, your diligence—it's been incredible."

Behind the flush of her drink, deep-seated sorrow stormed her eyes. "But not enough."

Her whisper brushed against his arm, the ache in her words against his heart.

"Ti . . ."

She blinked away any trace of sadness and raised her glass. "Merriment, remember?"

For her, he'd try.

Minutes passed with soft flashes of light from the TV flickering over Ti's smooth legs. Drew's muscles pulled taut every time a strand of her hair fanned against his thighs. If he had to sit here much longer, the TV's background noise wouldn't hide the inward groan barely restraining the urge to pull her up to the couch with him.

He let out a hard breath. He had to be smart about this. She'd pulled away when he advanced at the party. Had been pretending it had never even happened. He understood her needing to sort through things, but the clock was running out. How was he supposed to back off and fight for her at the same time? What if trying only pushed her further away?

Maybe he'd better wait till tomorrow. Give her another day to let the stress from today's setback at the shop wear off.

Ti nestled her bare shoulder under the crook of his knee. Her soft skin against him sent quakes from one tendon to the next. He swallowed. *Tomorrow. You can wait till tomorrow.*

If he actually survived tonight.

Drew stared ahead until a snort of laughter trailed up from Ti's spot on the carpet. He glanced from the screen to her. "What's so funny?"

She exaggerated a hand flutter at a couple on the TV. "That."

"Kissing?"

"No. Not kissing. *Movie* kissing." Soundless laughter folded her in half.

"Yeah, I think it's time to call it a night. You're getting delirious." Yet another reason to keep his cool right now.

"Oh, c'mon." She rose to her knees and turned to face him. "No one in real life sways their head all over the place while kissing someone."

He fought a grin. "They're just into it."

"No. I'm sorry. It doesn't happen like that." She covered his mouth with her hand, planted her lips on the back of it, and proceeded to illustrate how ridiculous it looked.

Watching her swivel her head around with dramatic flair had him laughing against her fingers. He finally cupped her shoulders to cut her off.

"Tell me that's not awkward." She dropped her hand and poked him in the chest. But instead of moving away, she stayed close. Too close. Her eyes gravitated to his mouth. "It's supposed to be slow, tender."

His pulse pounded in his eardrums. Sitting in such an intimate position with her, he couldn't think, let alone breathe. If he moved his hand from her shoulder to her neck, the self-control he'd failed to master all night would crumble in a second.

Ocean-blue eyes held his and deepened the yearning to explore them in every way possible.

This wasn't the right time. Not like this, when the day's disappointment left her vulnerable enough to drink more than usual. When she might not remember this tomorrow. Might not even know whether she truly wanted him.

Her thumb skimmed across his lips in a kiss all its own, the gentle touch awakening every dormant nerve in his body.

"Ti . . ."

Ignoring his husky warning, she searched his face. Slowly. Intently. He'd seen an array of emotions color her eyes since he'd known her. But the visceral longing enlivening those endless blues right now, he couldn't resist. Giving in, he unclasped her hair and ran his fingers through the strands waving down her neck—wild and messy and everything Ti.

Her chest expanded and contracted with rapid breaths, as if beseeching him to move faster. To relieve the magnetized tension holding them a heartbeat apart.

The strawberry scent on her lips overrode the last shred of resolve holding him in place. He kissed her hard. No space. No time. Just the essence of Ti Russo consuming him.

With her tight against his body, he absorbed the feel of her earring caressing the back of his hand, the silky skin beneath her ear, the openness with which she gave herself to him. The strain of waiting, wondering—the hunger spurred from almost kissing her before—crashed through him now without restraint.

She threaded her fingers through his hair, her affirmation inviting him deeper. Her touch ignited a familiar surge of heat inside him that he'd tamped down for so long. When she inclined her neck for his lips to navigate every crevice, he didn't hesitate.

The ache for more intensified as her warm hands traveled down his collar to the top button on his shirt. "Let me make up for today."

She whispered it so softly, he almost missed it.

His body tensed at her meaning, her words dousing the fire burning through his tendons. Was that what this was? What she still thought he wanted? Or worse, what she thought she owed him?

Hard breaths met his when he broke away. The physical pain of stopping was nothing compared to the fist of guilt slamming into him from the look in her eyes—questions mixed with longing and trust. Red marks left from his scruffy jaw trailed from her mouth to her neck, like the bruise that punk had left on her arm.

She studied him for an explanation. And when a haunted sadness bled into the confusion streaking her face, remorse shattered the last of his ribs sheltering his heart. He reached a hand to her cheek, yearning to protect her. Needing to make her understand.

The front door creaked open. Cooper stopped along the edge of the tiles with a girl under his arm. "Oh, sorry. Didn't realize you guys were here. We'll, uh, head back out." He pointed behind him.

"No, it's fine. We were just going to bed." Drew sprang to his feet. Catching Coop's telling expression, he cringed at how that came out. "Not together. I mean in separate beds. Rooms, actually." *Stop talking.*

Ti rose from the carpet with her arms hugged to her sides. "I was on my way out."

Cooper nodded without saying anything. Didn't need to. As soon as Ti rounded the doorway into the kitchen, a swell of emotions propelled Drew after her. How many times could he mess this up?

He caught the back door before it fully closed behind her. "Ti, hold on."

"I'm sorry." She stopped on the patio but didn't turn around. "The day got me all messed up. I wasn't thinking straight. I shouldn't have kissed you. I just wanted to show you how much I ..." She shoved her bangs off her forehead. "I shouldn't even be here. I need to go."

"Wait." Drew circled in front of her. "You're saying you don't want anything to happen between us? Because I do."

"No, you don't."

"Yeah. I do." He took her hands. "Just not like this. That wasn't how I wanted our first kiss to be. I mean, it was. The things you do to me ..." Why did she always have to make him tongue-tied?

His arms drifted to his sides. "What I'm trying to say is, that, in there—" He pointed to the house "—those were real desires, but that's not the way I want to treat you. You'd just finished telling me a kiss is supposed be tender." He glided a hand to her cheek over the marks his lack of restraint had left. "And I was anything but."

She dropped her gaze to her feet. "I'm not the kind of girl you treat with tenderness."

Did she honestly believe that? "Says who? Jamie? That guy's a world-class creep."

"It's not just Jamie." Eyes closed, she turned her head. "Forget it." She tried to skirt away, but he drew her back toward him.

"Ti, talk to me. We're supposed to be straight with each other, remember? Why would you say something like that?"

"Because it's what every drug dealer my parents forced me to be with said, all right?" Retracting her hand, she shrank away as if the unveiled truth erected an impassable space between them.

Her words punched through his gut, stole any attempt at a response.

The porch light reflected in her glassy eyes. "My parents were meth heads, Drew. They smoked every cent we had. When Mom got too sick to turn tricks, guess who they made stand in her place?"

Fragments of her story fused together. The way she'd withdrawn any time he'd brought up her family. The hurt she'd shown when she thought he'd only wanted a good time out of her. The way she equated affection with physical touch.

And he'd just made it worse.

A fury like he'd never experienced boiled from the pit of his stomach until he didn't trust the singed words that might come out.

She faced the dark sky when he didn't reply. "That's who you just kissed in there. The pimped-out daughter of drug addicts." A slow blink leveled a hardened gaze with his. "I already told you. You don't want to be with me."

Behind the courageous, tough-skinned New Yorker stood a broken girl bound by a past he'd sacrifice anything to rescue her from. Compassion for her overrode his anger at her parents. It made sense she'd turn to guys who used her. She didn't see her value beyond what they'd limited it to.

Without hesitation, he brought her close, cradled her head to his chest, and kissed her temple with the tenderness she deserved. "You're wrong."

The unanswered whisper hung between them, but he wasn't giving up. "Ti—"

The back door opened. In sweaty pajamas, Maddie stumbled down the steps.

Drew and Ti exchanged an uncertain glance and hurried over. "Sweetie, you all right?" Her forehead burned the back of his hand. "Maddie?"

Helpless eyes peered up at him. And with one labored breath, she collapsed in his arms.

CHAPTER TWENTY-FOUR

Undone

A flurry of ER staff joined the paramedics ushering Maddie through the receiving bay doors.

Drew clenched the edge of the gurney as speckled tiles streamed under his feet in a blur of scuff marks. The fast pace kept his legs from completely giving way. His heart was another story.

Flashes from the first time he'd taken her to the ER stormed in with each overhead light they passed under. Images of tubes tethered to his little girl's body constricted the grip of helplessness he'd vowed would never own him again.

Swallowing his fear, he covered Maddie's hand with his free one. "It's okay, baby."

Worried eyes looked up at him through a film of tears running into her oxygen mask. And suddenly he was back in the sound with Dad, broken by waves he was powerless to stop.

Orders and stats rang across the gurney as the team rolled her down the hall. He caught the words jaundice and biopsy right as a wiry-haired triage nurse stopped Drew with an outstretched arm. "I'm sorry, but we have to take her straight for X-rays. You'll need to wait till we come get you."

The heck he did. He shoved past her.

"Daddy?"

"I'm right here, Sea Monkey. Everything's going to be all right."

Another nurse blocked the double doors while Maddie faded out of reach. The small-framed woman set a consoling hand to his forearm. "Mr. Anderson, we can't take care of her unless you let us do our job." She gave his arm a gentle squeeze. "We'll find you as soon as we can. You have my word."

Glimpses of Maddie's gurney fanned in and out of sight behind the doors. Drew expelled a ragged breath, grappling for willpower to keep from plowing past the barrier between them.

A gentle touch pressed into his back. Quiet yet supportive, Ti stood by his side.

Another slow breath merged into a resigned nod. As hard as it was to wait on the sidelines, he had to let the hospital staff stand in where he couldn't. Right now, Maddie needed them more than him.

The nurse offered a supportive smile before turning to take up her post. And while the doors oscillated over the threshold, Drew weaved his fingers through Ti's and held on with all he had.

Ti pinched off a piece of Styrofoam from her empty hospital coffee cup and dropped it inside. Sitting in a waiting room's uncomfortable chair for three hours was torturous enough for anyone. Especially for a father like Drew.

Thankfully, he'd gotten to go back with Maddie shortly after her X-rays. But he hadn't sat down once since they made him wait while they took Maddie into surgery for a liver biopsy. Still pacing the tiles, Drew rolled and unrolled his sleeves for the thirteenth time since Cooper, Livy, and Grandma Jo arrived. They'd flocked together in a picture of family support that made Ti's heart ache and swell at the same time.

She hooked an arm around her legs and brought her knees to her chest. Livy was right. Maddie had the best family she could ask for. Ti needed to stop interfering with that.

But how was she supposed to let go of her feelings for Drew? His fierce need to love and protect reflected a gentleness she'd never known from a man. Same as his touch.

She lifted the back of her fingers to her mouth, reliving the sensations of his lips against hers. She'd been kissed with passion, yeah, but it was always empty. Drew held her with emotion, like he needed her—all of her—not just a fleeting brush with pleasure.

She couldn't bear to see his face when he realized that's all she was. He didn't believe it now, but he hadn't had time to process what she'd told him. How it would impact Maddie, the future he wanted. And when the rest of the family found out...

A soft melody of soulful prayers billowed toward her from Grandma Jo's corner chair. Ti cut a glance away from the motherly expression fixed on her as though tuned into Ti's thoughts.

A little longer. Be brave just a little longer.

Livy slid a cramped leg out from under the other and stretched up from the stiff chair. "I'm gonna get some more coffee. Anybody need a refill?"

As if answering for her, frigid air from the ceiling vent slithered down Ti's skin. "Give me a double." She'd take any intervention she could get right now.

"You got it. Coop?"

"I'll come with you."

Before they made it past the counter, the double doors leading to the bays opened.

Drew flew to the doctor's side. "How is she?"

He swiped off his blue surgical cap and lowered a chart. "She's stable."

Drew's muscles looked like they could've turned into putty with relief.

Visible exhaustion pulled at the doctor's tall stance. "We're still waiting on the results of the biopsy. But according to her symptoms and bloodwork, it appears Maddie's developed autoimmune hepatitis. Instead of her immune system attacking viruses and bacteria, it's targeting her liver."

"What? How? I don't understand." The frantic frustration splintering Drew's voice crushed Ti's heart.

"It's hard to say with these types of diseases. We pulled her medical records. Could be the result of genes interacting.

Could be overexposure from one of the drugs she's taking that might've caused too much toxicity in her liver."

A mess-up from the doctor's office? This couldn't be good. Ti sent Cooper a silent plea to intervene before Drew could react.

He clapped Drew on the back, made a confident stride forward, and extended a hand. "Thanks for all your work here tonight, doc. Is it all right if we see Maddie now?"

"We're treating her with medications to lower her immune-system activity and monitoring her vitals. Given her age, we'll keep her overnight for observation, but we moved her to a recovery room in Pediatrics. You're free to go up." He motioned to the elevator with his chart.

The double doors swung back and forth behind the doctor, but Drew didn't move. Body still frozen, he stared ahead as if peering across the ocean.

Not for the first time since she'd known him, Ti wished she had the answers he searched for.

Grandma Jo patted Drew's shoulders and jutted her chin at the elevator. "I know a little girl who's past ready to see her daddy."

Ti backed up a few feet, wanting to give Drew the space he needed, but he closed her hand in his and led her forward without a hint of hesitation.

Inside, a blurry mural of the close-knit family shimmered across the elevator's silver walls. Ti's reflection blended with the others as though she'd painted herself into a dream. She wiped a rogue tear and met another intuitive gaze from Grandma Jo.

Ti flinched at the elevator's *ding*. Twisting the fringes on her shirt into a spiral, she kept her head down and waited for everyone else to exit first.

"We'll go in shifts, sugar." Grandma Jo prodded Ti toward Drew and nodded them both down the hall. "Maddie will want to see you first."

Drew dipped his head in a bow of thanks.

Ti clutched her arms while shuffling forward. Her skin flushed under the fluorescent bulbs, zeroing in on her like an imposter. Cooper should be coming to see his niece. Or Grandma Jo to see her surrogate grandbaby. Even Livy had more right than Ti.

A sinking feeling bottomed out in her stomach. What if she'd played a role in running down Maddie's immune system? Had she kept Maddie up late too many nights preparing for Drew's party? Ti kicked herself. She should've been more responsible. Should've been—

Drew stopped in front of the hospital room. The vulnerability on his face turned her inside out and kept her in place. While whispering something she couldn't hear, he lowered his head as she'd seen him do numerous times in front of Maddie's bedroom door at home.

Ti pressed an encouraging kiss to the top of his bicep before thinking twice. "I'll wait right here."

Drew exhaled slowly, lifted his head, and walked over to Maddie's bed.

Beeping machines joined the IV bag's steady flow, releasing hope one drip at a time.

Maddie's groggy eyes fluttered open at the sound of his footsteps.

"Hey, Sea Monkey. What's this I hear about you winning all the nurses' hearts?" He eased onto the edge of her mattress. "I'm not sure they're gonna let me take you home."

"Dad."

"Well, I don't blame them for wanting to keep you." He rustled her bangs. "Who can resist falling for the world's cutest marine biologist?"

Ti leaned against the doorjamb, once again overtaken by their precious father-daughter relationship. Questions compressed around the pang she hadn't been able to shake since the party. How could his ex not be here? Did she even know about Maddie's autoimmune disease? Would it make a difference if she did?

Maybe it wasn't too late to help them. She backed off the frame.

"Ti, you're here." Maddie's tired voice strained against Ti's heartstrings.

"Of course I am, love." Ti tucked away her own issues and circled to the opposite side of the mattress. Right now, Maddie needed strength, whether Ti felt it or not.

"You're one brave chica. I have to admit, hospitals make me a little nervous."

Maddie looked from Drew to Ti. "Really?"

"Yep. I had to have surgery when I was your age."

"Were you scared?"

Ti leaned in as if telling a secret. "I made the nurses bring me *five* extra pillows so I could build a fort around my bed to hide in."

Maddie's sweet laugh rasped through a cough. "Did it work?"

"For a little while. But you know what really helped? A song my best friend and I wrote together. You want to learn it?"

Maddie inched up on her elbows, face aglow with intrigue.

It might not be enough, but it was all Ti had to give. "All right, I'll sing first and you repeat, 'kay?"

"Okay."

Ti stole a minute to hum the chords as if Cass where there, playing her guitar. "When the lights turn dark and the shadows deep, close your eyes and drift to sleep. To the place of dreams that sweep us away, together we run. Best friends, always."

She helped Maddie the second time through and then let her sing it on her own. From across the mattress, an expression holding more affection than Ti had ever experienced from anyone streamed from Drew's eyes. Sitting there with them like a family—the one she'd always wanted—was too much. Too hard. Thick tears stung behind her eyes.

She glanced away from Drew and rounded the bed, needing deflection. Fast. "Your dad can teach you the *Gilmore Girls* theme song next." She fake-whispered to Maddie over his head, "It's his favorite."

Before he could retaliate, Ti ducked out of the room. At least in the hall, she could breathe. Almost. Until the soft cadence of their good-night prayers drifted through the doorway and around Ti's heart. She leaned against the cool wall and craned her head back. Tears blurred the ceiling, lines too far crossed to see beginning or end.

Three breaths later, Drew closed the door behind him and dragged a palm down his face. Instead of a confident dad, a broken man stood before her. Drained. Weary.

Had she made things harder for him? "I hope I didn't overstep my bounds in there. As brave as she is, I thought she might be afraid. I just wanted to help."

Green eyes cascaded over her with a warmth no touch could match. Still without words, he closed her in his arms, buried his head between her neck and shoulder, and held on as if the floor had turned into the ocean, and she was the only thing that could anchor him. Hot tears soaked into her neck and hair.

The hospital corridor's noisy bustle dissolved behind the sound of a father's heart interceding for his daughter. Her throat closed. After all the years she'd invested in blocking out memories of her dad, she'd never realized she'd been numbing a yearning she didn't know existed.

Until right now.

All the feelings that being in Ocracoke had stirred came to light and chafed against the hollow space inside her. Tears streamed. Aches surged. She clung to Drew a little tighter, holding on to the very thing it was time to let go of.

CHAPTER TWENTY-FIVE

Resistance

Drew toweled his hair, wiped the steam off the bathroom mirror, and grabbed his razor. Looking at his reflection, he ran the back of his hand along his unshaven jawline. His five o'clock shadow had turned into a five-day beard. Maybe he'd leave it. With any luck, it would detract from the stress lines curving around his eyes.

He leaned on both hands and rotated his neck. Maddie was home, recovering like the trooper she was. Everyone was getting back to their normal routines. He'd finally gotten in touch with Lenny in time to meet Mr. Parsons's deadline tomorrow. Things should be fine.

Except they weren't. Not with Ti.

She hadn't left yet. At least, not physically. But she'd distanced herself again. Hadn't being at the hospital shown her how much she belonged here? With him and Maddie?

It had for him. More than ever. All the doubts and reservations he'd been wrestling since she walked into their life drained on that hospital room's floor. And he'd do whatever it took to make her see it, too.

Skipping the shave, Drew brushed his teeth, cinched the towel around his waist, and headed down the hall. In front of Maddie's room, he almost bumped into Ti as she backed gingerly through the doorway.

A gasp punctuated her flinch. "Sorry. I thought you were already at the shop."

"Yeah, I went in early to work on something." He picked at a dent in the wall. "I needed a break, but I'm on my way back now. Well ..." He motioned to his towel. "Once I get dressed."

Whatever momentary composure she'd gained a second ago evaporated further with each cascading glance down his body.

He wrestled a grin when her eyes finally made the trek back to his. The connection ping-ponged her gaze against every angle of the hallway.

"Um, clothes. Right. That's a good thing. I should probably do the same. Go, I mean. Not get dressed. I already have clothes on. Obviously." She bit her lip as though cutting herself off.

Man, she was cute when she blushed. And incredibly attractive.

As if following her skin tone's cue, his body temperature raised enough to need a second shower.

Ti nodded to Maddie's bedroom. "We were just finishing up a movie. She's asleep now."

Another step forward showed a glimpse inside the room. Welcoming the distraction, Drew did a double take at something on her nightstand that looked like a glowing hunk of rock extracted from an Indiana Jones movie. "What is *that*?"

A streak of the resolve he missed from Ti lately rose across her shoulders. "A Himalayan salt lamp." She raised a finger. "Don't mock. They purify the air and promote better sleep."

The kaleidoscope of blues in her eyes gleamed the way they did whenever she was riled up about something. Drew almost egged her on just to keep seeing it, but she lowered her chin, her countenance falling with it.

"I thought it'd be good for Maddie. Plus it's pink, so at least she'll like it."

The care in her soft voice drew him toward her. "She'll love it. Almost as much as she loves you."

Ti lifted a hand to her neck while keeping her focus on Maddie asleep in bed. "She has a big heart."

Tucked beside Maddie, Jasper popped his head up, his ears raised toward the sound of their talking.

Drew quietly shut the door before they ended up waking Maddie, too. Ti fiddled with the back of her earring. A stud. That couldn't be good. Maybe if he distracted her ...

"You'll never guess who I got a note of apology from this morning."

An undeniable grin fought for her lips.

"It'd have to take someone capable of putting Marcus in his place to get him to shake his pride." Just like she'd done for Drew. Why'd he have to be the slowest learner ever? He ran a knuckle under his chin. "You know anything about that?"

Shielding her mouth with her hair, Ti faced the ceiling. "Nope."

"Of course not."

Her gaze met his for the slightest moment and then flitted away. Not much longer, and she'd be flitting out of reach altogether.

One more shot. He had to break through to her before he lost the chance. He swallowed. "Can I take you somewhere today? There's something I want to show you."

"I can't." She pointed a thumb behind her, already backing toward the stairs. "I need to finish that painting for Carter."

Through everything, she was still fretting over helping him save the shop. "Don't worry about it." He started for her again. "I sold my dad's boat. We're gonna be fine."

Her head shot up. "You what? Drew, no."

"It took me a while to figure it out, but it's what he would've wanted."

She looked away. "But after this last trip to the ER, it can't be enough."

"It is for now." He angled around to face her.

Eyes blurry, Ti equaled each of Drew's forward strides with a backward one. "I have to go. Carter's flying out to San Francisco tomorrow. Today's my last chance to get him the painting."

"Ti—"

"Call whoever you sold the boat to. You're getting it back," she said on her way down the stairs.

"Ti, wait." He whirled around the corner, but she'd already made it to the front door. He slumped against the banister.

All this time she'd been fighting for them, never knowing what it was like to have someone fight for her in return. He raked his wet hair off his forehead and straightened. That was about to change.

Starting right now.

Drew weaved through the displays toward the back of the shop in search of Ti. "Hey, Chloe. Have you seen—?"

"She's outside."

He nodded at her behind the counter, grateful for women's intuition, and hustled through the back door.

Beneath a live oak's overarching branches, Ti mixed a series of paint colors on a palette. With her hair braided over her shoulder and a pale green summer dress flowing across her calves in the wind, she could've been a painting herself.

Drew evened his steps as he approached. The hard part was getting his breathing to do the same. "You have a way of capturing what few people see."

Her fan brush stalled over the palette. "Maddie has a good eye. She helped me pick out which photo to paint."

Her brushstrokes whispered across the canvas like music, each movement bringing the unassuming dimensions of the harbor to life. Same way she did with everything around her.

Himself included.

He took the paint supplies from her, set them aside, and grabbed her hand. "C'mon."

"The painting—"

"Can wait." He steered her through the shop to the front door. "We'll be back in an hour, Chloe."

"Have fun," she said with a wave.

"Where are we...?" Ti pulled her hand free and gawked at the four-wheeler parked at the curb. "What is that?"

"A little spontaneity goes a long way, remember?" Hopefully, far enough to break through her walls. Drew mounted the ATV, pulled on a helmet, and held one out to her.

The look on her face? Priceless. Just a little more haggling ... "I thought you were supposed to be up for anything. Not a fan of four-wheelers?"

Her tight lips strained to stay in place, and he knew he had her. She took the helmet with extra force and motioned for him to give her something else.

He raised a questioning brow.

"The key." She gestured for it. "If I'm gonna go all redneck, I'm at least going to be in the driver's seat." In classic Ti-fashion, she climbed on the ATV like a pro and cranked the engine.

Good thing the tinted helmet shield hid his grin. The bait worked better than he'd thought. Under the layers of hurts and fears, the free-spirited girl who'd resuscitated him without even realizing it still thrived. He just had to make her see that girl was who he wanted.

He reached for the handlebars. Ti's back fit against his chest, her arms under his. She stiffened for a moment but then relaxed into an embrace he prayed she'd know was home.

Once they took off, she didn't need any help driving. She mastered everything full throttle as usual.

Drew soaked in the comfort of having her near him again—the wind welcoming them, the ocean's fragrance blending with the essential oils lingering on her skin. He missed this connection, missed her. She had to feel it, too. Had to know he'd fallen so hard, he'd be lost if she left.

For an agonizing span of thirty seconds, the reality that he might not be able to convince her to stay etched the beginning of a wound that would be irreparable. The engine's rumble shook the lump out of his throat as he pointed to the opening for the off-road beach ramp approaching.

Slowing down, Ti peeked over her shoulder and lifted her face shield. "You want me to drive on the beach?"

Her smile only pulled him in deeper. "Hey, you wanted the full redneck experience, right?"

There was that glint of intrigue and adventure rising to a challenge. He held on tighter. This was about to get wild.

As expected, Ti punched the gas each time a dip in the sand resisted the wheels.

He directed her closer to the shoreline, where the wet sand evened out better, and called over the roar of the ocean, "Keep going."

Vacationers dwindled behind them as they gained ground on the more secluded end of the island, close to where the ocean met the sound.

Drew curved his fingers over hers on the handlebars and let off the gas. The four-wheeler slowed near the bank of rocks he'd grown up playing on. He helped Ti off, set both their helmets aside, and drank in the beauty of the expansive waves. A beauty that paled in comparison to the woman beside him.

"Wow, it's amazing here."

"It is now."

Her lashes dipped, and he had to burrow his flip-flops in the sand to keep from reaching for her.

She peered across the water as he normally did. No impressions of him this time. Just pensive thoughts she kept hidden. How could he make her feel safe enough to trust him without pushing her away?

"Before I ever owned a camera or knew how to paint, I used to dream up scenes like this. Pristine landscapes, where nothing but light and joy and safety existed."

Casting his reservations aside, Drew came up behind her and kissed the top of her shoulder blade.

She clasped her elbows across her chest. "When I was in bed with those dealers, I'd watch the ceiling fan circle 'round and 'round, pretending it was creating a portal I could escape through to somewhere like this."

A flare of anger over what she'd gone through spread from the bottom of his feet through every cell in his body.

She turned and brushed her fingertips through his hair. "To someone like you. Cowlick and all."

Her weak laugh broke his heart in ways he didn't know were possible. "Ti—"

"Please. Let me finish." She lowered her arm to her side and turned toward the sandpipers scurrying along the beach.

"They were dreams, Drew. Beautiful daydreams of being someone else. Of having another life."

He clenched the bottom of his shirt to hold in the response prodding him to interrupt. A faint flash of lightning streaked across the horizon in an echo of the storm brewing inside him.

"Cass and I started writing songs together in middle school, and it was like this whole other world opened up. I couldn't get enough. Music, photography, painting—anything to create something beautiful and untainted. That's all I wanted."

Waves agitated in the background, tears in her eyes. "I used to pride myself in never having done drugs, thinking I was so much better than my parents." She scoffed. "As if hiding in my make-believe worlds to escape real life was any different than getting high to do the same exact thing."

"You were just a kid."

"You can only use that excuse for so long. You know I ran the first chance I had to get the heck away from my roots?" A sad smile claimed her eyes. "My *other* life. Thirty-five hundred miles away in London on photo shoots I thought would color over the darkness for good."

She slipped out of her flip-flops and dragged her toes through the sand. "But all the colors in the world can't cover up a flawed canvas. Those flaws and scars will always be there. Seen and felt by anyone who gets close enough."

Drew curled his fingertips under hers, needing her to know he wasn't backing away. That he wanted her to open up to him fully and wasn't afraid to do the same.

A flicker of doubt snaked through his chest at the thought. Could he really give her all of himself? Even the wounded pieces? He should've thought about that before he kissed her the other night. If it didn't work out, she'd feel used again, abandoned. Maybe he should be more cautious—

Stop. Insecurities had ruled him long enough. He'd rather be broken with her than pretend to be whole alone.

"We all carry brokenness, Ti."

"I know. And after spending a summer in the Catskills with Cass and Ethan, I knew running away wasn't going to change anything. So, I finally went home. I thought if I found the courage to go back and open up an art studio, it'd be like facing my fears and proving my past didn't own me anymore, you know? That maybe I could even give hope to other kids in our neighborhood to do the same. But then he ..."

A seagull cawed overhead, garnering a frayed smile from her.

Drew moved closer. "Then what? Who?"

Her dejected expression speared him. His pulse lurched when tragically beautiful eyes found his again. "The reason I'm leaving."

CHAPTER TWENTY-SIX

Breach

Wind roared off the shoreline, light and darkness vying for the sky. Ti turned to the ATV. "We should get back."

The oncoming storm would have to wait. Drew jogged after her. "Ti, hold on. What reason?"

She faced the torn skyline. Lightning flickered across her eyes, highlighting the lies holding her in bondage.

He caught her hand. "Look, I might not know what's going on back in Queens right now, but I know the woman standing here on the beach with me." So full of beauty and value she couldn't see. He secured a wayward strand of hair behind her ear and struggled to reach the woman hidden behind this haunted brokenness he felt more and more helpless to rescue her from.

Drew tipped her chin toward him when she looked away. "Just because those guys treated you like you're worthless, doesn't mean you are."

"And just because you want to believe I'm something more, doesn't mean I am."

"Then let me prove it. Let me show you every day." He brushed his fingertips to the nape of her neck. "You said yourself you dreamed of being here."

Her lashes closed as she breathed in. "It was a fairy tale. That's not the way life works."

"And you think settling for creeps who hurt you is? You think that's all there is to reality?" He turned her arm over to expose the imprint Jamie had left.

Ti covered the bruise with her hand. "It's the way things are."

"It doesn't have to be."

"You don't know how much I wish you were right." With another wrecked smile, she peered toward two pelicans forging a path across the tumultuous waves. "You know why I love sunsets so much? All the grays and shadows from the day disappear. Color and beauty take over. And for one moment, I forget all that's marred and dark in the world."

As a cluster of ominous clouds shrouded the sun, she wiped at the tears collecting on her chin. "Escape only lasts a moment, Drew." She tugged on her helmet and straddled the seat.

He hopped on the ATV before she could take off without him. He'd relent for now, but he wasn't done fighting for her yet.

Raindrops splattered onto his helmet halfway down the beach. A trickle merged into a downpour, slashing them sideways in the wind. Drew steered the four-wheeler over to the lifeguard stand and helped Ti take cover under the wooden tower while frenzied vacationers scurried off to the parking lot.

"Where'd that come from?" Ti wiped her wet arms, looking frazzled and adorable and downright sexy.

The turmoil behind her eyes hadn't fully left, and they definitely weren't finished with their conversation, but the momentary interruption might actually be a good thing. Her tactics had certainly worked on tearing down his walls. Maybe they'd work on her, too.

He sauntered closer. "Just think of it as another helping hand teaching you how to be adventurous."

"You love making me eat my words, don't you?"

His mouth quirked. "Relish is a better word."

"Then how 'bout you *relish* some more of this rain." She shoved him into the storm.

Drew danced back under the tower, wrapped his soaked shirtsleeves around her, and nudged his dripping wet head into the crook of her neck.

Squealing louder than the downpour drumming onto the wooden planks above them, Ti squirmed to get away.

Like that was happening. He cornered her against a beam until their playful banter gave way to the same passion that had been sparking since day one. She felt it, too. He could sense it. If she'd just give it a chance, they could make this work.

With their clothes melded together, they breathed against each other, neither looking away. His pulse thrummed with desires he couldn't act on yet. Still, he wasn't ready to let go of her. Not when she was this close—when she'd lowered her guard, just for a minute.

Ti set a palm to his chest and froze. Panic stormed her eyes. "The painting!" Without hesitation, she pushed him back and bolted into the rain.

"Ti, wait."

But she didn't slow down. She sprinted up the beach to the road.

Drew banged the side of his fist to the beam and jumped on the ATV. She'd only made it to Lighthouse Road before he caught up and got her to hop on. As soon as the wheels breached the shop's gravel driveway, she dropped her helmet and bounded around back.

He darted off the seat and chased after her. But when he rounded the corner of the shop, Ti wasn't there. Neither was the painting. He ducked in through the back door to find her standing in front of the easel, a muddied puddle of colors accumulating beneath it.

"I'm sorry." Chloe propped open an umbrella in the corner. "By the time I remembered it was out there, it was too late."

Ti's slender shoulders rose and fell in quick, shallow movements.

Drew eased toward her. A step at a time, the painting came into view. Rivulets of undefined colors streaked the canvas like tears blurring the artist's vision.

Ti's chin sank to her chest, Drew's heart to the floor.

He nodded to the front door. "Chloe, why don't you call it an early night."

She nodded her understanding, grabbed her things, and flipped over the *Closed* sign on her way out.

Drew turned Ti around.

A new level of dejection looked back at him. "Your dad's boat. The shop. I ..."

"We're going to be fine. Promise. You're the one who always said that to me, remember? So many times, you drove me crazy." His inward chuckling waned behind the sobriety of the truth. "But that's because I had things all wrong." He threaded his fingers through hers. "Until you showed me what I was missing."

Her forehead crinkled. "I pushed too hard. Tried to force you to change everything. I shouldn't have—"

"Look around this place, Ti. Your creativity, talent, heart—you breathed hope back into this shop." He lifted her chin with all the tenderness he possessed. "And into me."

This close, minty breaths mingled with his and ramped up his heart rate beyond what it had been on the beach. More than physical attraction, the ache for her stemmed from somewhere deeper. Somewhere he'd kept closed off. Until now.

Words hovered beneath his Adam's apple—fear pulling from one side, hope from the other. Muscles caught in the middle, he strained in place until her earnest expression brought him a step closer. "I've spent my life trying to conquer the ocean. Spent weeks trying to resist the one I see right here."

Drowning in her blue eyes, he grazed a thumb over her temple. "And frankly, I'm still scared of what letting go of that fight means. I'm not even sure how, but I'm ready to try."

The confident gaze he'd fallen in love with wavered as she pulled away.

Slow, resolute strides brought him to her again. Ti didn't move. She held his intent gaze, eyes wild with fears he understood too well. His fingers slid behind her ear to the slope of her neck. One sigh, one dip of her lashes, and Drew had to coach himself to breathe as he leaned in.

With great restraint, he kept his lips slow and soft against hers, exploring every touch. The way their first kiss should've been. Simmering with emotion. With promises of commitment and safety.

Her heart raced against him as though begging the outward tempo to match the urgency raging on the inside. But he wanted to savor this. Her. The feel of her resistance crumbling in his arms, the release of finally trusting him. Trusting them together.

Every movement brimmed with desire to show her what love looked like. That it didn't have to be the way others had shown her.

He was about to pull back when she lifted both hands to the base of his neck and tightened their embrace. A visceral longing teemed through the movement drawing her deeper against him.

The skin on her back warmed under his palm as her heartbeat mixed with his. Her softness, her trust, the vulnerability in her affection—everything about her coursed through him until he lost himself in her kiss. Lost his fears, his brokenness. No past or mistakes. Just the future he wanted with her and the right-now moment heating every inch of his body.

Her cool fingertips slipped under his collar and traced the rigid muscle beneath his neck, the curve of his flexed shoulder. Her touch lit a path of fire to his chest. He breathed hard, the noise in his throat revealing more than he'd intended.

He broke away before he lost control. He wasn't going to treat her like other guys had. Wasn't going to make her feel anything less than worth waiting for.

Drew rested his forehead to hers and counted his breaths until his heart slowed and he could trust his voice. "It's more than a fairy tale, Ti." His hands framed her cheeks. "Stay," he whispered.

Tears he didn't understand ran into his fingers.

When he leaned back, she closed her eyes. "You'll regret it."

"That's not possible." He kissed her once more with reassurance. Salt blended with every live emotion running through him. His chest rose and fell with expansive motion, willing him to stop himself.

He slid his hands down her arms and entwined his fingers with hers. Pulse picking up again, he steered her toward the staircase. "There's something I want to show you."

She stopped at the first step. "Drew …"

"Please." He held her hand as they climbed to the second-floor studio he'd kept closed for nearly nine years.

At the top, Ti grabbed the banister and covered her mouth. Reflections of blown glass sparkled under the light. Bowls, vases, ornaments, sculptures—pieces he'd started decades ago, some he'd made since Ti had inspired him to begin again.

Drew picked up a turquoise star he'd made this past week and turned it over in his hands. "I started blowing glass when I was Maddie's age. First time I saw the way the light catches the colors, I was hooked. Couldn't get enough." Like time with her.

He returned the star to the shelf and sent a slanted grin Ti's way. "You'd be surprised what art can do for the soul."

Biting her lip couldn't keep her from giving in to a teary smile. "Don't tell me you've created a book of all my maxims, too."

"That's not a bad idea. It'd change people's lives." Before she could deflect, Drew led her from the staircase over to the center of the floor.

With her there, any remaining trepidation in inviting her into this part of his life vanished. She brought an energy to the room. Made it right, complete. Like she'd always belonged here.

"When Annie bailed for the city, I closed this place off, along with every part of my heart tied to art. I didn't want to face the reminder of what I thought it'd cost me."

He gave a wry laugh. "Then you came along and smashed right through that shield, awakening parts of me I'd buried for years."

"Drew—"

"You have no idea how bad I wanted to prove you wrong." Laughing, he roped an arm around her waist and pulled her to him. "But you weren't. Not about the shop. Business. Me. You've taught me more than you realize. Got me to start blowing glass again."

"This is where you've been sneaking off to? Why didn't you tell me?"

He tugged his ear. "Maddie doesn't even know yet. I guess I've been scared to reopen this part of myself and take risks on the things I used to live for. But not anymore. You've inspired me to do what I should've done ages ago."

"It wasn't me."

"Oh, it was exactly you." He held her gaze. "The way you revere art and hold fast to your convictions. The way you aren't afraid to call things like they are and push the borders I've tried to hide behind."

She shifted uncomfortably, but he wasn't letting her dodge the truth.

"I'm turning the shop into a gallery like I've always wanted to. We can both showcase our work. I know it's not as prestigious as a place in New York or California, but it'd be ours." He laced his fingers around her back. "I'm tired of living under regrets. Let's do this together, Ti. All of it." He whispered again, "Stay."

Competing emotions tore down her face. "I can't."

"Why not?"

The over-the-door bell chimed. "Drew?" someone called from below.

He snapped his head toward a voice he hadn't heard in nine years.

Ti straightened her shoulders, the corners of her eyes pulling in the opposite direction. "I'm sorry."

Sorry? Confusion drove him down the stairs until the sight of the woman standing in front of him froze every tendon and clamped a vise grip around his throat.

"Annie?"

CHAPTER TWENTY-SEVEN

Serrated

Drew stood at the base of the steps, his feet rooted in place. Ti bumped into his back as she soared around the banister, but he didn't move. He couldn't even if he wanted to, not until he understood what was happening.

Annie walked into the center of the shop as if she'd never left. Long red curls flowed above an ankle-length dress as she tilted her head at him. "It's been a long time."

"Whose fault is that?" A vein in his neck twitched. "What are you doing here, Annie?"

"Maddie was in the hospital."

"It's not the first time."

"No one ever asked me to come."

"As if it would've mattered." The floor finally released his feet. "Don't worry about being inconvenienced. Maddie's fine. I'll take care of her like I have since she was born."

"That's not fair."

The heck it wasn't. He stopped himself halfway to her. "You left us without looking back."

Tears he'd seen cloud her green eyes too many times resurfaced. "You don't know what it was like."

Being married to him was that unbearable? Old scars burned with enough potency to mock the nine years he'd spent letting them go.

Drew closed the last few steps between them, his chest heaving. "How could you walk out on your own daughter? On me?" His voice caught on the last word. "I loved you with everything I had."

"No, you loved a life you thought you wanted."

Fuming, he clenched his jaw. "At least I didn't run away." Something pricked his spirit, but he squelched it and turned.

"You think I don't know I've made mistakes? I regretted leaving as soon as I got to New York. But how was I supposed to come back after the way I hurt you?"

He shook his head. "Don't start. I came after you. I drove to the city, saw the life you chose over us. You wouldn't have traded that for anything."

"Like you can talk."

"What's that supposed to mean?" Blood hammered in his ears. "You know what? It doesn't matter anymore." He wasn't listening to this.

"It does to me." She grabbed his shirtsleeve when he turned. "Dang it, Drew. I messed up, okay? I'm the first to admit it. I haven't gone a single day without wishing I could make things right."

He scoffed. "And yet you never did. Not once have you even tried to contact your daughter."

"How could I face her after I let her down?"

"Then what are you doing here? And how did you even know she was in the hospital?"

Her gaze slanted past him. He followed her line of sight to Ti, standing by the stairs, witnessing the last encounter he'd ever wanted her to have to see.

His stomach dropped at the look on her face.

"I'm from New York. I know people." The ongoing joke she'd teased him with before now throbbed in the center of his chest like a bruise. "You contacted her?"

Ti hurried over. "Maddie needs her mom, and you need someone to walk through this with."

Someone other than Ti? The wound twisted in his gut, his own naiveté the worst part. Here, he'd been blubbering his heart to her, begging her to be a part of a life she obviously didn't want. Worse yet, she went behind his back to get someone else to take her place.

Rejection sank into betrayal and bottomed out in anger. "You had no right."

"I'm sorry."

The front door blew open, rain and wind spiraling inside. "Dad?" Maddie ran in with Cooper on her heels.

He shot Drew a look of apology. "Annie came by the house. I didn't let her in, but—"

"What's going on?" Maddie looked to each adult encircling the room.

"Maddie?" A teary-eyed Annie started for their daughter.

Drew glared at Cooper. "Get her out of here. Now."

Ti rushed to stop them. "Drew, wait. At least let them talk." Wrecked emotions splintered across her face. "Please."

Someone rapped a knuckle on the door, followed by Mr. California poking his head in. What was he doing here?

The dude glanced around the room filled with charged silence. "Sorry. I'm obviously interrupting something. I just came by to check on—"

"Your painting." Ti winced. "I'm sorry, Carter. It got ruined in the rain. It'll take me a while to replicate, but I promise to get it to you."

An assuring smile swept over her. "I'm not worried about the painting, Ti. More about my offer." He tapped what looked like a plane ticket in his hand. "Sue and I are heading into Hatteras tonight, but we can meet you at the airport in the morning if you still have things to wrap up here."

Wrap up? She'd already made plans to leave? Pieces fused together. This was why she said she couldn't stay. The realization thrust him into a storm of his own. How could he be stupid enough to ask her? She was a world traveler, been to places and seen things he couldn't dream of. She'd never be satisfied in a small-town life here with a family holding her back.

Rain pelted against the windows as Drew looked between Annie and Ti. One who'd demolished his heart. The other, he'd been foolish enough to give the leftover fragments.

When Ti didn't answer, Mr. California jutted the ticket behind him. "You know, we can talk later. Why don't you give me a call when you're ready?" With another awkward glance around the room, he backed outside.

The door closed, sucking the air out with it.

"Drew …" Ti's shoulders fell. Her blue eyes called to him until he couldn't take it.

He turned to a pile of mail by the computer. "This is your chance, Ti. It's what you always wanted."

"Please, let me—"

"Go." He dropped the mail and clutched the counter. "You have a plane to catch."

Footsteps stirred behind him. The bell chimed, but he didn't move. Wouldn't. His muscles quaked with tension, warring against his heart until Maddie's fractured voice broke the last of his resolve. "Ti!" she cried.

Drew turned at the same time the door swung closed. Two steps forward, he stopped. Breathed. He wouldn't follow, not this time.

He took Maddie from Cooper and cradled her close. "She has to go, Sea Monkey."

"Why?"

The response he'd suppressed since the first night he met Ti tightened his chest. "Because she never intended to stay."

"I thought she loved us." Maddie nestled her head to his neck, her whimper a spear.

"She did, sweetie." He cupped the back of her head. "But sometimes love's not enough."

"I don't understand."

"I hope you never have to." He glared at Annie, shielded Maddie from her, and flicked his chin at the door.

A live wire of determination prompted Annie toward them until something unseen slowed her steps. Head lowered, she hoisted her purse strap to the top of her shoulder and started to take another stride forward but turned and left them instead. Again.

Within minutes, the door reopened. This time, by a force he didn't want to reckon with.

He transferred Maddie back to Cooper and dodged Grandma Jo's cut-through stare. "Let it be."

She marched up to him. "I've been speaking into your life for thirty-two years, young man. I'm not about to stop now."

"There's nothing to say."

"You mean, nothing you want to hear." Ignoring his arched brow, Grandma Jo pulled Drew off to the side and lowered her voice. "Like it or not, Annie is Maddie's mama."

A curt laugh barely suppressed the retort he wanted to make, but Grandma Jo didn't bat an eye. "She's been watching Maddie grow up since she left."

He stiffened. "What'd you just say?"

"She contacted me that first year she was gone. Asked me to send pictures and keep her filled in on Maddie's life."

A muscle on his neck flexed. He walked away to keep from saying something he'd regret. Facing the ceiling, he unclenched his fingers and released a hard breath. "Did you?"

"Wasn't my place."

Drew turned and leveled her with a gaze. "But you just said—"

"Her parents still live here, sugar."

"The Barretts?" She had to be joking. "They cut ties with Annie before she ever left." Marrying him had been the last straw for them.

Grandma Jo covered his taut forearm with a weathered hand. "People make amends, Drew. Something you shouldn't be so quick to write off."

He cut away from her sage-like brown eyes and forked his fingers through his hair. "So, you're telling me Annie was willing to swallow her pride enough to contact everyone—even her estranged parents—before she'd come to me."

How many more blows could she pummel through him?

Pictures. Updates. His shoulders tensed at the thought of her keeping tabs on Maddie without involving him. Had everyone else known? One glance at Cooper's shocked expression ruled him out. Drew wouldn't put it past the Barretts. But Grandma Jo?

"Why didn't you tell me?"

She cocked her head the way she did whenever he'd tried giving her sass as a kid. "Because the conversation would've gone about as well as it's going now."

"I had a right to know."

"You're darn right you did. And Annie should've been the one to tell you." The parenthesis-shaped wrinkles around Grandma Jo's eyes softened. "I'm not trying to justify any of this. But a mama staying away from her own child out of guilt? A daughter never knowing her mama cares about her? It's wrong, Drew. They deserve a chance at healing. You all do. You'll never be able to move on without it."

"Move on to what?"

"You know what."

His gaze skimmed over the front door. Ti was probably already gone, leaving another empty reminder of where opening your heart left you. He stalked into the back room before his inward scoffing became audible. In front of the counter, he yanked open a box of tea.

Grandma Jo strode up beside him. "Ti belongs here."

"Not my call." The coffee next to the tea canister sneered at his efforts to prove her wrong. "You can't give a wildflower roots. Trying only breeds loss. For everyone."

"Garbage. That girl's been fighting for you since she got here. You tout around like you're willing to do the same, but you give up on the first trial?"

He tossed the tea bag into his mug. "What am I supposed to offer a girl like her? A monotonous life constricted to a four-mile radius?" He jerked the electric teakettle's cord from the socket. "We've all seen how that ends. Maddie doesn't need to relive history." Neither did he. It was a moot point, anyway. He couldn't compete with Ti's dreams.

A sigh brought Grandma Jo a foot closer. "Ti isn't Annie. If you keep letting pride blind you from seeing that, then she's not the only one who'll lose."

"You don't get it. You can't lose what you don't have."

"Look at me." She turned him toward eyes of compassion he didn't want to face. "It's time."

"For what?"

"To let go." She nodded. "You're allowed to hurt, Drew. We all are. It's okay to grieve for the life you thought you were supposed to have. Fall to your knees, if you have to. Cry, yell, do whatever you gotta do to release the heartache."

She grasped his hand. "But there comes a time to stand up again. To breathe deeply and choose the life that's right in front of you." She squeezed his fingers. "Ti didn't just blow into your world on accident, sugar. She's been part of the plan for your life all along."

Some plan. Look what it had cost him.

A motherly glint tinged her eyes. "All those mornings, feeling like you've been yelling to an earless sky… You think you've been chasing God for answers, but He's been the One after you. Waiting for you to be ready."

"Ready for more pain?" Count him out.

"For you to trust He makes all things new."

Lightning flashed outside the window as the sound of the water hitting his mug filled the quiet space. "Maybe He asks too much."

"No more than what He gives." Grandma Jo's bracelet clinked against the counter. "You just remember what your daddy taught you. Sacrifice doesn't build character. It reveals it." Leaving the impact of Dad's words behind, she shuffled out of the room.

Cooper took her place before the bell had a chance to chime. He reclined against the counter on his forearms. "And Grandma Jo's words of wisdom strike again."

"I'm not in the mood, Coop." Drew took a cautious sip of his steaming drink.

"Annie's as beautiful as ever, isn't she? And just as piercing."

Apparently, Drew was the only brother who'd learned caution. Cooper would back away from Drew right now if he knew what was good for him.

Instead, Cooper plowed through the tape Drew had strung around the demolition zone Grandma Jo left in her wake. "You know, I used to think you and I were romantics. Both sitting around, clinging to the past instead of moving on."

Drew's knuckles whitened around his mug handle.

"Then Ti came along—"

"Don't." Drew didn't need another lecture, especially from him.

Cooper pushed off the counter. "All this time, you wouldn't admit it, but you wanted Annie to come home, didn't you? You wanted things back the way they were when you were kids. For life to go the way it was supposed to." He pointed at the door and shrugged. "Now's your chance. She's here. You wanna try another round? Go for it. I'll be here when it all falls apart again."

"You don't know what you're talking about." Drew banged his mug down to keep from slamming it in his brother's nose.

"Yeah?" Coop edged forward. "I know you lost yourself when Annie left. I know you gave up everything that used to drive you. Buried yourself in this old shop, like you could freeze time, trying to take care of everyone and everything but yourself."

Teeth clenched, Drew squared his shoulders. "One of us had to be the responsible one."

"You're not Dad."

Drew got up in Coop's face, grasping at control. "At least I'm trying."

"Trying to what?" He equaled Drew's intense stare. "Be someone you're not?"

Thunder clamored outside, the war inside Drew raging even louder. "You think I should be more like you instead? Gallivanting around as America's favorite bachelor. Just forget the shop and jump on any whim that blows my way?"

"Ti wasn't a whim. You can lie to yourself, hoss, but I watched her tear off that armor you wear to convince the world you're not broken—that you've got everything together without anyone's help." His voice softened. "She brought you back to life—"

Drew chucked his spoon on the counter. Pulse pounding, he jerked an arm in front of him. "Take a look around, Coop. *This* is my life. Past, present, future. Right here. Nothing else."

"No. It's Dad's."

"And I'm the son failing to honor it." Drew's hands drifted from the back of his neck to his sides. Dad had taught them to persevere, provide for their families, and build a legacy of security, not loss. Drew had let him down on every account. Risking hope to change that had only magnified it more.

The truth burned. "You know what it's been like to spend this last year, fighting to keep his shop from closing? You have any clue what it's like to sit with your baby girl in the hospital, knowing you can't pay her bills." He advanced. "Don't talk to me about the future when—"

"Stop it!" Reddened cheeks and bleary eyes shot up from behind the front counter.

"Maddie?" Hadn't she left with Grandma Jo?

"Stop fighting. Both of you." Tears streaming, she darted for the door.

"Sea Monkey, hang on a sec. I didn't mean—"

For the fourth time tonight, the door swung behind yet another serrated piece of his heart.

CHAPTER TWENTY-EIGHT

Sabotage

Like a piece of driftwood trapped in the waves, Ti staggered against the cool sheets of windy rain hammering from all sides. The raindrops stung, but no worse than the truth she was trying to outrun. Every effort she'd made to do right by Drew had fallen short. Bringing Annie here was her last chance at helping him find what was best for him and Maddie. And that failed, too.

The part of her wishing she could've been enough burned with her lungs the harder she ran to Livy's apartment. Up two flights of stairs, Ti fled inside and backed against the door. Stillness pressed in from all four corners of the empty room until the echoes she'd worked so hard to shut out this whole time broke through with full force.

"She's not worth it."

"Do yourself and every guy you're with a favor. Remember who you are."

"He ain't gonna go for a girl like you."

Voices pummeled. She had to move. Had to regain the control she'd lost in Drew's shop at hearing him tell her to leave. She knew that was best, knew he deserved more. But the slightest glimpse of feeling whole with him now laced every fractured piece of her with an all-consuming hatred of her past.

She yanked her suitcase up from the floor and dumped dresser drawer after drawer into it. The overhead fan pulsed above her, sending an assault of memories crushing against her sternum with the gravity of how real they still felt—the body weight on top of her, the smell of sweat, the ragged pain of robbed innocence.

Waves of nausea continued to roll in, despite the hand clutched to her stomach as if she could block it.

Anxiety slammed against her temples. She shoved away from the dresser and turned to her art supplies and the need for escape. The pounding of rain outside shot her gaze to her camera instead. No. Running to art wouldn't make it better. Nothing would.

The room closed in on her. Grabbing only a rain jacket, Ti bounded outside and straight into someone around the door-frame.

Livy grabbed her by the arms. "Whoa. Slow down."

"I'm sorry. I can't." Ti pushed past her.

"Can't what? What's going on?"

Livy's voice trailed down the staircase as Ti ran into the rain.

Across the street, Jamie and his buddies huddled under a golf cart with brews in hand and raucous laughter competing with the storm's constant rumble. Something inside her prodded her to them, calling her to the identity she knew best.

Scenes with other guys crashed into moments with Drew. *"I know this isn't home, but you're safe here. With me."*

He *was* home. The only one she'd ever found. And lost. She couldn't go back to a hollow second place now.

Shaking in restraint, Ti searched the grounds until she spotted Livy's beach cruiser. She swiped it from the bike rack and pedaled with all she had in her. Past the general store. Beyond the last hotel. Windy rain lashed at her, but she didn't slow.

When the tires breeched the beach access ramp, Ti dropped the bike and tore through the wet sand to the waves raging against the shoreline. The cold water's first strike drew a sharp intake of breath. She held it in as white foam climbed her calves.

"You think you can just walk away?"

Stop. She covered her ears. Behind the charcoal shadows, a glimpse of a bleeding sun cast warm colors across the ocean. She kept pushing, needing to keep the sunset in reach.

Grainy water beat into her thighs. Voices struck with the waves, one after the other, ending with Grandma Jo's. *"He's got a way of working out the unexpected. Even when we think He's forgotten us."*

Forgotten.

The yearning for a father's protective embrace collided with the emptiness left from a stranger's callous touch. Ti craned her head to the dark heavens and banged her palms against the top of the water. "Why weren't You there for me?

All those nights in my bedroom. Where were Your plans then?"

A clamor of thunder echoed her cries. "Where *were* You?" She yelled louder. Again and again until the rain drained her tears, and the rage of the storm surrendered to a whisper of memories rivaling the nightmares: Laughing at sleepovers in the safety of Cass's home, writing music under the bleachers at school, singing with the only one who knew how to make it okay.

Scenes with Cass blurred into ones alone creating art. The passion that watching *The Joy of Painting* had awoken, the beauty she'd uncovered the first time she looked through a camera lens, the peace she'd found breathing life across a canvas.

Rain coursed from her hair into her lashes. She blinked through them, too frozen to look away from an answer she hadn't expected to receive. All this time …

Sand caved under her feet, her grasp wavering with the tide. Waves rocked her balance.

Arms closed around her. Livy dragged her out from the water and onto the sand under the lifeguard's tower. "Blimey, Ti." Livy searched her face. "You okay?"

Hunched on her side, Ti gave her a weak nod. Livy released a sigh of relief, cradled Ti's head, and rubbed circles over her back. And for what felt like hours, Ti simply held on.

The storm blowing across the water continued to battle, but with each slow breath, the one inside her gradually began to calm.

She hugged her knees to her chest. Though the sun might've faded, the truth she'd been too scared to admit never would. "I love him."

"I know." Livy twisted Ti's wet hair over her shoulder. "It's a lot easier to give love than to accept it."

Ti sniffled through a smile. "When'd you become so wise?"

"Since I had no choice."

Damp gusts of wind blanketed Ti's goose-bump-covered skin. Liv stroked Ti's arm as though debating saying more until a shaky exhale finally turned into a pained whisper. "I have a son."

"You what?" Ti sat up, fumbling for stable ground.

"I found out I was pregnant the year you left London. And don't bother asking who the father is because, truthfully, I don't know." Livy stared ahead, whether from shame or regret, Ti wasn't sure. "The glamorous life of a model."

Yeah. The parts no one saw. Liv didn't need to go into details. Those days were branded in Ti's memory along with all the others.

"Murray told me to terminate or leave. That he couldn't afford to bust the summer photo shoot." She flicked a shell across the sand. "Heartless prat."

That was one name for him. Ti covered a ragged moon-shaped mark left on her forearm from one of their fights. Bruises healed. Scars didn't.

"I couldn't go through with it, but I couldn't be a mom either. My modeling career was over. I had no way to provide for him. No clue how to take care of a baby." She twisted the belt on her apron. "So, I came home, stayed with my parents until delivery, and then gave him up for adoption."

Ti rested a comforting hand on her knee. "Liv, that took a lot of courage and sacrifice. There's no shame in that. Why didn't you ever say anything?"

"Guilt. Pride. I don't know. It's been two years, and it still feels so raw." Her belt unfurled, her emotions with it. "I send money every month. It's not much—and his parents never asked for it—but it makes me feel like I'm still connected to him, you know?" She ran a finger under her nose. "That's probably stupid."

"It's not stupid. You're a better mom than you think."

"I just wanted him to have the best life he could." Livy lifted her head. "His parents are good people. I know he's loved and taken care of. But sometimes, I can't help wondering if I made the right choice. How different things would be if I'd given it a chance."

No wonder she'd said not everything was black and white. She may have relinquished parental rights under different circumstances than Drew's ex, but Livy must've empathized with her.

Head down, Ti scraped the sand out from under her nails. "You think I was right to contact Annie?"

"I think it should've been their call."

"Meaning, I overstepped my bounds."

"More like you keep sabotaging the things you think you don't deserve. From someone who's done the same thing, believe me, I know." Liv turned a broken shell upside down in her hand. Smooth, liquid-like colors ran into each other without beginning or end. "Who you are isn't what holds you back, Ti. It's who you think you're not."

Ti stared across the tumultuous water and into what she couldn't hide anymore. "I'm scared."

Liv leaned an arm into hers. "Then it's a good thing you're not in this alone."

Barks echoed behind them. They both turned toward Drew's Jeep roaring up the beach. Cooper hopped out of the passenger's seat, his face a sheet of white against the dark sky.

Livy helped Ti to her feet. "What happened? What's wrong?"

Through the Jeep's rain-coated windows, a glimpse into the driver's side showed Drew with his hands gripped around the wheel and Jasper's paws propped on the dashboard.

Cooper raked a hand through his hair.

Heart rate jumping, Ti bounded forward. "Coop, if you pause a minute longer, I swear, I'm gonna—"

"It's Maddie." He looked from Livy back to Ti. "She's gone."

CHAPTER TWENTY-NINE

Choice

The windshield wipers smeared a blurred view of Ti striding toward the Jeep. Drew gripped the wheel harder. Why he bothered, he'd never know.

Ti yanked the door open. "Move over."

His stare jumped to the center console and back. "Excuse me?"

She unbuckled his seat belt and waved him to the passenger seat with the flick of her hand. "You're in no position to be driving. Now move."

Even with her hair a tangled mess and makeup in streaks, she upheld enough New York grit to usher Drew out of the Jeep without argument.

Around the bumper, he slid into the passenger side, set Jasper in his lap, and clicked his seat belt in. "Why are you soaking wet?"

"Not important."

Livy and Cooper hopped into the back seat. "She decided to have a date with the ocean." Liv swung her door shut. "That's why."

"You did what?"

"Not now." Ti punched the gas and gunned it off the beach. "Did you make sure Maddie wasn't with her friend Winnie?"

Drew leaned an elbow on the door panel and braced his forehead against his hand. "Yeah, along with anyone else I could possibly think of." Even the last people he wanted to talk to.

Ti veered onto the street. She kept her eyes on the road, but the slump in her shoulders said she was reading his thoughts. "And Annie?"

Despite how softly she said it, the hurt and concern in her voice reverberated throughout the car like distant thunder.

"She's at her parents' house." Drew stared out the side window. "Maddie's not there. I checked every room myself to be sure." Annie had lost his trust a long time ago.

Why did she have to come back now? Of course Maddie would be upset. He banged his hand against the armrest.

Ti brushed a consoling touch to his knee, comforting him without condition. The knot already seizing his throat scaled up another notch. He grazed the side of his finger against hers, needing her through this more than he understood.

Cooper landed a solid grasp on Drew's shoulder. "It's not the first time Maddie's overheard us fight. She probably just needed a little space. I'm sure she's fine."

Ti snapped off the wipers. "What were you fighting about?"

About Drew not wanting to admit how much he loved her.

He sent a thanks-a-lot glare at Coop. Now wasn't the time to get into it. They needed to concentrate on Maddie, not him.

Drew rubbed at the familiar throb of guilt building between his eyes. "I was blowing off steam about everything. The shop, trying to honor my dad, not being able to afford her medical bills." All the taffy in the world couldn't relieve the tension of thinking he caused Maddie to blame herself for any of this.

Ti whipped the Jeep to the left, tires screeching.

"Easy." Drew palmed the dashboard and restrained Jasper from falling into the floorboard. "Where are you going?"

"I think I know where she went."

"What? Where?"

The Jeep skidded around a curve. "Did Lenny come and pick up your boat yet?"

"He's coming Monday. What does that have to do with anything?"

She gestured to the ominous sky. "It's lightning right now."

"Yeahhh . . .?"

Ti jerked them to a stop in front of his buddy Jacob's house.

Cooper and Livy got out while Ti twisted in her seat toward Drew. "This morning, when we were watching *Sweet Home Alabama,* Maddie said something about you going to the inlet during storms. That you were waiting for lightning to strike the sand."

"Okay, slow down. That's not why I went to the inlet. You're not making any sense."

"I'm talking about lightning creating sea glass."

Drew unbuckled his seat belt. "Yeah, that's not how it works."

"I know that, but she doesn't. To her, the movie was true. Don't you get it?" Ti opened her door. "She's trying to save the shop. And you."

His stomach sank. Agitated laps of water beat into the dock where his boat should've been. He bolted out of the Jeep, Jasper on his heels. "We have to get there."

"Already a step ahead of you, hoss." Cooper tossed him a set of keys to Jacob's boat as he and Livy came back down from the house. "Jacob said the tank's full."

Drew hastened to undock the speedboat. "You guys don't have to go with me."

Cooper helped Ti and Livy aboard. "As if that was ever a question."

Not for the first time in his life, Drew was glad it wasn't.

The nose of the boat dipped and rose while carving a white path through the water. Lightning flashes illuminated the deep violet sky with dangerous beauty. His knuckles whitened over the gearshift. *Please, let her be okay.*

Ti curled an arm around his. A single touch shouldn't be able to hush the storm inside him. But with her there, his panic followed the rain's transition into a slow, tapered drizzle.

Cooper was wrong. Drew hadn't spent all these years waiting for Annie to come home. He'd been waiting for Ti.

No doubting could deny it. She was an answer to a prayer he hadn't known how to pray.

Swallowing hard, he slowed the engine as they approached the shallower water.

Ti gripped his sleeve. "You hear that?"

The faint sound of singing whispered in the wind. "When the lights turn dark and the shadows deep, close your eyes and drift to sleep."

A sniffled laugh feathered against him. "She's singing the song I taught her in the hospital."

Jasper's ears perked up. One beat, and he dove off the edge of the boat, barking like he'd just chowed a pallet of Mighty Dog. Drew would've been right behind if Ti hadn't kept him grounded in place.

He maneuvered the boat to the shore alongside Dad's skiff and sprang out. "Sea Monkey?" He sprinted through the sand on Jasper's trail.

"Dad?" Tucked between two bushes on the far end of the inlet, Maddie hugged Jasper to her chest.

Drew scooped them in his arms, never more relieved to hold her. "Are you okay?"

"I'm sorry."

He kissed her head. "Me too, baby."

Jasper licked every last raindrop off her face, clearly not wanting to share her.

Drew set them both down but kept Maddie close. Kneeling in the wet sand, he cupped both sides of her face. "Listen to me. I didn't mean what I said back there. Everything's going to be fine. I promise."

"I thought if I could bring back—"

"I know." He encased her in a hug and glanced up at Ti. "But how about we make some glass together back at the shop."

"Really?"

"Yeah. I have something I want to show you." Something he should've brought back into their life a long time ago.

Ti beamed at them, and Drew had to shove the relentless knot back down his throat when Maddie flung her arms around Ti's waist.

"I knew you'd come." She squeezed even tighter. "The song you taught me... It really worked. I felt courageous like you."

Ti brushed Maddie's wet bangs away from her eyes and fluttered a glance out to the sound, stumbling over a compliment as usual. What would it take for her to see how much she had to offer?

A similar question rippled back to Drew in a familiar voice he would've sworn was Dad's.

Cooper swept Maddie into the air when they reached the boats. "I thought we agreed you could only do crazy things with me, Freckles."

"Sorry, Uncle Coop."

He set her down and rustled Jasper's ears. "Well, if Jasper forgives you for leaving him out, I guess I can, too."

Maddie returned Cooper's wink as he lifted her into the skiff.

Ti headed for Jacob's boat instead. "We'll meet you two back at the house."

"Ride with us," Maddie pleaded.

"I think you and your dad probably need a little time alone, love."

Not anymore. Drew grabbed Ti's hand, hoping everything reeling inside him came through his eyes in place of words.

Ti glanced over at Livy, who gave her a prompting nod.

Cooper cranked his engine. "Beat you home."

Drew looked between the two boats. "In what world would that be a fair race?" And how was he able to play it cool so easily?

"It's the driver who makes a boat. Not the other way around."

"Spoken like Dad."

Shifting gears, Cooper grinned. "I did end up with a little of him in me, you know."

More than Drew had realized. He waved them off and eased the skiff into gear. Ti and Maddie sat in the back, glued at the hip once again. The way it should be.

A steady pace kept the skiff charging through the waves and Drew's thoughts through all the things he needed to tell Ti.

If she'd give him the chance.

Would she leave as soon as they got back?

The dock approached much too soon. He navigated into the harbor, not ready to trade one storm for another.

They all piled into the Jeep with Maddie sandwiched between the girls in the back seat. Drew drove through his hometown on autopilot as vacationers careened through puddles in their golf carts.

A peek in the rearview mirror showed Ti staring out the window, lost in thoughts he'd pay a thousand pennies for. Then again, maybe he didn't want to know.

Familiar insecurities cropped up as he downshifted around a curve.

No. No more doubts. He needed to man up and fight for her, no matter the risk. As soon as they parked, he'd pull her aside and tell her—

"Stop the car."

Drew darted his attention from the street to the mirror.

Ti flipped the lock on her door. "Stop the car, Drew."

He swerved to the side of the road. "What's going on?"

"I have to go."

What? Drew tasked Cooper to man the car and hustled after her. "Ti, wait. Slow down. Can we just talk a minute?" He caught up and stopped her by the shoulders.

Standing in the glow of his headlights, she looked away but couldn't hide the tremor shaking down her arms.

He peered behind him to the shadows. "What's wrong?"

She pushed the matted hair off her forehead. "You need to go. Please, take Maddie and get out of here."

"I'm not leaving." He reached for her hand. "I'm sorry for being a royal jerk at the shop earlier. Excuses don't matter. Truth is, I was scared. Of losing you. Of the things you make me feel." He edged in. "I still am, but I'm not walking away."

Eyes closed, Ti turned her head. "You have to."

"No, I don't."

"Drew, I can't." She tried to sidestep him, but he kept hold of her hand.

"Can't what? What are you running from?"

"From hurting you." When she whirled around, the wounds in her expression seared into his heart over the ones he'd placed there himself. Grandma Jo was right. It was time to heal.

"None of us can avoid pain, Ti. It's part of life." He pulled her close. "And love. That doesn't mean we give up on either." It had taken him much longer than it should've to learn that.

"I know." Ti took in an unsteady breath, silenced the tremble in her shoulders, and met his gaze with the ocean-blue eyes he'd come to rely on. "And this is me, loving you." She lifted on her tiptoes and pressed a lingering kiss to his cheek.

Drew kept her close, wanting her to feel safe, loved. She inhaled against him as if about to say more but then let go. Crestfallen, he stood, watching her leave one choice for another.

CHAPTER THIRTY

Waves

Breathe. Everything around Ti slowed, every noise amplified. The rain's steady patter against the ground. Distant murmurs in the wind. Tree branches rustling, footsteps nearing.

How'd he find her? She wrenched her eyes shut, but fears kept taunting. An unsteady breath traveled through her lungs, her pulse through her ears. Darkness clawed all around.

Breathe.

She had to face him, had to end this. She loved Drew and Maddie too much to hide this time. She wouldn't let him near them. Ti straightened her spine. "I know you're h—"

A hand covered her nose and mouth from behind and pulled her deeper into the shadows. Rough fingers absorbed her cry as hot, shallow breaths strained against the barricade she couldn't break free from.

"Don't be scared." A deep voice rumbled over her hair. "I just want to talk. I'm letting go, okay? Just take it easy." He slowly loosened his hold.

Ti shoved away from him. Chest heaving, she glared at her nightmare standing in front of her. Weathered. Gaunt. Aged by the effects of his lifestyle.

He grimaced as though hurt by her expression. "It's me, Trina. Dad."

"My name's not Trina anymore. And I don't have a dad."

The vehemence in her words furrowed his brow. "I deserve that."

He didn't have a clue what he deserved. Her nails dug into her palms with the force of all the emotions boiling inside her.

Taking hesitant steps forward, he stared at the ground, as if searching for a boundary line to tell him where to stop. "Honey, I'm sorry. I know what you must be thinking. If you'll just hear me out, I—"

"Hear you out?" Her clenched jaw started to shake. "I spend every day trying to forget the way you never spoke up for me. Don't you dare ask me to listen now."

"You think I don't want to go back and change that?" He tugged off his newsboy cap and wiped his sweaty face. "You know what it's like to spend eleven years in a six-by-eight cell, wishing you could rewrite the life you screwed up?"

Traitorous tears clouded everything around her. "I had a jail cell, too. In my own bedroom." Her prison of memories closed in.

He touched her arm. "Tri—"

"Don't." She recoiled and tried to square her shoulders, but the broken little girl inside her came undone. "You never even checked on me after your dealers left. Was I that worthless to you?" She charged him. "Just a means to a temporary high. Is that all I was?" Ti pounded the side of her fist to his frail chest. "Tell me!"

"No." He held her wrists down. His burly voice dwindled to a hoarse whisper. "You never should've been caught in the middle of our addictions."

Ti pulled free, regaining her balance and what remained of her faltering composure. "It's a little late for that."

The age lines around his worn blue eyes sank deeper. "I know I can't change the past, but I'm not the same man I was then."

"No?" She huffed. "You get out of jail and come chasing my money for no reason?" It might've been a long shot for him to get into her bank account, but that had to be what he was after, desperate for his next score.

"I'm not looking for your money."

"Then what are you doing here?"

A reluctant pause intercepted another unsure step forward. He leaned away from her and coughed with the abused lungs of a long-term smoker. Eyes fixed on the pavement, he clutched his cap to his chest. "I came to make amends."

Heated paralysis channeled down her body until she couldn't move. Couldn't speak. Whether from anger, shock, or cynicism, she wasn't sure. "A ... mends?" The word circled around her brain in a failing attempt to register. "By breaking into my studio and stalking me?" Did he think she was stupid?

Emotions she didn't have the energy to decipher pulled at his eyes. "You shut me out. I couldn't get a hold of you. What did you want me to do?"

"The same thing you need to do right now." She clipped his shoulder on her way past him. "Stay out of my life."

"Please, baby. Your mom's gone," he called through the raspy cough of illness. "And I will be soon, too."

Ti halted on the sidewalk with her back toward him. Raindrops funneled from her hair down her arms, the cold not penetrating. She'd spent too long learning to become stone. She wouldn't crumble now. "Good."

He deserved the consequences of the life he chose. Something pricked her heart, but she kept walking. Away from giving him what he'd never earn.

The salt lamp glowed on Maddie's dresser in place of the sun yet to come up. Drew feathered a kiss to Maddie's forehead, lifted quietly off the mattress, and cast one more look over his little girl, safe in her bed, before reaching to turn off the lamp.

"When's she coming back?"

Drew stalled with his hand on the switch.

Jasper stretched and yawned at the sound of Maddie's sleep-heavy voice while Drew searched for his own.

"Ti. She'll come to see me today, won't she? I mean, before she leaves?"

Her tender questions burrowed into the ones that hadn't stopped festering since last night. She had such insight for her age. Maybe more than him.

Drew brought the covers up to her chin. "I'm sure she will, Sea Monkey." Ti may not want to see him, but if he knew her at all, she'd at least say goodbye to Maddie.

"Can we leave it on?" She stopped him as he went to turn off the lamp again. "Please?"

Nodding his understanding, Drew left on the light he prayed Ti wouldn't forget about and gave Jasper and Maddie both a kiss. His shoulders sagged once he eased the door closed behind him.

In the dark hallway, he backed against the wall and hung his chin to his chest.

There was so much he didn't understand. But if Ti had to leave because she loved him, then maybe loving her in return meant letting her go. She'd dreamed of having her work in a gallery, and San Francisco was her chance. He wouldn't hold her back from that. She deserved it.

The clock in the living room echoed up the stairs while beams of passing headlights stretched across the hallway. A break in the shadows hinted to the promise of a new day coming. One he needed more than ever.

On instinct, Drew grabbed his surfboard and left for the beach and another sunrise.

The waves' soothing rhythm greeted him on the cool shore. Foamy water peppered with gritty sand flowed around his feet in a welcome he knew as home. This was part of him. The island. The beach. The shop. Even Annie. It was part of his heritage, his identity.

Water crept higher up his calves, luring him to a race he swam every day since losing Dad. Waves churned. His pulse echoed—one beat, another. The board's edges sawed into his hands as his feet lost their grip on the shoreline.

He'd messed up so many times, had tried to carry everything on his shoulders. Blinded by pride, afraid of failure. Through all the ways he'd fought to shelter himself and Maddie from the risk of getting hurt, he'd lost sight of the truth Dad had instilled in him.

Drew wedged the end of his board into the sand. No more racing. No more searching. He was done trying to be someone he wasn't. Done striving on his own. He'd spent years chasing the horizon. Demanding answers, desperate to cling to control. But maybe Grandma Jo had been right the whole time about needing to let go. Of bitterness. Of the defenses binding him to the things that had broken him.

Was he finally ready?

Orange-dusted clouds gradually gave way to a sliver of sunlight. Inch by inch, warmth stretched across his face in an embrace waiting for a response.

With a long breath of surrender, he lifted his eyes to the heavens. Even if he didn't know how, he had to believe Dad was right. Perseverance built character, character hope.

The kind worth risking.

"Still slaying the ocean at sunrise?" Annie's familiar voice blended into the sound of the beach as it had done a million times since they'd met.

He laid his board aside. "Not anymore."

"And I thought some things would never change."

"Sometimes they have to."

Head down, she dragged her feet in the sand. Long red curls caressed her shoulders the way his fingers used to. Memories washed over him. But for the first time, they didn't stem from a place of grief or bitterness. They rose from a place of release.

"I didn't mean to intrude."

"No, it's fine." He sat on the cool sand. "I'm glad you came."

She joined him on the dry shoreline.

Arm to arm in a pose he'd gone years missing, Drew sat beside one answer he didn't have to search for anymore.

"Drew, I'm sorry—"

"Not as much as me." He unburied a cockleshell and wiped the sand from inside, the truth so much harder to purge. "I always thought you were my first love, but you and Coop were right. It was the life I always envisioned having here."

"Your dad's life." Her freckled arm grazed his with insight.

No wonder their daughter brimmed with intuition.

Drew's smile dimmed. "He had everything."

"So do you." Instead of bitterness, a sense of admiration hung on her words.

He looked across the waves. Had it always been enough?

The truth eased out with a slow exhale. "I'm sorry for trying to force you to fit that life, Annie. For trying to make you someone you didn't want to be." And here, he'd been doing the same thing to Ti—asking her to stay and give up who she was. Could he be any more selfish?

"We were kids. I didn't even know who I was myself." A sad laugh flittered over him. "Still don't, half the time."

"I know the feeling." It shouldn't take this many mistakes to figure it out.

"Are you joking? You've known who you wanted to be since we were five. I always admired how sure of yourself you were. It's one of the reasons I fell in love with you."

Drew tossed the shell in the water. "Maybe I got it all wrong."

"Not possible."

Confident as ever. He laughed. "What makes you so sure?"

"Our daughter." Annie twisted what looked like a non-traditional wedding band on her ring finger. "I got remarried a few years ago," she said slowly. "Have really tried to turn things around. Do them right this time."

After an uncertain shake of her head, she faced him. "Maybe we both lost our way, Drew. But you've never stopped being an anchor for Maddie. If you ask me, that one right choice trumps a whole lot of wrong ones."

It wasn't about being right or wrong anymore. He had to let go of his pride. "Annie, Maddie deserves the choice to know her mom. And I know I can't protect her from every hurt she'll experience. But I only want to open this door if you're going to keep it open."

"Does she want it open?"

"That's for you to ask her."

Annie curved a curl around her ear. "What if she says no?" Her voice barely crested the splash of the waves.

"Luckily for both of us, she inherited my dad's compassion." Drew wiped the sand from his palms as he rose and then helped Annie to her feet. "The better question is what happens when she says yes?" He nudged her on. "I'll let Cooper know you're coming."

Fiddling with the hem of her shirt, she dawdled a moment longer. "For what it's worth, your dad would be proud of who you've become."

He dipped his head without replying.

"And Drew?" A few steps away, Annie turned. "Don't let the right girl slip away. Ti left you something in the shop."

He stumbled over his board and the words he had to have misheard. "Wait, what? You talked to her?" The girl who hated getting up before noon had already gone to see Annie, of all people, before seven o'clock? This was bad.

Annie spun and waved behind her. "Don't take all day."

Thirty seconds of standing there, blinking, finally launched Drew toward the parking lot. He didn't slow down until he crossed the shop door's threshold.

From behind the counter, Chloe didn't bother thwarting a grin. "About time you got here."

Had Ti seen everyone today but him?

Chloe motioned to an easel in the corner with her eyes.

Drew had sprinted the entire way here. But now that the gift Ti had left was only a few feet from him, it might as well have been an ocean's length away.

Chloe grabbed her purse. "I'm gonna go get some coffee."

The door must've closed behind her, but his heartbeat overpowered every other noise. Uneasy strides brought him to a painting wrapped in brown paper on the easel and a photo album beneath it. An envelope taped to the front read, *Open painting first.*

He ran his fingers along the canvas' top ledge and tore into a corner of the paper. Strip after strip unveiled the sunset's myriad colors blending into the ocean's endless layers. In the center of the painting, Drew stood, gazing across the waves with Ti in his arms as they'd been the night he first took her to Springer's Point.

He padded beside him for a chair and folded into it, unable to look away from the moment she'd freeze-framed in time. Her back nestled into him, her soft hair billowing against his skin, the longing to care for her. It all welled up from a place inside—where she belonged.

Drew slowly opened the photo album in his lap. Ti's gift of seeing what others missed danced from each page with images he wanted as more than just memories.

A spiral of nerves and desires kept him turning the envelope in his hands until the urge to hear her words trumped the fear of what she'd say.

Drew, I've spent my life capturing moments I wished I could be a part of, always from behind a distant lens. Until this summer. Thank you for giving me moments I can paint from memory. Not as an artist, but as a girl who found love for the very first time.

The note sank to Drew's lap. The real-life details in the painting awakened every thought and feeling from that night. Including the choice he'd known was right even then.

Not wasting another second, he grabbed his cell and tapped the last number he ever planned to call. "Marcus?" He didn't wait for a response. "You still interested in buying my shop?"

CHAPTER THIRTY-ONE

Home

Ti scanned Livy's room one more time. Clothes, toiletries, jewelry. She'd packed everything, hadn't she?

In front of the dresser mirror, Ti laid down the plane ticket Carter had given her and dodged her reflection. Good thing Livy had an early shift. Ti could hardly face her own sad eyes. Forget Liv's. She turned the sea glass bracelet she'd made with Maddie around her wrist, the ache of already missing her twisting with it.

One deep breath followed another and finally steered her focus to her suitcase at the foot of the bed. Shoes! How could she forget her shoes?

A gentle knock on the door drifted into the room. Grandma Jo poked her head inside. "Thought I might find you here."

Ti clutched the closet door handle. "Please don't make this any harder."

"Oh, I think you and Drew are doing a good enough job of that on your own."

Ti froze at her words but then squatted to the bottom of the closet and piled pairs of shoes in her arms. She stilled when she came to her flip-flops. She braced the doorframe with one hand, her balance lost in so many ways.

The shoes in Ti's arms clattered to the floor. Competing emotions drove her to her knees in a scramble to keep the broken pieces inside her from scattering across the carpet, too.

Grandma Jo knelt beside her and helped her gather up the mess. "You know, when Maureen died, I questioned whether I had any right to stand in her shoes. Took me a while to figure out I wasn't. I was stepping into my own." She raised a brow at the spiky pair of heels in her hands and smiled. "Thankfully, mine didn't come with a death wish."

Laughing softly, Ti took them from her and tucked them into the side of the bag.

Grandma Jo sat back. "I've wrestled my share of doubts through the years, sugar. Not saying I still don't question life at times. Might even be tempted to run when things get hard. But I'll tell you what's as true now as it was the day the Andersons took me in."

She covered Ti's forearm with an age-spotted hand. "You sure enough can't outrun the Father's love. You get a hold of that truth, young lady, and you won't be running no more."

The dam in the center of Ti's chest finally broke. She darted up from the carpet. "I have to go." She couldn't let this woman who'd blindly welcomed her like a daughter see she was a child no father wanted.

An echo of the assurance she'd felt in the ocean yesterday swept in as if countering the thought. But the harder she tried to soak it in, the harder the scars around her heart resisted. She grasped at Grandma Jo's words like a life jacket. So many times, she'd almost given in to Drew's pursuit, accepted a place in the family she'd always wanted.

But how could she? Even if she wasn't abandoned all those years, that didn't erase them. Nothing she'd done since coming here had changed that. They followed her, lurking in the shadows as her dad had last night. She wouldn't let guys like him near Maddie. She'd do anything to protect them.

Chin down, Ti toyed with the clip on her bracelet again. "I know you don't understand, but this is best for Drew and Maddie. That's all I've ever wanted for them."

"Then take it from someone who wants the same. You're what's best for them. Your sins don't change that. Neither do your daddy's."

Ti whipped her head up. "How do you ...?"

Grandma Jo patted Ti's hand, rose, and strode toward the picture frames on the windowsill. "You don't get to be my age without gaining a few insights."

While wedging the last sandal into her bag, Ti scoffed at the image of her dad having the nerve to show up here. "He said he came to make amends."

"And you don't believe him?"

"Hard to believe even a decade of jail time could change the only thing that ever drove him. Doesn't matter, anyway. He doesn't deserve amends." Ti shook her head and stood. "Regretting his mistakes shouldn't keep him out of prison."

"And you think holding onto bitterness is going to release you from your own?"

"It's not that easy."

"Forgiveness never is."

Ti clenched her bag handles. "You don't know what you're asking."

"I'm not asking anything. I just want you to remember this." At the dresser, Grandma Jo set a picture of Ti with Drew and Maddie from the day at the harbor on top of the plane ticket. "No one earns love, sugar. That's what makes it a gift." She gave Ti's arm a good squeeze, turned, and left the imprint of her motherly touch behind.

Ti gripped the edge of the dresser and pressed her lashes together. But instead of seeing the scene behind the picture frame, she saw it behind her eyelids as if reliving the day. Maddie's sweet laughter blending into Jasper's splashing in the water. Butterflies mixing with the safety of being in Drew's arms.

Livy's words from the beach pressed in with Grandma Jo's. Was she the one holding herself back? Ti had tried to do everything she could to love this family, but maybe she didn't even know what love meant. She'd been too afraid to accept their affection. So certain she wouldn't be enough to keep it. Even now, fear raged against hope.

"No one earns love, sugar. That's what makes it a gift."

Light stretched through the windows and curled around Ti's shoulders with another answer she hadn't expected. The Father's love had been with her all along, hadn't it? In the sunsets. In art, friendship. Even in ... bringing her to Drew.

Tears coated her cheeks as she looked from the plane ticket to her bags. Breathing in, she grabbed her cell and scrolled to the unknown number that had been calling her. No matter what happened next, she at least knew where she needed to start.

"*Slow as midtown traffic.*" Drew didn't fully appreciate Ti's annoyance at how slowly people moved around the island until today.

In his Jeep, he let up on the gas before he ended up bulldozing the van in front of him. Wasn't a bad idea, actually. He stuck his head out the window to get a look around the Toyota.

Drew slumped back in his seat and banged the steering wheel. "Come on, already."

The radio clock practically laughed at him. He could tease Ti all he wanted for being free-spirited, but a lot of good his anal retentiveness was doing him now. He should've gone straight to the ferry first thing this morning, not to the beach. Now, he might miss her.

Another glance out the window to the second lane revealed enough space to make the pass. Drew didn't flinch. Gunning it, he swerved around the family van and cut back in front of them. "Sorry," he said to the rearview mirror, as if they could hear him.

With less than half a mile separating him from the ferry docks, Drew's stomach groaned with his Jeep's overworked engine. Even if he hadn't missed Ti, would the things he came to say make a difference?

A flock of seagulls trailed the edge of the island like they always did when following a ferry leaving port. The horn blew. He was too late.

His Jeep coasted into a parking space, his heart somewhere behind him on the highway. Stomach still lurching, he left his door open and jogged up to the dock, where a state worker stopped him with an outstretched arm. "Sorry, sir. Can't have you crossing that white line there."

The strip of faded paint stared at him from the concrete, but all Drew saw were the stains of missed opportunity.

"Sir? You all right?"

Drew blinked up from the ground, forked a hand through his hair, and backed away. "Fine. Sorry."

The man returned to his work while Drew scoured the docks for some means to get on the water without being arrested.

"I hate to break it to you," someone said from behind him. "But you probably won't score a very successful ferry heist without a skilled partner."

An inch at a time, his feet managed to turn his legs around.

Blonde again, Ti clipped her hair to keep it from blowing in the wind. "New Yorkers make the best accomplices. Especially when they're hopped up on coffee. Gives 'em an edge."

"Is that right?" He sauntered toward her.

"So I hear." Her smiled stretched as wide as her giant hoop earrings.

Maybe all hope wasn't lost.

Drew ran a knuckle over his jaw. "I'm kind of in a hurry. Know where I can find one?"

"I might have some connections." A gradual frown ransacked the sassy look in her eyes.

Why wouldn't it? He'd transferred his resentment of Annie's choosing New York over him onto Ti so many times. In nursing his own wound of inadequacy, he'd unintentionally fed Ti's. His shoulders fell. "Ti—"

"My father was here."

"What?"

"Last night, I saw him when we were driving back from getting Maddie."

His jaw ticked at the thought of the man anywhere near her. "Why didn't you tell me? I would've gone with you."

"It's my battle."

Drew knew those words inside and out. Had carried them around his neck for years. Staring at the reflection of what they cost had never struck deeper.

Ti bit her lip and looked out toward the sound. "I worked so hard to prevent my past from owning me. Even moved back to Astoria to open my art studio like I was really brave." She released a terse laugh. "One phone call. One sound of my dad's voice. That's all it took for me to run again."

Everything in him wanted to hold her and make it all right. The pavement barely kept him in place.

"I came to Ocracoke to hide, Drew." She faced him then, hints of shame trapped in her blue eyes. "I never meant to dump my baggage on you."

Seeing the consequences of her dad's choices taint her self-image stoked the slow burn already building in the pit of Drew's stomach. If anything, it was the reverse. That two-hundred-ton ferry couldn't hold all of *his* baggage.

Ti ran her hands along her arms. "I thought he was looking for drug money, and if I stayed away for a while, he'd give up and move on. I should've told you from the beginning. I'm sorry."

She wasn't the one who should be sorry. The veins on Drew's arms throbbed above his balled fists. "What was he doing here? Did he hurt you? If he's still here, I swear I'll—"

"He came for forgiveness."

Drew almost fumbled his keys. "What?" Of all the four-letter words that tore through his mind, that was all that came out.

Ti nodded toward the distant ferry. "I just sent him off."

"What'd you say to him?"

"You don't want to know." The ghost of her usual cheeky grin flitted across her lips. She stared at the water, sobriety taking over. "I told him I didn't know where to start or how long it'd take, but..." A slow exhale through her mouth lowered her shoulders. "I'd pray for the strength to try." She shook her head. "Grandma Jo's words of wisdom can be annoyingly convincing."

She had no idea. But Grandma Jo wasn't the only wise one. Strong and heart-achingly beautiful, this amazing woman stood before him, unaware of how courageous she truly was.

It was past time for him to be the same. A deep breath closed the last few feet between them. He held out a hand. "Can I see your phone?"

Ti cocked her head. "Why?"

"I have some notes to make." He motioned for her to hand it over.

Reluctantly, she set it in his palm, still eyeing him like he was a crazy person. Maybe he was. Crazy enough to risk everything for the girl he loved.

Drew scrolled to the voice recorder app, lifted it to his mouth, and flaunted the impish look she'd given him dozens of times. "The artist is one seriously bossy New Yorker who can't pronounce coffee to save her life. She challenges everything the owner says, always knows what he's thinking, and is infuriatingly right all the time."

Ti perched her hands on her hips and scrunched her face at him.

Forcing his gaze off her lips and back to her eyes, he inched nearer. "Her hippie-chick, free-spirited drive presses the owner's buttons in every way possible. And heaven knows she drives him crazy, singing to herself nonstop."

When she gave him a shove, Drew kept her hand on his chest and edged closer still. He studied her face, his heart racing. "But he can't imagine a day without her voice in his life. Without arguing over who has better dance moves, or watching her care for Maddie as her own daughter." He swallowed hard. "Because no matter how scared he's been to admit it, the truth is, the owner's in love with the artist."

His ribs barely restrained his heart when he returned her phone. He brushed back the untamable strands of hair dancing across her cheeks in the perfect picture of who she was. The woman he wanted to spend the rest of his life with.

Drew searched her watery gaze filled with questions about all the unknowns. "Queens is your home, Ti. I respect that. And I know this opportunity in San Francisco is important to you. I'm not asking you to give any of that up. We'll move wherever you decide to go. I'm selling the shop."

"You're what? Drew—"

"The shop was my dad's dream. I took it on, trying to live his life, when really, he wanted me to find my own." Sunshine warmed the back of his neck. "You know the real reason I chased the sunrise every morning? Because I needed to know how it got to start over every day when I couldn't. I wanted to figure out my past. Why things happened the way they did."

He inhaled slowly. "Honestly, I don't know why we've had to go through the things we have. I still haven't found all the answers, but I know I'm not ready to let go of the one that matters most."

He angled his head and tipped her chin. "I'm sorry for the times I failed to love you the way I should have. And I can't swear I'll never make mistakes in the future, but I promise to spend every day learning to be the man you need me to be." He curled his fingertips under hers. "For our family. Through every storm."

Tears overran her ocean-blue eyes. She lowered her head, and his pulse thundered in her pause. Was she still worried about her past?

"We've *both* let the past limit us, afraid it'd always brand us or wouldn't be enough. And yeah, some of it's messy. But it's part of what's shaped who we are. Even part of what brought us together." He wouldn't be able to love her so completely the way he did if he hadn't first experienced the kind of grace that met him through all his failures.

"But there's more than the past." He cupped her neck with assurance. "I don't want to just walk in my parents' footsteps. I want to write our own legacies, go wherever our story takes us. All in." A breath. "I want to rebuild my life with you, Ti Russo."

A slow smile caught the tears slipping down her cheeks as she found his eyes. "Even when I make inedible peanut butter sandwiches?"

Laughter joined the exhale freeing the tension from his muscles. He rested his forehead to hers. "Even then."

"What about when I switch your grass tea with coffee?"

Drew pulled her simpering grin close to his. "As long as you promise to let me dress however I want."

Eyes glinting with mischief, Ti slid her palms up his chest to the back of his hair. "Negative on the wardrobe, Poster Boy. We all have our limits."

And not kissing her right now was testing his.

Her gaze drifted to his cowlick, her expression turning pensive. "You don't have to compete with Queens or San Francisco, Drew. My home's right here. With you."

He leaned in a smile at a time. "That's good. 'Cause Grandma Jo's fixing a welcome-to-the-family barbeque right now."

"How did she ...?" Ti shook her head. "Never mind." She glanced down at her jean shorts and fringe sweater. "I should probably change first."

"Not for me." He wanted her exactly as she was.

Sunlight filtered through the clouds with the promise of new beginnings, and Drew brought his lips to Ti's with a love that would always be home.

EPILOGUE

Awe

Six Months Later

Ti dropped her third suitcase in the entryway by Drew's front door and repressed a grin. It might've been a bit much for a four-day trip. But if Drew was going to share the same house as her soon, he might as well get used to dealing with all her clothes now.

"Babe, we're going to miss our plane," she called up the stairs. "Everything's taken care of. Chloe knows how to reach us. The gallery will be fine while we're gone. Stop worrying."

"Who says I'm worrying?" he called around a toothbrush in his mouth.

"Then what are you dragging your feet for? Coop isn't rubbing off on you, is he? 'Cause you know that cowlick's a lost cause, right?"

The water in the bathroom ran. "Very funny."

Ti slung the coat she couldn't fit in her bags over her arm. "I know you don't like the cold, but the Catskills are gorgeous in December. You're gonna love it." She strained to keep a straight face. "It wouldn't be so bad if you'd just let me get you in a Hen—"

Drew rounded the top of the stairs in a pair of low hanging dark jeans and a hunter green Henley, looking every bit as ridiculously sexy as she knew he would be in it. His mouth quirked above his scruffy jawline. "You were saying?"

Speaking would require a functioning diaphragm. Or at least a head not fogged over by an image of masculinity and love that still left her in awe most every day.

Looking down so she could breathe again, Ti spun the ring on her left hand and played it cool. "I was just saying, you're pretty lucky to have a fiancée who knows what looks good on you."

Drew moseyed down the stairs with two plastic bags in his hand and sass in his dimples. "The same fiancée who's suddenly conscientious about sticking to a schedule?"

Ti crossed her arms. "Well, maybe you shouldn't have fixed the clock in my car if you didn't want me to actually use it."

He swaggered toward her. "Now, how'll you ever learn to roll with life that way?"

"We're going to be an old married couple, and you'll still be making me eat my words, won't you?"

"Every day." He nestled his unfairly adorable grin to her neck and kissed the skin beneath her earlobe.

She gripped his solid shoulder to steady her legs. Her heart, not so much. "Or we could just skip New York and get married right now. A Christmas wedding could be nice."

Drew leaned back but not far enough. His eyes were doing a serious number on her today. "How about we settle for a prelude?" He lifted the two shopping bags. "Zimas with Jolly Ranchers and a *Gilmore Girls* marathon."

She busted out a laugh. "The ultimate bad-boy package, right there."

"I warned you I knew how to be edgy."

"And I warned you I was a bad influence." She checked her cell. "We're gonna be late."

"Not for tomorrow." Drew set the bags down and led her over to the couch. "I changed the flight."

"What? Why?"

"Can't blame a man for wanting to spend part of the holidays alone with the woman he's about to marry."

Marry. The word still warmed her as much as the blush no other man but Drew could ignite in her.

"We deserve a vacation after all the work we've invested into paying off the shop and opening our gallery." He untangled a tress of hair from her hoop earring. "And I can't wait to meet Cassidy and Ethan and tell them all about it. But tonight, I want to celebrate alone."

She pulled her leg up on the cushion with her. "What about Maddie?"

"She and Livy are playing referee between Grandma Jo and Mr. Fiazza tonight."

Of course they were. And with Coop living in Lake Gaston now, that meant…

"All alone." Ti ran the tip of her thumb along the emerald-shaped diamond on her finger. "So, how would you like to celebrate, *Mr. Anderson?*"

Under the glow of the Christmas tree lights in the corner, he set a large present on her lap. "With seeing you smile."

She cast him an apprehensive look but couldn't deny her curiosity. She slid a nail under the tape holding the box together and removed the lid. Wide-eyed, Ti peered back and forth from Drew to the painting, her heart trapped between them.

She traced the path leading into the fall forest that had started her journey as an artist. "How did you ...?"

Drew removed the canvas from the box and admired the Bob Ross painting with as much awe as it had stirred in her the first time she turned on *The Joy of Painting* as a kid.

"At the barbeque, when you told me about how this painting inspired you, I knew I had to find it." He laid it on the cushion and took her hand. "You inspire me every day, Ti. Push me past borders I don't even know are there. I'll never stop looking for ways to do the same for you."

Eyes on his, she brushed a thumb over his dimple and held on to her evidence that good truly could come from heartache. "You already have." She kissed him with every ounce of the love she never thought could be hers.

Erratic breaths melded together. Ti clutched his Henley and rested her forehead to his. "So, about moving up that wedding date ..."

Raspy laughs washed over her. "Don't tempt me."

"Then at least take me dancing tonight."

"Only if I get to wear the trilby hat. I mean, I am kind of the reigning champion."

"Oh, you're ready to do this, are you?" She marched two fingers up his chest. "You just remember who the teacher is here, buddy. I'll leave you in the dust on that dance floor."

"Not possible." He leaned close, grin hitching. "Because … where you go, Ti Russo, I will follow." With far too much amusement, Drew belted out the most off-pitched version of the *Gilmore Girls* theme song she'd ever heard.

Between laughs, Cooper's words from that night on the beach filtered to mind. *"My dad used to say we'll never find where we belong until we're willing to admit we're lost."*

Yet even when she'd kept running, love hadn't stopped pursuing her. Ti let her soon-to-be husband gather her in his sturdy arms, grateful to finally find the home that had been waiting for her all along.

A WORD FROM THE AUTHOR

Make no mistake about it. Your voice matters. If you enjoyed this story, please take a moment to leave a review on Amazon and Goodreads to help new readers discover Drew and Ti's story. Even if it's just one sentence. Reviews are a tremendous help to authors, which in turn allows us to keep writing more stories for you. I can't do it without you!

If you haven't already read Ethan and Cassidy's story, pick up a copy of *Write Me Home* and see Ti try to hack it in the mountains!

Ready for Cooper's own book? Grab a copy of *Just Maybe* and enjoy a southern sweet romance full of small-town laughs, memorable family members, and the heartwarming treasure of second chances.

Enjoy all the books in the Home In You Series:

Still Falling: A Prequel
Write Me Home: Book One
Begin Again: Book Two
Just Maybe: Book Three
Chasing Someday: Book Four

ACKNOWLEDGEMENTS

Dave, I'm so grateful to share in a love that continually calls us home no matter where we run or how we fail. Thank you for embracing new beginnings in that love with me every day.

Erynn, thank you for sowing into yet another piece of my heart … and for humoring my love of the word "sow." For refraining from shipping a wood chipper to my house to grind up the "devil door" constantly interrupting Drew and Ti's intense moments. For keeping me engaged with visual reminders of Drew's eyes and dimples. And for rescuing me again and again from my own awkward phrasing. I'm beyond blessed to have one of the best editors around.

Melanie, girl, I'd be a hot mess without our hundreds of emails. And chocolate … and essential oils … and salt lamps. Did I mention chocolate? I'm so thankful God paired me up with a kindred spirit for a critique partner. Thanks for sledging through the quagmire of first drafts with me and offering encouragement during the many days I feel I'm sinking. Here's to crossing over into hippie land.

Victorine, thanks for fine-tuning a cover I'm head over heels in love with, and for offering input on the storyline.

Rachel, Julie, and Mom, thank you for lending your proofing skills to give this story a final polished touch.

To my awesome launch team, thanks for rallying behind this series. Your support and enthusiasm have been a huge blessing.

To each of my readers, I was so thrilled when you asked for Ti to get her own story. This book wouldn't exist without your nudge. Thank you for letting Drew and Ti share in a small part of your life, and for joining me along this journey of grace.

Made in the USA
Middletown, DE
13 February 2020

84706746R00205